The OTHER MAN

WITHDRAWN

ALSO BY
FARHAD J. DADYBURJOR

How I Got Lucky

The OTHER MAN

FARHAD J. DADYBURJOR

LAKE UNION
PUBLISHING

Text copyright © 2021 by Farhad J. Dadyburjor
All rights reserved.

No part of this book may be reproduced, or stored in a retrieval system, or transmitted in any form or by any means, electronic, mechanical, photocopying, recording, or otherwise, without express written permission of the publisher.

Published by Lake Union Publishing, Seattle

www.apub.com

Amazon, the Amazon logo, and Lake Union Publishing are trademarks of Amazon.com, Inc., or its affiliates.

ISBN-13: 9781542031554
ISBN-10: 1542031559

Cover design by Philip Pascuzzo

Printed in the United States of America

To my family

CHAPTER 1

"Sir . . . Punjabi Clooney, may I leave?"

Ved looked up from the neat stacks of paper on his desk to find his secretary, Sheetal, standing in the doorway to his office with a big-dimpled smile. She hung back, with one foot placed slightly beyond the door's frame.

A quick glance at the clock on the wall confirmed what Ved had been dreading all day—the weekend had officially begun. Realizing that his failure to respond immediately was only making Sheetal feel more awkward, Ved scrambled with a rising blush coloring his cheeks on being likened to the rakish Hollywood star. "Err . . . yes, Sheetal. Thank you, that's all for today." As an afterthought he added, "Have a nice weekend."

"You too. May I offer some advice to my very hardworking boss?" Without waiting for him to answer, Sheetal continued, "Ved, you practically own this company. Shut off your computer and get out of this cursed building! I'm sure whatever work you have can wait until Monday. It's not like you have to impress your boss or anything. If I were a millionaire businessman, I would be outta the office on Friday as soon as the clock hit five." She gave a quick wink before shutting the door.

Ved leaned back against the plush cushioning of his swivel chair with a deep sigh, pushing himself around in slow circles, wishing he could share some of Sheetal's bubbliness. He briefly considered stepping out to see who else remained in the office, but he knew he was the last one left. Just like always. Who in their right mind would spend their Friday night trapped in this soaring glass prison working for Mehra Electronics—building and company both owned by his father—with only the hum of sleeping computers for company? Not when there was so much potential for fun: families and friends and clubs and movies and restaurants . . . even Sheetal had ditched her demure daytime sari for Friday-night "fuck me" attire, a short black dress with a plunging neckline.

Well, at least someone was going to have a good time in Mumbai tonight. He had met Sheetal's boyfriend, Rahul, once or twice and quite liked him—the way he was around her, fussing and fawning, as if she was the best thing in his life. To make him feel welcome at their office party last year, Ved, abandoning the boss card, had fetched two glasses of wine for them, and with much charm and flourish offered the drinks to them, saying, "Cheers to you two." Rahul had been so taken aback that he took one gulp and spilled the rest on his shirt.

Ved's presence could be intimidating, with his tall frame. The full head of soft, floppy hair with just a hint of salt and pepper on the sides, with eyes a shade of swirling caramel. Always dressed in a sharply tailored suit, usually Armani or Brioni, often accessorized with a silk tie or kept relaxed with the shirt's top two buttons open. When he walked into a room, you noticed him.

He looked back up at the clock. He had maybe thirty minutes before the night cleaning crew would come in, and he didn't think he could bear their looks of pity another week in a row. Home it was, then. As he packed his briefcase, he turned back to his desk and groaned. While the neat stacks of paper gave the illusion of organization, organization couldn't be further from the truth. By Monday, Ved still had to write up departmental monthly reports, plans for product development, a presentation on the future of electronics for the board of directors. He had no option. Ved would have to complete the work at home. He sighed. Doubtless, this would prove to be another long night with just his laptop and countless lukewarm cups of black coffee for company.

From the time he had joined Mehra Electronics right after college as a trainee on track to becoming vice president, Ved had done everything he could to prove he was more than just a "daddy's boy." From daily factory visits to eating lunch with his coworkers to even dealing with the union and its increasingly raucous meetings, Ved hadn't been afraid to get his hands dirty. In fact, he took every chance to do so. There was satisfaction in earning his workers' trust, in knowing that his work was actively contributing to the company's growth. Moreover, he was able to learn how the company truly operated, all the way on the bottom floors of the building, beyond the glass walls of his cushy office. Even as Ved rose through the company ranks, he always ensured that he was available to his employees whenever they needed him.

Ved never let himself forget that someday in the not-so-distant future, he would be in line to take over Mehra Electronics after his father, as was the case in every other business family in India. This was not something to be taken lightly, not to Ved. It had taken him years to earn his peers' respect, their trust, and now that he was lucky enough to have it, Ved knew he had to work harder than anyone else to hold on to it, including on weekends.

With a sweep of his arm, the neat piles were destroyed and the papers stuffed into his briefcase, along with a laptop that would surely already have emails outlining more work to do. Yeah, working through the weekend *every* weekend wasn't ideal, but if Ved was being honest, what else did he have to do? How many years had it been since Ved had looked forward to "weekend plans"? How many years since Ved had had someone to share his weekends with? Drinks, pizza, movies, late-night walks . . . anything? All Ved knew now was that working through the weekends, Friday through Sunday, was normal. Frankly, having all the work to keep himself occupied was really a relief. At least this way he could tell himself that he was just dedicated to his job, not a loner without a single plan during the two long days stretching between him and Monday.

Stepping into the glass elevator, Ved stared at his reflection. Sheetal wasn't the only one who said he looked like George Clooney, though Ved wasn't sure his salt-and-pepper hair really warranted the compliment. Did George Clooney have thick-ish eyebrows and an unflattering bump of a belly? It really was time for Ved to put a lid on those late-night binges at the refrigerator. He couldn't rely on his height to balance out his weight forever.

The city below him slowly approached. Sleek, glossy skyscrapers with the demeanor of runway models, slim new constructions coming up over old heritage Bombay houses, luxury fashion boutiques, and exorbitantly priced health food cafés. With the offensive amount of glass, everything and everyone—expats, hipsters—was on display. At all times. This narcissism reeked of the nouveau riche, and while Ved was technically a member of that group, that didn't mean he could forget the good ol' Bombay he'd grown up in so easily.

Gone were the clear skies and starry nights. Gone were the days when a "night out" entailed nothing more than a simple and easy traffic-free drive on Worli Sea Face with a stop at the *kulfiwala* for a cold sweet treat. Now, in upwardly mobile Mumbai, where plenty of families owned at least two cars, the roads were always gridlocked with traffic, and a blanket of smog perpetually hung over the city.

Closing his eyes, Ved could remember the horse-drawn carriage rides he would take with his parents at the oceanfront promenade along the Gateway of India, the bump of the carriage wheels across the uneven stone pavement. He could remember the Chinese food at the Taj Hotel's Golden Dragon restaurant as a special treat on birthdays and all the crisp plates of fish and chips at the Sea Lounge with his father to celebrate yet another acquisition at Mehra Electronics. His family would drive his dad's first car, a white Ambassador, back to his grandfather's colonial cottage in Prabhadevi every month. Ved would always roll down the windows, enjoying the soft breeze that caressed his face, while his parents would (lovingly) argue over which station to listen to on the radio. Unsurprisingly, Mum always preferred old Bollywood classics, while Dad preferred contemporary English pop. Back in those days, Dad switching the radio station while Mum wasn't looking had been life's biggest problem.

Everything changed after Mehra Electronics suddenly became a sprawling empire.

A new elite school, a palatial house in an upscale suburb, constant bickering at home between his parents, Ved finding himself more and more in the company of the many servants hired to attend to the Mehra family. Soon enough, conspicuous wealth was the new order, and everyone spoke a language of important brand names. Even the thought of *kulfi* was offensive, long replaced by the gelato that came both sugar- and dairy-free.

Like the Mehra family, the city had long since embraced a new visage—gaudy Mumbai. The small clump of old heritage Bombay houses that remained looked like dolls' playhouses next to the new, shiny monoliths.

Just as Ved was stepping out into the dusk, his phone started ringing. A quick glance at the caller ID confirmed his worst fears. "Dolly Mehra" was requesting to FaceTime. After ignoring her for a week, there was no way he could get away with not answering. If he did, he knew the police would be knocking on his door later that very night with a hysterical Dolly in tow, claiming she had filed a missing person's report in his name. So, knowing he would regret it, Ved accepted the call. Dolly's high cheekbones and hazel eyes filled the screen.

"Hello, Mum."

"Hello, Mum? *Hello, Mum?* Really? After not answering my calls for *an entire week*. Do you know how worried I've been? Do you know how many messages I've left you? You could have been dead for all I bloody knew!"

". . ."

"Ved! Do you have anything to say for yourself?"

"I think Dad would've told you if I was dead."

"Don't be smart with me!"

"You're right," Ved sighed. "I should've texted you at least. Work has just been so hectic this week."

"I know, Vedu," she said, calming down, "but just focusing your life on work is bound to lead to an isolated, pathetic existence. Just see what happened to Prem."

"Mum. Dad's life turned out fine."

"But I want *the best* for you, dear. You need to be social, get out of the house. Why don't you come over to my place tonight?"

The proposal didn't come as a surprise. Ever since Ved was a child, he had preferred his own company. Nevertheless, Dolly had taken a particular interest in making sure his social life was as bustling as hers. It didn't matter that Ved didn't have many friends—he wasn't interested in going out and playing cricket with the other boys, preferring to play on his own with his mini kitchen set—or siblings of his own to have fun with; she would find the friends or have him tag along with her friends. That was how it had always been.

"I told you I'm busy."

"Enough of this busy-shizy. I've invited Guru Askahvanii to give my friends and me a special session at home."

"The astrologer who defrauded a bank? Mum, no. You know I don't believe in all of that. Adding an extra *d* in my name or rearranging the furniture in my room isn't going to miraculously improve my life."

Since her divorce, Dolly Mehra had gotten into the habit of having "spiritual cleansing sessions" at her place for her "kitty friends"—all well-to-do ladies who were either divorced or married, many of them deeply unhappy. A few months ago, it had been an aura reader; before that, a feng shui expert. There had even been a notorious crystal gazer who was later arrested for murdering her husband.

"Stop it. Have some respect. There are greater forces above you and me, planning our destinies. Plus . . . Pamela Singh, the London socialite, is coming specially from Hydy Park just to meet you, *beta*."

"You mean Hyde Park."

"Yes, that only," she snapped, her irritation rising.

"Did you already tell her I was coming?" Ved suddenly felt nauseated.

"Well, she wants to meet the successful son I've been telling her so much about. She might have someone in mind for you. The *perfect* girl we've both been waiting for."

"Mum, you know, you've been searching for a girl for so long . . . it's probably just best we let the matter go. I'm fine on my own. Really."

"For such a handsome boy like you? What nonsense. You should hear the things I have to hear from my kitty group. 'Oh, Dolly, it's such a shame that Ved isn't married yet.' 'Oh, Dolly, Ved is such a catch; why isn't he married yet?' 'Oh, Dolly, what a tragedy that your son isn't married. All of *my* sons are already married.' How do you expect me to answer these questions, Ved? What am I supposed to say?"

"Mum—" Ved knew what it was like. The one time he had dropped in at his mother's house unannounced to collect some delicious *pakoras* she'd made, he had found himself bang in the middle of one of her kitty parties. "My, my, Ved, you're all grown up. Looking so tall and dashing. I still remember how you used to hide behind your mother's *saree pallu* out of shyness as a child every time I was over. Good thing you lost those plump cheeks and all that belly fat, my little roly-poly," said Mimmy aunty, his mother's oldest friend. "Tell me also your secret; I could use some of it." She winked, holding her stomach laughingly, while Sheila aunty chirped in, "Just look at your handsome son, Dollyji—how is he still single? I'm sure there's a line of women rushing after him. Come on, Ved, tell us, anyone you fancy? There are so many beautiful girls I know who would love to be married to the Mehra scion. I can arrange it quickly; just tell me when you are ready. It's about time you gave Dollyji some cute grandchildren, no?" Before he could even think of responding, Seema aunty butted in: "Oh ho, don't worry about him. Look at all the dark circles below his eyes—we know what you've been up to with all those 'late nights,'" she chortled, pinching his cheeks naughtily while the rest laughed along. Ved quickly grabbed the packet of pakoras and left, vowing to never *ever* go over to his mother's place unannounced.

"You're thirty-eight. You know that you should've been married years ago. It's time to settle down with someone who can look after you. No one is fine on their own—not you and certainly not your father."

"I'm still not coming over to meet Guruji," Ved insisted, hoping that it would end the entire matter.

"Well, in that case, you will meet whichever girl Pamela aunty has in mind for you."

With that, his mother hung up the phone.

CHAPTER 2

When he finally arrived home, Ved threw down his briefcase and curled up on the couch, still fully dressed in his custom-tailored Armani suit. He knew his father would disapprove of him putting his fancy Gucci Horsebit crocodile loafers on the couch, but at the moment, Ved couldn't care less. His head hurt, and just thinking about having to go on a date with "Perfect Girl #24" deepened the cavity Ved felt was rapidly cracking open in his chest, turning the contents of his stomach upside down.

Ved tried to will his eyes shut, hoping that he could calm himself down. Even the fancy breathing exercises his father had recommended last month to "relieve" his "work stress" only managed to make him feel worse. Mum was right. He was alone. Alone. Alone. Alone. He was in an apartment without a single companion. Dad didn't count. Doubtless, he was eating dinner in his study, just down the hall, slowly making his way through the weekend work. His mother didn't count. Doubtless, Mum was having a jolly good time with her kitty group and Guruji, elated by the prospect of her aging son finally settling down. Thirty-eight and still unmarried. Oh, what horrors were destined to befall his mother's cursed life.

Turning to open the large french windows for some fresh air only made Ved feel worse.

Right through that window, Ved could just make out the faint outline of the wrought-iron park bench below. He and Akshay used to meet there after work, hidden from view by thick shrubs and the fast-thickening darkness. Just to talk, maybe let off steam. Akshay always knew how to make Ved laugh after a bad day at work. "You really need to stop taking yourself so seriously. Remember, you're not the prime minister of India. In fact, you're not even the president," he would say with mock seriousness. Ved always knew that would be Akshay's closing line. Never did it fail to make him smile.

And they could talk about anything. Office politics, parents, shitty food for lunch, the state of the country, trashy Bollywood gossip—nothing was off limits, not between them. Ved's favorite moments, however, were the ones they would spend in silence, sitting next to each other, happy in the terrible weather, watching people go by. Ved didn't need words to enjoy Akshay's company. Just sitting with him, being in his presence, was enough to melt away whatever stress or anxiety had hardened in Ved during the day. Akshay was bold too. He would openly reach for Ved's hand right there on that bench. Until their very last time together, Ved still couldn't fathom how Akshay so readily showed affection, openly for the world to see. Akshay would smile when Ved jumped at the physical contact and would smile even broader when Ved used the folds of his suit jacket to cover their loosely entwined fingers.

Ironically enough, it was Dolly who had introduced Ved and Akshay during one of her famous dinner parties. They were the only two men at the party who weren't interested in watching cricket with the husbands. As such, they both sulked in opposite corners of Dolly's living room, and if there was one thing Dolly couldn't tolerate, it was unhappy party guests. It had only made sense for her to push the two loners together.

They had laughed about that meeting all the time, how they were pushed together at the very times in their lives when both their mothers were anxious to marry them off to "respectable" women. Akshay, being that he was older and far more experienced in the gay-relationship department, had made the first move by asking Ved for his number. Yet it was only after Akshay had asked three times that Ved reluctantly handed it over. He had read enough stories in the newspapers about blackmail or abusive calls to gay men to make him wary of sharing his mobile number.

After that, everything else was a whirlwind. First, they met openly on Saturday nights for drinks and dinner, holding hands under the table. Then, they were a couple. Just like that, in mere weeks, they had been able to develop the kind of intimacy usually reserved for married couples.

Ved wouldn't even be at his apartment during the weekends, spending the hours at a desk in front of a screen, like he was destined to do now. He would spend the hours, instead, at Akshay's place. They would laze in bed until the afternoon, reading the stack of morning papers with mugs of steaming bitter black coffee before making love again. Then, Akshay would cook lunch for them in his tiny square kitchen. Once, Ved had tried to cook lunch. To no one's surprise (except Ved's), the neighbors came banging on the door about the fumes billowing through the kitchen window.

For dinner, they would order in the greasy takeout food that their diets couldn't accommodate during the week. Sometimes they would watch a film, though it didn't matter which one because they usually ended up talking through it anyway. They sometimes took long walks through the sparse greenery they could find in the city, both trying to inhale the smell of grass underneath the omnipresent haze of pollution. By late Sunday evening, Akshay would hold Ved against his chest, unwilling to let him go home. Ved would cling to Akshay right back, breathing in the scent of his clean linen detergent. Leaving was the worst part. Eventually, realizing that they both needed to be up by six the next morning for work, they would detangle their arms from each other.

Ved would never forget the look in Akshay's eyes during those moments, the adoration. No one had ever (or had since) looked at Ved that way. Looking into Akshay's eyes, Ved could never feel alone. How could he? Impossible when someone loved him *that* much. Ved would be the one to reach in for one final, deep kiss, stopping only when Akshay pulled away. Akshay would smile and give a short nod, and Ved would shut the door behind him as softly as possible, dreading the click of the lock.

For four years, weekends were Ved's escape. He left his life during the week for magic with Akshay. He would spend most of his Fridays stealing glances at the clock in between meetings, willing the hour hand to just *speed up*.

Look at Ved now.

Lying on the couch mourning over bliss he'd already paid for a long time ago. Mum was right. She really was. Being alone was pathetic; it made Ved *feel* pathetic. He couldn't resign himself to spending the rest of his night here, staring at an empty park bench. Akshay was gone. He wasn't coming back. That was it.

Ved felt silly, really, looking back at everything, He'd been a mess, both socially awkward and lacking ambition. Akshay had been so put together, both personally and professionally. He swept into Ved's life, and suddenly, everything seemed sharper, clearer. It had never bothered Ved that Akshay liked to check his text messages periodically or that Akshay never wanted to share dishes at restaurants. It was far easier for him to let Akshay remain in control, and Ved had no problem with that. To Ved, he and Akshay couldn't have been on a more equal plane. They were both still in the closet, and not a day passed when Akshay would forget to remind him that they would come out to their parents "soon."

"Soon," however, came and went, and Ved, for some reason, continued believing Akshay.

In many ways, it still felt like "soon" was impending for Ved, even though Akshay was long gone. He'd grown so used to staying in the closet that he didn't really want to find his way out anymore. What would be the point now, when there was no one worth risking it for? No one needed to worry about Ved's hookups besides Ved.

Ved's phone suddenly beeped. He read the message. Thank God. After walking to the front door briskly, he left the house, shut the door behind him, and stepped into his BMW.

Thirty minutes later, he arrived at the luxurious five-star hotel, House of Maharaj, by the Arabian Sea. Room 144 was opened by a man with a set of hard eyes that assessed Ved, direct, expectant. A thick moustache nearly concealed a sideways smile, and black wiry curls circled a bare chest over a thick, taut stomach, ending with a wrapped white towel. Ved hastily brushed past the man and walked into the orgy, neglecting to return the smile.

Ved climbed onto an available bed, lying on his stomach. The man who had opened the door approached and placed a bottle of poppers under his nose, which Ved greedily pulled on. The vapor crept through his nostrils, filling his whole body with warmth.

CHAPTER 3

Ved awoke the next morning at six. What a joke. On weekdays, his 6:00 a.m. alarm was fiery, relentless hell on earth, yet on weekends, his body couldn't seem to break routine. As tired as he still was, there was no point wasting his time in bed. With a huff Ved sat up and stretched, horrified by the creaking in his joints. His body was sore, and his head was already pounding. The start to a great Saturday. Ugh.

On his way from his wing of the colossal apartment to the main wing with the breakfast table, Ved checked his phone, seeing two unread messages. What did the people at the office want him to take care of? Surely, they had personal matters to worry about on the weekends. Of course. The messages weren't from the office—they were about H&M's Great Indian Sale. Everyone from the office *did* have better things to worry about. Obviously.

Another message chimed in—this time from Grindr—the cheerful noise doing nothing to raise Ved's spirits. Seeing that the message was from Rohit, Ved quickly deleted it. It really didn't matter what Rohit wanted to say. They'd already slept together on Wednesday. That meant they were done. One night of sex. Period. Ved could never afford to let it become familiar by putting himself out there and being vulnerable, risking the pain of lame excuses and blocked numbers he'd endured in those miserable months after Akshay. He'd learned to play the game since then, how to shut himself off completely. That distance had been exactly what Ved needed after Akshay. Casual sex was far easier to deal with because that was all it was: sex. No need to worry about love or sharing a life with another man or about coming out of the closet. Seeing that Rohit was now trying to call him, Ved swiftly blocked the number.

Before Ved could sit down, a ball of fur leaped straight into his arms and began licking his face, causing Ved to nearly drop his new iPhone.

"Hi, baby! Oh, you missed me, my love. You missed me. I missed you, too, yes I did," Ved said in the singsong voice reserved only for his darling dog, a Cavapoo. Ved rubbed his nose against Fubu's, cradling him against his chest. Fubu squealed and jumped down, circling Ved's legs and licking his feet. Ved laughed. "Okay, baby. Come have breakfast with me."

As usual, Ved reached for the stack of newspapers after sitting down. Half the stack that contained business newspapers was already gone, presumably with Dad in his study, but he had left all Ved's favorite papers on the table. Ved reached for *The Times of India*, expecting the usual diatribe about the stock markets and pollution. What he actually read was nothing short of paralyzing. "Supreme Court Agrees to Hear Plea Seeking to Decriminalize Homosexuality" was the headline, in bold text. Right there. In a national newspaper. Ved didn't even bother with the other news. He read the article, and then he read it again to make sure he had read it right the first time, unable to let the words on the page fully sink in. His heart thudded in his chest, faster and faster.

Could this *really* be happening?

After all these years, all the men who had been forced to mold themselves into what was comfortable for Indian society . . . there had never really been any hope before. Not a realistic drop of it. Now, there was a chance. Yes, there would be bigots who'd get on cable television and do everything in their power to instill fear over the constitutionality and morality of the potential decriminalization, but there was still hope. That meant something. Ved swallowed hard against the tightness in his throat. It *did* mean something.

Fubu, in the meantime, dozed on Ved's right foot, unaware of the intensity with which Ved was flipping through the next paper to see if the story would also be reported by other news outlets.

"*Saab*, should I get breakfast?" asked his father's longtime servant, Hari.

Ved quickly turned to the business section of the paper, as if he'd been caught in some minor act of indiscretion. "Err . . . yes, Hari. Please. Could you also bring out some black coffee now and the bottle of aspirin?"

As Hari prepared Ved's usual egg-white omelet with toast, Ved found articles with similar headlines in the rest of the newspapers, each allocated different amounts of space but essentially saying the same thing. Gay activists and a legal team were adopting a strong legal case to ensure that this time, *finally*, the reprehensible Section 377 in the Indian Penal Code would be struck down—once and for all.

Ved's head didn't hurt so much anymore. While squishing an obscene amount of ketchup on his omelet, just the way he liked it, Ved found himself able to smile. Things were finally changing. But before he could mull on those prospects for much longer, his phone rang: Dolly Mehra. This time, Ved didn't think twice about answering.

"Good morning, Mum!"

"Oh wow, Vedu? You sound so upbeat!"

"Well, it's a good day." Ved still couldn't shake the smile from his face.

"Very happy to hear that. We all missed you last night."

"Mum, your kitty group did not miss me, trust me."

"Well, in any case, *I* missed you. I never get to see you anymore, beta. You should visit me this afternoon. I've invited an aura reader!"

"Mum." Ved knew where this was going.

"I'll make you your favorite chai and pakoras," she said, sweetening her tone.

Damn. That was tempting. He *did* miss Mum. Maybe the aura reader wouldn't even be that bad . . .

"Plus, beta, we need to discuss the girl Pamela Singh found for you—her niece, Disha."

"Oh." Of course there was a catch.

"Oh?" she mocked. "Vedu, this girl is absolutely *perfect*. I think she's going to make you very happy."

"Mum . . ." Ved hesitated. "Do I really need to get married?"

She inhaled sharply. "Why are you asking me this? I thought you wanted to get married."

Ved was incredulous. "When did I ever say that?"

"How about from the time you met the first girl I found for you, Ved, hmm? What has suddenly changed now?" All the sweetness was gone from her voice.

"But I never said that. I've got to go. Bye." Ved hung up. He knew the gesture was rude and that he would have hell to pay for it with Mum later. Maybe at least he could try to enjoy his breakfast now. No such luck. Mum immediately called back. Twice. Ved didn't have the energy to explain his thought process to her right now. Or ever. He'd just do what he always did: go out on a single date with the girl to humor his mother and then say that the girl wasn't right. Eventually, she just wouldn't be able to find any more "perfect" girls, and they could give up. Hopefully sooner rather than later.

His phone pinged again. What now? Naturally, it was Mum. Seeing as she couldn't tell him the information about this girl, she'd decided to message it all to him. Better to get this over with now. He could at least tell Mum he'd set up a date to get her off his back.

Disha Kapoor. Age twenty-two, degree in fashion design from the Parsons School of Design, currently owns her own company custom-making Indian wedding outfits. Beautiful, smart, young—perfect, right?

Setting his phone down next to him, Ved absentmindedly fed Fubu a piece of his buttered toast. Ved didn't care much for whole wheat bread. He only tolerated it because Dad insisted that they must remain heart healthy to continue their active lifestyles at work. Yeah, like *that* was going to be what made the difference despite all the crazy levels of stress they encountered at work seven days a week.

Ved was so tangled up in his own brooding that he almost didn't register Prem striding up to the breakfast table with his chipped blue coffee mug. Seeing his father sit down in the empty seat after years of eating his meals in solitude was enough to make Ved choke on a sip of his coffee, the liquid scalding his throat. Prem helped himself to some coffee and settled into the chair, picking up the copy of *The Times of India* Ved had just read. They sat like that for God knows how long—Prem contentedly sipping his coffee with his ankles crossed out in front of him, and Ved desperately trying to figure out why Prem was drinking a cup of coffee with him. Finally, Prem set his wire-rimmed bifocals on the marble table right next to Ved's phone, turning his face to return Ved's gaze.

"Who was that on the phone with you earlier? Your mother?"

His tone was casual, as if he sat down with his son in silk navy-blue pajamas to chat over cups of coffee all the time. That was rich. Ved couldn't even remember the last time he'd seen his father in pajamas, much less shared a conversation with him outside the office. Despite living together, their interactions were limited to the occasional polite "hello" and recommended breathing exercise as they passed each other in the halls. Work wasn't much better. There, Ved was little more than an employee to Prem, deserving of only the most curt professionalism. Now, Ved didn't know how to react. He went for the composed option: staring at Prem in absolute silence. Maybe seeing his son taking over more of the reins of the company had helped him to finally relax, cut back on a workaholic existence, and free up some morning time, which would allow them to actually share a regular conversation over breakfast like every other father and son.

Prem did love Ved. Ved knew that. The awkwardness arose in how to express that love. Ever since his parents' divorce, Prem and Ved's relationship had grown distant. Ved had spent most of his time with Dolly, only seeing Prem for an hour or so every weekend. Even the few days that Ved did spend with Prem consisted of Ved sitting outside Prem's office at Mehra Electronics while Prem worked behind closed doors, and then Ved sitting outside Prem's office at home while Prem (again) worked behind closed doors.

"Ved?" Prem asked, a small crease of concern appearing between his two very bushy gray eyebrows.

"What? Um, yeah. Yeah. I was talking to Mum." That certainly made Ved seem composed.

"Hmm."

Was that it? Ved couldn't stand another eternity of silence. "She wanted to tell me about Pamela Singh's niece," he blurted.

"Pamela, the heiress from Hyde Park?"

"Yeah."

"Well, that certainly sounds like a match Dolly would approve of."

"And you don't?"

"I never said I didn't approve of the match, Ved."

"Well, you never said you did either." Ved hated how this conversation was making him sound like a child.

"What do *you* think of the match?"

How was Dad's tone so even all the time? Ved tried for a deep breath. "I don't know yet, Dad. You know I'll have to go on a date with her to make Mum happy."

Prem crossed his arms across his chest, considering. He shrugged. "It's your life, Ved. You're a grown man. You can go out on dates with whomever you choose."

Ved smiled. "That would be the ideal life. But tell that to Mum. If I'm not married by the end of this year, she might just have a heart attack."

"Well, do you want to get married?"

"What do you mean?"

Prem only continued looking at Ved. As if this conversation couldn't get any more uncomfortable. Ved should sever it right now. Get up and return to his room. Why did it even matter to Dad what he thought about marriage?

"It's your life," Prem repeated, pushing his chair out from the table. Before returning to his office, he refilled his mug and slid *The Times of India* over to Ved—open to the article on gay rights. "Did you see the headlines today?"

Prem strode out of the room before Ved could muster a response.

CHAPTER 4

They were polar opposites, Mum and Dad. Oxford educated, Dad had gone from the conservative world of his Punjabi family to the thick of the British swinging sixties, a time of free love, the Beatles, and hippiedom. To study in London was a big deal in those days. Very few got the opportunity, and even fewer could afford the plane fare from India on top of the university fees. Prem, however, was an exceptional student who studied day and night, working himself to exhaustion to receive the full scholarship he knew he needed in order to have a chance at that coveted education. Prem's father had dipped into his own retirement savings to pay for the plane fare, and Prem was off. With only a few clothes and a box of *ladoos* packed into a dirt-brown trunk, Prem had stepped onto the campus of Oxford University.

Once he was there, Prem knew he had no choice but to make the most of the opportunity. So, while some other students smoked pot and chased girls, Prem studied. And studied. And studied. He graduated third in his class and went on to run one of the most successful technology companies in the world.

But before Prem Mehra became that technology mogul, he was a man with a degree from a foreign country, returning home to get married and start working. It was that degree that had enticed Ved's mother, the prospect of an internationally educated husband "from Oxford, no less." Prem was full of ambition, and Dolly had enough of her own to match. In fact, it was her creativity and ideas, built from her own job managing a fashion boutique, that helped put the Mehra name on the map. More importantly, Prem and Dolly had really loved each other.

Ved could remember how it was when his parents were happy.

They would eat dinner as a family. Every single night. Mum would cook meals that put professional chefs to shame: her famous pomegranate chutney with sizzling lamb kebabs, light *naan* infused with plump dried figs, warm eggplant *bharta*, crab cakes cooked in curry leaves with tangy mango chutney. Knowing Mum's sweet tooth, Dad would always pick up fresh *kaju katlis* or *jalebis* on his way home from the office. They would eat the sweets after dinner on the living room's Kashmiri carpet to avoid staining the expensive beige-and-gold Viennese furniture. Nestled against Mum's side, Ved would listen to Dad mull over the day's business with her, seeing him smile whenever she found a solution to a seemingly impossible predicament.

Things quickly changed when Ved turned ten and Mehra Electronics took off.

Dad started eating dinner in his office, leaving Ved and Mum alone at the long dining room table. Though the table was meant to seat twenty, the three of them together had been enough to fill the room. Yet without Dad sitting at the head of the table, and the only noise coming from the clink of Ved's cutlery against his antique fine china plate, the room felt painfully empty. Soon, it wasn't just meals.

Dad started spending *all* his time in his office. No more surprise vacations to the white beaches of Goa. No more vanilla ice creams on the balcony during unbearably hot summer days. No more bedtime stories about gods and heroes. Dad worked and Mum drank wine.

Mum would stand outside Dad's office every night, sobbing insults at the thick wood door. Ved, creeping out of his own room, would hang on the railing of the staircase and crouch out of sight, trying to listen but afraid of what he would hear.

"I'm not dumb, you know, just because I didn't go to some fancy university!"

"Running this house is harder than running a company, let me tell you!"

"Don't forget that without my father's money, you wouldn't even have a company at all!"

Dad never responded.

Eventually, Mum would finish the bottle of rosé and go up to bed. Ved would remain on the staircase waiting for, willing, Dad to come out of his office. No matter how late he forced himself to stay up, Ved never saw Dad leave.

By the next morning, Mum would wake Ved up early, gently coaxing him out of bed with promises of ketchup on his eggs. She was fresh faced, like nothing had happened the night before. Dad would already be long gone for work.

Their divorce wasn't a surprise, but it still made Ved feel like his heart had cracked—not jaggedly, but perfectly down the middle. These two had once made up the whole of his heart, welded together by the warmth of his childhood. After the divorce, there was a clear division. Because the break wasn't messy, Ved always had the chance, the hope, that the two halves would be brought back together again, restored to their rightful state. As it turned out, such hopes were foolish.

The divorce had left Mum with nothing. Literally nothing. She had no husband, no job prospects, and no friends. Her so-called society best friends had quickly ceased to associate with her. Her social net worth, once featured prominently between the pages of society newspapers, plummeted to zero—below zero, if that were even possible.

Dad continued working in his study, just as he had before. That door always firmly shut.

His parents had married for love, and all that had brought them was misery, years wasted. Ved wished he'd had the sense to learn from their mistakes with Akshay. Now he knew the truth. Love—true, burning love—was synonymous with self-inflicted pain, and there was only so long that pain could be endured.

For many years, Ved had enjoyed casual one-night stands with men, mostly tourists visiting Mumbai. He was a different person in and out of the hotel rooms. In the confines of hotel rooms, he was comfortable with his sexuality, more open to experimenting to satisfy his own needs. When he stepped out of the hotel rooms, he was discreet, cautious to the extent that he would go months on end without meeting anyone. He couldn't stand to have his parents find out, to disappoint them by not being the ideal Indian son, especially Mum. Not after what she had been through with her divorce and the humiliation she endured.

He was well aware how people viewed homosexuality in this country—as if it were a disease that could be cured like any other. He would become the object of ridicule at work, and he could imagine all too easily the way Mum's friends would sneer about his "abnormality" behind his back, offering their sympathies to Dolly while secretly relishing the downfall of the once-mighty Mehra name.

After all those years of letting Mum think that *someday* she would find the perfect bride for him, letting her dream that he would have a normal family with a horde of children running around, he couldn't rob her of that dream. The only time he'd even considered it had been when Akshay had come along and changed everything.

Ved had fallen into the same trap as his parents, sacrificing the best years of his life for a man he loved with all his heart, a man he thought could make his heart whole again. And what did Ved get in the end? Misery.

CHAPTER 5

Ved knew he should text Disha Kapoor. He knew he had promised Mum he would and that the soonest way to move on would be to take her out for dinner, yet he couldn't bring himself to do it. Not now. Every time his finger hovered over her phone number, Ved felt bile rise in his throat and the air catch in his chest, compressing painfully. He could just as easily text her tomorrow, he reasoned. Nothing would change by tomorrow, of course. Ved would still be gay. Taking Disha on a date when he had no intention of marrying her would still be wrong. Ved tried to press her number again, with no success. Feeling like he couldn't breathe, Ved shut down his phone and leaned back against his bed frame. He tried Dad's breathing exercises again. Still no effect.

Doesn't matter. Doesn't matter. *Doesn't matter.* It's just one date, Ved reasoned. He would buy her dinner and tell Mum he didn't feel the connection. Surely tomorrow Ved would be able to perform the simple task of typing out a text message. For now, he had work to do. Piles of it, in fact, still crammed in his briefcase.

The time passed easily. Between the mundane, like testing which fonts seemed the most professional on PowerPoint, and the strenuous, like preparing a financial summary of the quarter to present to the board of directors, Ved didn't even notice that he hadn't moved from his spot against the headboard in hours. That is, until Hari softly knocked.

"Saab . . ."

Ved continued drafting the email he planned to send to his team the following morning.

"Saab," Hari tried again.

This time, Ved did look up, blinking wearily and looking over to the clock on his nightstand: 8:00 p.m. No wonder Hari was worried. Usually, Ved's hunger sent him to the kitchen by 7:00 p.m., and here he was, unaware even that the sun had long set and that he hadn't eaten since early morning. How had he not noticed the enchanting scent of Hari's famous chicken *biryani* until just now?

"Saab, would you like dinner?"

"Yes, Hari, please. I will be out to the table in a few minutes."

Hari quickly nodded his head and left the room. Ved finished drafting his email and put away his laptop in his desk drawer before immediately pulling it out again. He still had more work to do. Multitasking between completing work and eating dinner would be a more efficient use of his time. Besides, eating a meal in silence and alone while Hari watched him from the kitchen door, like he usually did, his eyes filled with concern, would be unbearable. No wonder Dad always ate dinner in his study.

As it turned out, Ved was *too* productive on Saturday. Not only had he burned through all the work set aside for the weekend on Friday afternoon, but he had also burned through the work delivered to his inbox on Friday night and the extra work he'd created to get a head start on next week. That meant Sunday would be wide open. A whole day of nothing was what Ved could look forward to then. Great.

After dinner, Ved crawled into bed, still wearing the pajamas he'd worn the previous night. Mum had always hated when he showered and immediately put on the same clothes as before, but she wasn't here right now to reprimand him. She also wasn't here to reprimand Ved for lying down immediately after eating. He closed his eyes and rolled onto his stomach. Yep, she would definitely hate that.

Sleep remained elusive for hours. How was it possible that Ved could feel the fatigue collecting in his bones, weighing him down more and more each day, and still couldn't fall asleep easily? He flipped onto his back and stared at the ceiling, squinting in the dark, straining to make out the stars in the skylight. It was no use. The pollution clouded the stars just like it had for every other night of Ved's life.

When Ved had told Akshay he missed seeing the stars in the sky, Akshay had laughed, asking when he had ever seen the stars in Mumbai skies. Ved hadn't been talking about Mumbai, though. He had been talking about Goa.

When Dad took him and Mum there over the weekends, they always stayed in a hotel room that had huge windows, so big they practically took up the whole wall. Curled up on his side, Ved would stare at the stars until his eyes couldn't remain open any longer. Seeing that Ved wasn't joking, Akshay had gone to a kids' toy store the next day and purchased glow-in-the-dark rubber stars that he stuck all over his bedroom ceiling as a surprise for Ved. Ved wondered if those stars were still on Akshay's ceiling now. Ved wondered if he held his wife's hand, just like he'd held Ved's, and stared at them until he fell asleep.

Ved turned onto his stomach again. There was no point wasting time trying to fall asleep. With a huff, he rolled himself out of bed and put on his fuzzy bunny slippers, then headed straight for the kitchen. The white light of the freezer temporarily blinded him. Blinking wearily into the blasting cold air, Ved clawed out his favorite ice cream in the world: Baskin-Robbins' Honey Nut Crunch. Akshay had always teased him for that, saying Ved had chosen "the most boring guilty pleasure possible." That had made Ved laugh. Once.

Ved knew himself too well. He could already see the end of this night: he would eat half the pint (or the whole thing if he was feeling especially sad), shed some tears, and eventually fall asleep. How was it that he still missed Akshay? The close companionship they shared every weekend? After all these years, it was pathetic.

Ved couldn't spend his entire night moping over Akshay again. Akshay was married to a woman and certainly not standing in the kitchen at midnight opening a pint of ice cream to cry into. Ved knew he needed to do something to make himself happy. Besides eating the pint of ice cream, that is.

Walking back to his room, Ved realized what he would do. He would watch his favorite movie of all time—a movie that wouldn't remind him of Akshay: *Love Actually*. Ved had always been too embarrassed to tell anyone how much he loved *Love Actually*, even Akshay. He'd seen all the rom-coms, everything from *When Harry Met Sally* to *Just Go with It*. Truly, Ved was a sucker for anything romantic. He was a sucker for love, for seeing people so reluctant to fall in love, despite themselves. It gave him hope. If all those people in the movies could find "the one" without even trying, Ved could too. In five or ten or a hundred years, Ved could. Maybe if he weren't so shit scared of loving someone again. Maybe then.

Yes. *Love Actually* would help Ved forget all about Akshay tonight.

Ved could not have been more wrong. The movie didn't make him feel warm or hopeful or comforted. He wasn't still waiting for "the one," the way Aurelia and the prime minister and Sarah were. He had already found "the one"—Akshay. He *had* experienced the kind of love in *Love Actually*—better even—because Ved and Akshay had fallen for each other in the real world, not the movie's magical version of England.

Something in Ved's chest began to tighten, just like what had happened when he'd tried to text Disha earlier. That same stab of pain, straight into his heart. If his parents' divorce had broken his heart clean in two, Akshay breaking up with him had been the hammer that shattered Ved's heart into tiny bits so small that if you ripped open his chest, the fragments would blow away with the slightest breeze.

Why did things turn out the way they did? *Why?* They could have lived the dream, he and Akshay. The ending of every rom-com movie. Made a great life together. Ved had been willing to do anything. If being with Akshay meant going against everyone in his family, so be it. If it meant being made a mockery of in the closed-minded business community he inhabited, so be it. If it meant breaking the law that criminalized gay sex, so be it. So bolstered was he by this love—this love he shared with Akshay—that Ved had been ready to come out to his family, after all these years. Even risk hurting Dolly, shattering her dream of repairing her own family through Ved, giving him the chance for the loving spouse and horde of kids she could never have.

And then Ved learned that Akshay had different plans.

CHAPTER 6

Ved remembered that night so clearly, even though it had been four years and twenty-nine days ago. He had been on top of the world. He loved a man who loved him back. He had been promoted, had worked his way up Dad's company on his own merit. That very night, Ved had won *Biz World* magazine's "Young Business Achiever" award.

Ved had called Akshay immediately after the ceremony. It was well past midnight, but Ved knew Akshay found it hard to sleep without him on the other side of the bed. Akshay was awake. But Ved could tell that something was wrong from the moment Akshay took a heavy breath before saying "Hello" or "Congratulations," as if bracing himself for something. Akshay had said, "We need to sit down and have a serious talk soon. Are you on your way to my apartment?"

My apartment? Since when was it Akshay's apartment? It was *their* apartment, *their* home.

Ved had rushed there like a madman, ignoring the glasses of champagne raised to toast his victory and the heavy congratulatory pats on the back. He drove himself from the south end of the city to the suburbs of Andheri in a daze, likely breaking an inordinate number of traffic ordinances, even for Mumbai.

You're overthinking things, Ved had kept reassuring himself. Maybe Akshay had decided that they needed to make a more serious commitment. Maybe he wanted Ved to move in! Or maybe this was all just Akshay's idea of a sick prank, and he would laugh when Ved burst through the door, taking him into his arms and kissing him on the forehead, teasing him for being so gullible, reminding Ved how much he loved him . . .

No. Akshay wasn't going to do any of that. Ved could feel it in the pit of his stomach, the ticking timer on their relationship. The bomb would detonate any second. He had to get to Akshay *now*.

When Ved burst through the door, panting and sweating as if he'd run the entire way, Akshay had embraced him, standing still and clutching Ved's back, pressing him close to his chest. Then, without warning, he had stepped back, looked Ved straight in the eyes, and said, "We need to end things between us. It's not my decision. My parents want me to get married."

Ved had stepped away as well, pushing his back against the door, closing his eyes, trying and failing to breathe air into his collapsing lungs.

Akshay had stayed rooted to the same spot, pity tempered with sadness filling his eyes. "I'm sorry, Ved."

Ved couldn't move, much less open his mouth to respond. He tried to focus on the solid wood of the door behind him, the solid tile of the floor, the solid trophy that he'd brought to show Akshay clutched in his right hand. Ved's black three-piece cashmere suit was soaked entirely through with sweat. He could not stop shaking.

"I'm sorry, Ved. I really am, but there's nothing I can do. I've racked my brains to figure out some way, but there simply isn't one." Akshay sank into the couch next to him. "I can't let my parents down. You know that, don't you? They're my whole world. They've sacrificed everything to see me happy. Please try and understand. Please, Ved."

Why was the ceiling tilting like that? Ved sank to the floor, clutching the trophy even tighter, hugging it close to his chest.

"You, too, are my entire world, love, you know that, but I can't put them off any longer. I've already postponed the engagement for far too long. Let's not make things difficult between us."

Now Ved met Akshay's eyes. Ved's voice was hoarse.

"Me? You're asking me to not make things difficult?" He pushed himself off the floor and walked right in front of Akshay. His entire body was heating up, his face reddening, but his voice was now steel. "How long have you been engaged? How long have you known that you would leave me? Who gave you the right to manipulate me like this? Who the *fuck* gave you the right, Akshay?"

Akshay had stood up and brought Ved to his chest once again. He leaned in to whisper in Ved's ear, lips brushing the lobe: "We can carry on. Quietly. Just like before. Just like always. Nothing will change, I promise. No one needs to know."

Then, Akshay rubbed Ved's back, slowly going up and down, exactly like he always did whenever Ved was angry. "No one needs to know, love," Akshay repeated.

Ved had shoved Akshay away, the disgust clear on his face, his tears dry. He didn't need to be comforted by Akshay. Not ever again. "Don't use your parents as an excuse, you coward! Your parents know about us. They know you're gay. Don't delude yourself! They know I stay over at your house every weekend. They call me their 'second son.' They *know*."

How much of what he shared with Akshay had been a lie? For how long had Akshay planned this breakup? From the very beginning? Ved didn't want to know the answer to that question. How could something so beautiful, so intimate, be erased into oblivion by the decision of one man? How *dare* Akshay suggest Ved become a part of his sick manipulation in the name of love? As if things could ever be the same after this. Akshay was getting married. Ved would no longer fulfill Akshay's need for love. He would fulfill Akshay's need for sex.

"Ved, I'm also in a terrible position. You understand that, don't you?"

Understand? Oh, Ved understood perfectly.

He flung the heavy silver award straight into the glass table, not caring where the broken glass landed. Ved looked at Akshay one last time and left. Leaving had always been hard before. It wasn't hard that time.

For God knows how long, Ved had sat in his car and cried. For the pain. The anger. The frustration. The betrayal. Just when he thought his tear ducts had finally run dry, he would remember something small, like how Akshay kept a pint of Honey Nut Crunch in his freezer "just in case," how he hugged Ved from behind when they did the dishes together, how he lit eucalyptus candles during dinner, how he had smiled when Ved said "I love you" for the first time.

No. This can't be happening, Ved had thought. Akshay loves me. I love Akshay. That can't suddenly change. Not in one night.

Akshay had tried calling him several times after that. When that failed, he had bombarded Ved with text messages. And when that failed, Akshay had stopped trying. Ved should've known that Akshay would be a "dutiful son." He'd always believed that he had to overcompensate, be the extra-perfect son because maybe then it would be okay for him to be gay. Ved should've known that Akshay wouldn't change his entire mentality, that, like so many other gay men in India, he would marry simply to please his parents, even if it meant enduring a lifetime of lies and misery. There would be no breaking off the engagement in a fit of undying love. That only happened in the movies.

Sunday slouched past just as expected —completely uneventful. Ved created some work for himself, this time prepping two weeks in advance (a new personal record), made excuses to not text Disha Kapoor, and cracked open another pint of Honey Nut Crunch. Good thing Hari always kept the freezer well stocked. Ved filled the rest of the day with a healthy combination of lying down, snacking on ketchup-flavored potato chips, and drinking mugs of black coffee.

Come Monday morning, Ved knew it was time for him to hit the gym. It was getting harder and harder to firm up his slight belly, especially as he aged.

Ved had been bullied growing up for his weight. Being double the size of most kids his age, he had endured being called Fatty or "Motu Mehra" for years. Really, Ved knew the taunts weren't just about his weight. There were plenty of other chubby kids running around on the playground. At least those kids had some sort of connection to the broader student body, whether through academics or sports. Ved was fairly smart, although no genius, and certainly never within the top fifty students. His athletics were even worse. He never made any of the teams in school, was an embarrassment at track and field, and would be out of breath after attempting to whack a cricket ball with a bat he could never quite hold right. Years later, his time working out at the gym would make him feel good about himself.

He headed to Pulse Nation, a gym so exclusive that people could become members only if they had recommendations from three of its older, well-heeled clients and could cough up the money for the steep annual fee. Excessive, yes, but convenient, being that it was only a ten-minute drive from his apartment.

The place was crammed with designer-outfitted bodies doing more networking than actual exercising, like always. Ved ignored them all, walking straight to his favorite treadmill in the corner, positioned directly above the air-conditioning vent. In all his four years as a member, Ved couldn't actually remember the last time he had spoken to anyone while working out. He jammed his Bose headphones into his ears, fixed his eyes on the wall in front of him, and increased the speed as much as he could bear. Then, he increased the speed a little more. No eye contact and no chitchat. Just the way he liked it.

After an hour of running and half an hour of lifting weights so heavy he knew his arms would ache for the rest of the day, Ved was drenched in sweat but feeling happier and more alive than he had all weekend. He downed a cup of raspberry-infused water and went into the men's changing room to shower and grab his bag. While toweling off his hair, he caught sight of a familiar face in the mirror. Although the bearded guy had his head bent, Ved was sure he knew him.

Friday at the House of Maharaj. He was the one who had opened the door. The man must've felt the force of Ved's stare because he jerked his head up, making eye contact in the mirror. They both stared at each other's reflections, still not turning to face each other. His heart suddenly pounding again, Ved quickly turned and shoved his towel into his gym bag, practically running out of the room, ignoring the man as he got up and started walking toward him. He struggled to steady his breathing, and his hands shook uncontrollably as he reached up to wipe away the beads of sweat that dripped down his forehead.

This was the first time Ved had ever seen someone from Grindr in real life, the life he had outside anonymous hotel bedrooms. The guys he hooked up with were supposed to remain in a separate world, one that Ved could quickly escape. Seeing the worlds suddenly collide made him feel hopelessly exposed and out of control. This man could do anything. Make a scene, touch him, blackmail him by telling everyone in the gym about the orgy . . . things like that happened all the time. Gay men made such easy targets. Ved read the paper often enough to know stories about the unfortunate men who had been outed in a collision of their two worlds. Exactly like the kind Ved was experiencing right now.

CHAPTER 7

Walking through the office was easily the worst part of Ved's morning—even worse than his 6:00 a.m. alarm. To get to his personal office from the elevators, Ved had to walk past the large cubicles that were filled with people talking on the phone and rushing around, heads buried deep in computers.

Through it all, there was a sense of office camaraderie: people discussing an episode of a new Netflix show, making plans for the weekend, chatting simply to get out of doing work. As the son of the company's owner, Ved had always been isolated from the other employees. Sure, he'd worked his way up the corporate ladder over the years like any new recruit, just as Dad had insisted, but no one wanted to risk getting on the bad side of the person who would eventually inherit the company. There was no way around that fact. Ved's surname—not the surname of any other employee—was the one in the company name. It was no secret who would inherit Mehra Electronics one day. That had been all too clear for Ved, even from a young age. Wondering whether he truly wanted a life of monthly review reports and marketing presentations was never to be indulged. There would be no point, not after what Prem had sacrificed to build up this company, effectively guaranteeing Ved a prosperous future.

Whenever Ved walked past the cubicles, the other employees would pretend to continue whatever they were doing. Still, Ved could feel the way their eyes all turned to look at him, to scrutinize him. At least he had his own office now. The staring had been much worse when Ved worked in the cubicles right alongside the others.

As soon as Ved made it into his office, he shut the door. Sheetal had left a stack of papers on his desk with a Post-it note attached, detailing what he needed to work on.

Just as he'd settled into his plush desk chair and pulled his laptop from his briefcase, Ved received a text from his mother.

Vedu! When are you meeting Disha?

Right. He'd promised Mum that he would take Disha Kapoor out on a date. If he put off texting Disha any longer, he knew Mum would show up at his apartment later that evening, demanding that he text her right there and then. It was time. Anyway, she would be just like all the other girls, he was sure, and he could pretend to be straight for one evening.

He sent a text introducing himself and received a response instantly. The date and location were set soon after. They were to meet at Le Cinq, the fine-dining French restaurant inside a very posh mall, on Tuesday night. Of course the meal had to be dinner; lunch was far too casual. In Dolly's words, they needed to get to know each other "intimately" as soon as possible. That even though it was the prospect of an arranged marriage, he was bound to fall in love with her at first sight. From all the girls whom Dolly had made Ved meet over time, she said Disha was "simply perfect." Ved had been through this routine so many times before, simply to please his mum, that he was certain that, at the end of it, he would reject her based on some missing characteristic or other. And his mother would be left looking for *another* potential bride for her son. Although, in this case, Ved loved the restaurant with its cozy, private ambience and mouthwatering food so much that he was almost looking forward to the date. Almost.

Ved put his head down and got to work. Later, as the sky darkened outside, he heard the familiar sounds of the office shutting down for the night. He heard laughing and the sound of eager, heavy footsteps. Those people really couldn't wait to leave. Ved spun around in his chair, waiting for Sheetal to inevitably come in and ask if he wanted her to order dinner for another night hard at work in the office, just like she did every night. While he waited, his phone chimed. Probably Mum. Who else would be texting him on a Monday evening?

Ved rubbed a hand over his face and reached for his phone. The message read: send me ur dick pics. Okay. That was not what he had expected. The message was from StudGuy on Grindr. His profile picture was that of a beefy, hairy guy, and his bio simply stated "TOP."

In the world of online gay dating, "top" and "bottom" were your calling cards, your sexual preference being of paramount importance as to whether you were active or passive in bed. Ever the romantic, Ved's bio was more elaborate—"38, single, discreet, well-educated, loves to cuddle, No Strings Attached . . . but surprise me"—accompanied by a headless shot of himself back from when his belly was a little firmer. He had no "dick pics" of his own, so to speak.

Ved's phone chimed again: a dick pic from StudGuy.

Maybe Ved shouldn't have been surprised by the crudeness. After all, Grindr existed to help people hook up. Sending a dick pic was how you said a friendly hello. Ved logged on when he needed short-term companionship. Tonight, his options were sorely limited. He could work alone in the office eating Thai food with Sheetal until she went home, work alone at home eating ice cream, or have sex with StudGuy.

Ved sent him his chest shot.

As he waited for a response, Ved's phone chimed with a message from another man, JaipurVisitor, saying hi!

Ved opened JaipurVisitor's profile to a picture of a guy in his twenties wearing a white T-shirt, a black leather jacket, faded blue jeans, black Ray-Bans, and a big goofy smile that stretched across the entire screen. He was standing in front of the Jaipur Palace and giving a thumbs-up. His skin was slightly pink, as if he'd forgotten to put on sunscreen. Like Ved's profile, JaipurVisitor's said nothing about his sexual interests, only "27, single, love traveling, food, and fashion!" He was sweet, for sure.

Ved's phone chimed again, this time with a message from StudGuy: nice. Let me be ur slave, daddy. That didn't sound like something a "top" would say. Most men, especially Indian men, were still confused about the meaning of those terms. They bandied them about because everyone else did too. Now, Ved was irritated. His reply read, u sound like a bottom. Are u top or bottom?

Ved was now toggling between two chats.

JaipurVisitor: would you like to chat?

Huh? "Chat"? Which dating app did this guy think he was using?

StudGuy: versatile but for u I want to bottom.

JaipurVisitor: I'm Carlos! Right now, I live in Jaipur, but I was born in New York City.

StudGuy sent a picture of his ass, wearing only a pair of thigh-high plastic black boots. Ved quickly texted back not interested and blocked the number.

JaipurVisitor: would you like to be friends?

Just as Ved was about to respond, he heard a soft knock on his door. He lifted his head sharply. Sheetal walked in. "Ved, you in the mood for Thai food tonight? I could really go for some drunken noodles."

CHAPTER 8

The next day, Ved went to the gym again. Though he'd been too tired to consider consoling himself with another pint of ice cream when he got home the night before, he had eaten more than his fair share of dumplings in peanut sauce with copious amounts of coconut curry and rice. It was time to burn off some of the excess calories. Thankfully, Ved didn't run into anyone he knew this time. He just got on the treadmill, completed his run, and showered in peace. It was only when he got in his car to go to work that his peace was shattered by, what else, a call from his mother. Ved was sure he couldn't ignore the call. Mum knew his routine too well, always calling when he couldn't use work as an excuse to avoid speaking. He sighed and accepted the call. "Yes, Mum?"

"Oh, excuse me, *Mr. Mehra*, am I disturbing you?"

"No, Mum, of course not."

"Come now, Ved. The least you could do is show a little respect for the woman who brought you into this world."

"Sorry." Ved's tone remained just as sullen as when he'd first picked up the phone.

Her voice was sharp. "Some days, you really seem like a sullen teenager again, you know that? God, those years were awful for me."

"Why are you calling, Mum?"

"Well, if you want to be brisk with me, so be it—"

"Mum, I'm almost at the office. What is so important?"

"I'm going to pretend I didn't hear that irritation in your voice, Ved. I simply wanted to see if you were prepared for your date tonight. With Disha."

"What? What do you mean 'ready'?" Now Ved was worried.

"Oh, I don't know," she mocked. "Did you tell your secretary to buy a bouquet of flowers? Did you tell Hari to iron you a nice button-down shirt? Did you do something about all those bags under your eyes?"

Ved knew Mum wasn't going to like his response. "Um, actually I was just planning on wearing my work clothes."

Dolly scoffed. "Ved, I must ask that you put at least *a little* effort into this date. I know I don't need to remind you that the Kapoors are a very, *very* influential family. This is such a good opportunity Pamela Singh has given you. Take it seriously. You know they would be the perfect partners for diversifying *your* company. What ties do *you* have to the entertainment sector? You know how your father used to tell me all the time how we need to get Mehra Electronics associated with Bollywood? This is your opportunity, your chance to take your company to the next level. Think, Vedu: Mehra Productions. Picture the big, bright Bollywood lights!"

Ved didn't know what else to say besides, "I will." The affirmation sounded meek, even to his own ears.

Dolly said, "You'd better, Ved," and then hung up.

Ved slouched back against the seat, finally breathing normally again. It was a single date. If his mother wanted him to buy flowers and change his clothes, he could. The demands were simple enough. Dolly could have had a career. In anything. She was one of the hardest workers, one of the most creative people, Ved knew. But she didn't choose to have a career. Instead, like a good Indian wife, she had dedicated herself to her household and raising Ved, giving him all the attention her parents had been too busy working to give her. After all that she had done for him, this date seemed like a small request, minute in comparison. For now, Ved would do what he could to make sure she was happy. Later in the week, he could gently break the news about it not working out.

As soon as Ved arrived at the office, he stopped at Sheetal's desk. "Good morning, Sheetal."

She looked up from her computer screen and raised her eyebrows at seeing Ved standing before her, instead of speed walking into his office. "Hi, Ved. What's up?"

"Sheetal, you needn't act so surprised."

"No, sir. I'm not surprised at all. You stop by my desk every morning to exchange pleasantries," she teased with mock seriousness, a smile growing on her face. Why was she so goddamn happy on a Tuesday morning?

Ved kept his tone all business. "I'm not here to exchange pleasantries. I'm here to ask you to order a bouquet of flowers for me."

Sheetal smiled even wider. "Ooh, Ved. Does someone have a date tonight?"

"Something like that," Ved said and then quickly stepped into his office, shutting the door.

It took all of thirty minutes for Sheetal to knock on the door with the flowers. How she managed to knock while balancing a huge bouquet of red roses in one arm and a thick stack of contracts in the other, Ved would never know. He rushed over to help and took the heavy bouquet. "Sheetal, where on earth did you get a bouquet like this on such short notice?"

She winked. "I have my ways."

Ved set them down on the floor and moved to return to his desk, but Sheetal quickly snatched them up and turned to look at Ved incredulously. "Ved, what do you think you're doing? You can't just leave an expensive bouquet of red roses lying on the ground! Honestly, here, you just take these." She handed him the stack of contracts. "I'll take care of the flowers until the end of the day *with the love that they deserve*."

"Thank you, Sheetal." Ved truly was grateful. "What are these contracts for?"

"The new manufacturer we signed on in Delhi. I left tabs where you need to sign."

"And the legal team already looked over these?"

"Yep. They just need your stamp of approval."

Ved sat down at his desk and began signing. He expected Sheetal to take that as her cue to leave, but she stood there with her head tilted, looking at him.

He looked up again. "Sheetal, can I help you with something?"

"Ved, you really need to do something about your appearance."

Ved must've heard her wrong. *"What?"*

"I'm just saying that even your dreamy hazel eyes can't save the general haggardness of your face. Maybe go home early and take a nap? Use a cucumber face mask?" She gave him a tentative smile. "You don't have any meetings after three p.m., and you're weeks ahead of work, so . . ."

Ved relaxed and smiled back. "The nap is out of the question; however, if you can get me the face mask, I promise to use it." Maybe the lack of sleep really was catching up to him.

Right as Sheetal left, Ved's phone chimed. It was JaipurVisitor again: I'm visiting Mumbai for work soon. Maybe we can meet for coffee or a drink?

CHAPTER 9

Ved arrived early, mainly because he wanted to take a quick look at the mall's loo. The loo here was legendary in gay folklore. Before the luxury designer stores came in, the mall was a train station, making it prime cruising ground for gay men. There was no one in the loo besides the bathroom attendant—not that Ved was really interested in hooking up with some stranger in a bathroom. He couldn't even imagine how gay men in the city during the eighties and nineties had put up with looking for sex in foul-smelling train station loos, seedy massage parlors "for gents," or the promenade at the Gateway of India in the wee hours of Saturdays.

Meeting another man like yourself was a pure stroke of luck, proving that fate had dealt you a good hand. Most of the time, players lost it all in the game of chance that was gay dating in India. The guy you met could end up being a petty blackmailer, a truck driver, or an incomprehensibly horny Arab looking for a quick jolly. No long-term love. No way to find your life partner.

All of that seemed to change with the invention of online dating apps. Suddenly, the possibilities seemed endless, and the game of chance seemed much less perilous. After having been in the world of online gay dating for years, Ved wasn't so sure that he was more likely to find a future with another gay man in the era of technology. On Grindr, guys sporting pictures of a hairy, ripped body turned out to be hairless, horny eighteen-year-olds. When a man claimed he had an eight-inch monster, Ved never expected anything more than a weasel. Gigolos posed as students; students posed as experienced lovers. Flabby old men described themselves as "muscular and gym fit." The app made it easy to deceive. What was worse, it was Ved's only option. At the very least, Ved was able to find short-term companionship. Before the apps, even that had been tricky.

Ved soon stepped into the high-ceilinged, art deco interior of Le Cinq. Some said it was a carbon copy of Eleven Madison Park in New York City, though Ved thought this restaurant was much cozier, with all the tables allocated their own corners of privacy. Mild chatter surrounded the space around him. The clientele was clearly very wealthy, members of India's "rising rich" class. Men gorged themselves on caviar and truffles while reclining back in their chairs, clothed in custom-tailored Italian suits. Women were surrounded by shopping bags from Chanel, Dior, YSL, you name it. A mix of expensive colognes filled the air. There was such a variety of Birkin bags in the room that, together, they would've made a rainbow. All the faces smiled, stretched free of any indications of age. While he was dressed in his own designer clothing, Ved couldn't help but shift uneasily in his seat as he waited for Disha. The pressure his mother was putting on him that night didn't help either.

It was weird. Ved had no interest in marrying Disha, yet he knew he had to perform well on this date. If he didn't, he would risk incurring his mother's disappointment, and that was so much worse than her wrath. What kind of son would he be if he embarrassed her further than the divorce already had? What kind of son would he be if he denied her the one thing she had dedicated her life to: His future happiness? Disha couldn't be the one to say that she didn't enjoy Ved's company. After all, her aunt was the London-based busybody socialite, the "loo paper heiress," whose father had made a fortune by inventing wet wipes for the butt. To make things worse (or better, in Dolly's opinion), Disha's father was Dharmendra Kapoor, the founder and CEO of Kapoor & Co., the most prestigious investment firm in the country. He was ranked number five on the *Forbes* billionaire list and owned offices all over the world, including in London, Dubai, and Mauritius.

More than a marriage proposal, Dolly viewed this as a business deal to help Ved expand Prem's company. It didn't matter that Dolly had lost all financial stake in Mehra Electronics after the divorce. What mattered was that her son still *did* have a stake, more than a stake. Her son was to inherit the entire weight of the company, and she'd be damned if he didn't inherit a successful one that would secure prosperity and comfort for his future. And for his future family. So, just as Dolly had done everything in her power to help Prem make the company successful for Ved's future before the divorce, she'd continued doing everything in her power to reach the same goal after the divorce.

Yes, Ved had to be the one to say he didn't enjoy Disha's company. That was the only way he could get out of this situation without hurting anything, besides perhaps Dolly's pride. Oh, Dolly would certainly push back on any excuse Ved presented, but if Ved insisted he would be unhappy with Disha, then Dolly would eventually drop the issue. She always did wherever Ved's happiness was concerned. Not that there had to be anything wrong with Disha. From what he'd seen on Facebook, she seemed lovely. For all her money, she was not at all flashy. Her taste was classy. She clearly loved to pose in front of the camera in a variety of different outfits: a downcast halfway smile while wearing a gray V-neck T-shirt and ripped white jeans; a regal, tall posture while wearing a pink *salwar kameez*; a close-up that flaunted large diamond earrings and red highlights in her long, dark-brown hair. Slim, with expressive almond-shaped eyes and full lips, she was a conventional Indian beauty.

Ved looked down at his phone, where he'd prepared a list of questions to ask Disha. He had already memorized them, as if he were studying for an exam, but he needed something to do while the people all around him ate their dinners. Then, a message came in from Disha: Ved, I'll be there soon. Hope you haven't reached!

Ved quickly typed out a response: Don't worry, take your time.

She texted back: Haha! Sorry. Give me 10 minutes, followed by two smiley-face emojis.

Ved sent a thumbs-up and put his phone in his pocket. Staring at his list of questions was only making him more fidgety. Pulling the skin down from his hangnails was not helping at all. He settled for observing those around him again. Something caught his gaze. Above the left shoulder of the woman sitting at the table in front of him, Ved could see a man staring at him intently. Once he met the man's stare, Ved couldn't look away. His stomach dropped and his heart thudded painfully in his chest, somehow too fast and too slow at the same time. Was it really him—Akshay?

This was the first time Ved was seeing him after all these years. He looked worn out, as if age and unhappiness had ravaged him: wrinkles prominent along his brow line, his once-full thick clump of hair having thinned and grayed with abandon. He now had a thick black moustache straight across his upper lip and chunky framed black glasses perched on his long nose. He was dressed formally, like Ved was, with a suit jacket and a tie. Akshay gave a shaky smile and a nod. Ved wasn't sure what the expression on his own face was. He probably looked like he'd just gotten hit by a car. No, a truck. He quickly broke eye contact and buried his face in the leather-bound menu closest to him, pretending to consider his options. In his panic, Ved had reached for the wine list. Wine was Ved's least favorite type of alcohol, yet here he was reading the list like it was the most interesting piece of literature in the world. If Akshay could see what Ved was reading, he would immediately see that Ved was acting like a fool. Ved didn't know what to do. His heart was still thudding too painfully in his chest for him to calm down.

The waiter's presence with a glass of water forced Ved to lift his head out of the wine list. He could feel the burn of Akshay's gaze as he shifted his eyes to Ved in between nods of conversation and mouthfuls of food. Ved refused to return the looks, instead keeping his eyes firmly on literally anything else in the restaurant. It was clear that the woman with Akshay was his wife. She looked pretty from her side profile, with long, black flowing hair and a gold-embroidered burgundy sari. Even as he contemplated returning to the loo to throw up, Ved could see the irony of the moment. After the man he loved had broken up with him to marry a woman, Ved had arrived at the same crossroads in his life: to continue his bachelor lifestyle as it was or to make his parents happy by marrying a nice rich Indian girl. The pressure from Mum only built up every day. What Ved was doing right now made him just as bad as Akshay, as much as it pained Ved to admit. They were both hypocrites. Who was Ved to judge Akshay for taking his wife out for dinner when Ved was taking a potential wife out for dinner at the very same restaurant? What right did Ved have to judge Akshay? It was as if—

"Ved! I'm so sorry!" Ved turned and saw Disha Kapoor hurrying toward him. Before he could respond, she leaned in to hug him and sat in the opposite seat. The scent of her expensive floral perfume made Ved's nausea even worse.

CHAPTER 10

"The traffic was absolutely crazy from Malabar Hill onward because of a workers' march against rising prices. I've been stuck in my car for almost two hours, if you can believe it! God, it was mad." She paused to take a large gulp of water and to catch her breath. "I know I've kept you waiting a long time, Ved. Please forgive me?" She smiled, showing all her teeth.

Ved found himself smiling back, despite his earlier unease. "Don't be silly," he said with a dismissive wave of his hand. "There's nothing to forgive. Mumbai wouldn't be Mumbai without its traffic woes."

Disha laughed. "Yeah, that and the constant backlash against the government, right?"

Ved chuckled along with her.

Disha was laughing fully now, with her head thrown back and her mouth wide open, without any self-consciousness, even when the other people at surrounding tables turned to glare. And Ved was laughing, too, gasping for air. Mum always said his laugh made him sound like a dying man gasping for air, but in this moment, Ved couldn't care less. The joke wasn't *that* funny either. After a certain point, they were just laughing from the fact that they couldn't stop laughing.

When they finally were able to stop, Disha took a deep breath. "Well, now that we've thoroughly embarrassed ourselves, I guess we should order before someone complains and the restaurant kicks us out."

"Let's do it," Ved responded. He watched her as she perused the pages of the menu, her hand gently sweeping her falling hair over the side of one ear. She was dressed in a well-fitting white jumpsuit that fell into a deep V. On her neck, she wore a simple gold-chain necklace with a circular pendant. To Ved's surprise, she wasn't wearing any makeup.

Disha looked up at Ved and said, "Wow, all the options here look great. Reminds me of the little bistros in Paris."

"You've been to Paris?" Ved asked.

"Yep. I studied abroad there for a semester while I was at Parsons."

Ved was impressed. "That must have been an amazing experience."

"It was! I designed European-style clothes, ate my weight in croissants, and spoke French twenty-four seven. I really hope to go back soon."

"So, you speak fluent French?" Despite Prem's constant urging to learn Mandarin Chinese, since they planned on opening an office in Singapore soon, Ved only spoke Hindi and, of course, English.

"I do! It's a real passion of mine. If I ever go back to school, I would want to study the language more in depth."

"Can you say something in French?"

She gave a breathy laugh. "Sure. *J'adore le restaurant que tu as choisi, Ved. J'ai hâte de manger.*"

"Well, I recognized my name."

Disha nodded. "Mm-hmm. Understand anything else?"

"I wish. What did you say?"

"I said 'I love the restaurant you chose. I can't wait to eat.'"

Ved smiled, the nausea he felt just ten minutes earlier completely forgotten. It turned out that he didn't even need to use his prepared list of questions. "I'm glad. Since you're the French expert, maybe I should be asking you what to order?"

"No, no. You're the one who's been here before. What would you recommend?"

"The coq au vin and the duck confit are excellent, though you can't go wrong with the beef tartare."

Disha laughed again. "I would love to, but I'm a pure vegetarian. Except on Sundays. Papa loves his chicken biryani, so every Sunday afternoon, we make an exception. You go ahead. I'll live vicariously through you and keep it classic with zucchini ratatouille."

They placed their orders, and Disha leaned back in her chair. "So, Ved. Down to business. I've been hearing so many great things about you. Pamela aunty was praising you to the sky. She said you remind her of a young Colin Firth."

"I've actually never gotten Colin Firth before. People usually say I look like George Clooney."

Disha raised an eyebrow, failing to hide her smile. "I didn't realize you were so humble, but I can see why people say you look like the very dreamy Clooney. You know, if Pamela aunty were fifteen years younger, I'm convinced she would've bagged you for herself."

Ved laughed—it was strange how often that was happening tonight—and then abruptly stopped, craning his neck to look at the restaurant entrance. Akshay had gotten up from his table and left hand in hand with his wife, again making eye contact and smiling at Ved. The smile didn't seem friendly anymore, more mocking, as if letting him know he knew what he was up to. What a bastard.

Disha shifted in the ensuing awkward silence. "Ved . . . don't worry. Pamela aunty is already married, I assure you."

Ved forced a laugh and tried to bury the twinge of pain deep within his heart.

CHAPTER 11

Ved and Disha kept up steady conversation for the rest of dinner without any more awkward silences. Soon, Ved began to feel more at ease. The pain currently burying itself deeper and deeper into Ved's heart, desperately trying to dig its way out of him, was not forgotten. Rather, Disha was able to distract Ved, to make Ved smile more times than he had in the last month combined.

He learned that she loved hot yoga and made sure to do it every single evening. He learned that she loved dogs and had always wanted a puppy, but that her parents had never let her have one. He learned that she had dreams of designing Western-style wedding outfits as well as Indian ones. He learned that she designed wedding outfits because she loved to make people happy on the most special day of their lives. That, and she was a big romantic.

By the time they'd finished eating their profiteroles for dessert and had scraped the rich chocolate sauce off the plate, Ved couldn't stop himself from asking the question that had been nagging him in the back of his head all night. "Disha . . ."

She met his gaze, seeming to sense the shift in his demeanor. A crease of concern formed between her brows. "Yes?"

"I just . . ." Ved took a deep breath. "What made you choose to go out on a date with me? Out of all the other guys I'm sure have asked you?"

Disha took a long sip of her espresso, as if not sure how to word her answer. "I have to be honest, Ved, you were the guy my parents chose. They are eager for me to get married soon, and they view you as ideal marriage material."

"Oh." Ved pushed his cup of espresso away, suddenly worried. Talking with Disha that night, he'd afforded himself the luxury of forgetting how he was deceiving her. He had no serious intention of getting engaged to her, much less marrying her. Yet here she was saying that she had every intention of marrying him. *Marrying him.* The nausea was back with a vengeance.

Disha tried for a tentative smile. "I hope I didn't offend you. I really didn't mean to. In fact, when I saw your picture and heard about how successful you've been at Mehra Electronics, I couldn't believe you were still available."

"Yeah, well," Ved mumbled, staring at his shoes.

"Do you mind if I ask you the same question?"

Ved met her eyes. "Honestly?"

She nodded. "Honestly."

Ved sighed. "Same reason as you. My mother liked you and said you were perfect."

Disha started laughing. Ved was confused. "What's so funny about that?"

Disha wiped a tear from the corner of her eye. "We really are quite *bechara*, aren't we? Sitting here, as grown adults, still listening to our parents like children?"

Ved's posture relaxed—just a little. "You'd think that by now we would have the judgment to pick our life partners, but no. Our parents do know best."

"I really hope you're being sarcastic, Ved."

Ved was incredulous. "Of course I'm being sarcastic!"

"Ved. Listen. You have to change your tone. You need to *exaggerate.* Follow my lead. You'd think that by *now* we'd have the judgment to pick our *own* life partners, but noooo. Our parents really *do* know best."

"Okay, that's fair. I see your point."

Disha laughed again. Ved couldn't fathom why.

Her expression then became more serious. "I really shouldn't be the one to say that, though. When I was still at Parsons, I met this guy who had gone to Columbia, Hemant. He was twenty-five and I was nineteen. He didn't have a job. All he wanted to do was go out partying every night. For some reason, I was completely head over heels for him. When my parents found out, they were furious and threatened to bring me back to India for good if I didn't break up with him. They said all they wanted was the best for me."

"I was in a similar sort of situation. Years ago. Except, I was the one being broken up with."

"I'm sorry that had to happen to you, Ved."

Ved shook his head and raised his half-full cup of espresso. "Let's forget about the past and cheers to the happy times ahead."

Disha raised her own espresso cup. "Here's to the future."

CHAPTER 12

When Ved got home after dropping off Disha, he went straight to bed, lying down in his fleece blanket with Fubu, who curled against him, licking his arm. This "date" had been different. The other girls he'd taken out were sheltered or spoiled or stupid. Never had a girl been worldly and grounded and intelligent. As much as Ved hated to admit it, he'd had a good time with Disha, talking and laughing with an ease that had become unfamiliar in recent years. He truly didn't want to hurt her. But he knew he would have to, and that made him feel worse. Ved hugged Fubu closer.

And seeing Akshay had shaken Ved. Of course, the first time Ved sees him, after all their years apart, is when Ved is on a date with another woman. Of course. Akshay can get his sick satisfaction that he was right to submit to his parents, that Ved was going to do the exact same thing.

Ved's phone beeped. Even at 11:00 p.m., Mum couldn't wait to hear how the date had gone. Ved didn't have it in him to speak with her tonight. She would have to wait. What was worse, Ved knew deep down that Dolly had been right. Disha was as perfect as possible, everything that would make a great wife for Ved. He didn't know what he could possibly tell Mum that would get her to forget Disha and give up on marriage for him. How could he avoid making Akshay's mistake?

CHAPTER 13

Ved had true hell to pay on Wednesday morning after ignoring his mother's calls the previous night. Not only did she call at 6:00 a.m. sharp, right when she knew Ved's alarm would be going off, but she demanded that he come over for tea *and* dinner to make it up to her. Being that he was still half-asleep, Ved had agreed before later realizing as the pit in his stomach rapidly expanded that he hadn't come up with a way to avoid getting engaged to Disha yet. All day at work he was distracted, unable to complete the most menial of tasks. He ran through scenario after scenario in his head. Just like he'd done after every single one of those dates Mum had sent him on.

Scenario #1

Ved: "Hello, Mum."

Dolly: "Vedu! I'm so glad you're finally here for dinner. I prepared all your favorites."

Ved: "Thanks."

Dolly: "So, I spoke to Disha's parents, beta, and since the date went so well, we have already started preparations for the party!"

Ved: "What party?"

Dolly: "Your engagement party, silly! You're engaged to Disha."

Ved: "Don't I have any say in this?"
Dolly: "No, don't be silly."

Scenario #2

Ved: "Mum, how are you?"
Dolly: "Fine, fine."
Ved: "So . . ."
Dolly: "No, Vedu. Listen to me. You don't need to get married to Disha. I don't want to force anything onto you. Be free."
Ved: "Really?"

Scenario #3

Ved: "Mum, I can't get engaged to Disha."
Dolly: "What do you mean you can't? Of course you can."
Ved: "No, Mum, I can't. I'm gay."
Dolly: "What?"
Ved: "I'm gay!"

CHAPTER 14

For the first time in years, Ved left the office at 5:00 p.m., just like all the other employees.

Sheetal gasped so loudly that everyone turned to watch Ved shuffle his way awkwardly into the elevator, pretending to use his phone. For once, he didn't have the elevator all to himself.

The day had gone to waste. He hadn't completed any real work, and he still hadn't figured out what he should tell Dolly. He could feel a tension headache developing right between his two eyes. When he got in the car, he sank back into the plush leather seats, closed his eyes, and massaged his temples. The company driver (who often drove him to and from work) seemed shocked that Ved had left work so early as well. At least he did a better job hiding his surprise than Sheetal had. Ved's phone beeped, making him sit upright. It was a Twitter alert from *The Times of India*: Activists Hopeful of 377 Being Scrapped Very Soon. Ved scrolled through the feed, where several prominent names, gay and otherwise, had commented on why they were optimistic about the draconian law being removed. The tension he had been feeling earlier suddenly dissipated, and Ved rested his head back calmly. His phone beeped again. It was a message from JaipurVisitor. How are you today?

What was with this idiot? Why did he keep messaging Ved? Maybe Ved should respond to him. Just to get him off his back, of course. Ved replied, This is a hookup app! Most guys here only ask for dick pics.

Ved received a response immediately.

JaipurVisitor: ha ha ha, don't worry. I'm not.

Ved thought for a second. Ok, bye then.

JaipurVisitor: LOL.

Before Ved could respond, another message came in. What's the weather like in Mumbai? It's so hot here.

Ved smiled: Is that your idea of flirting? *Hint*

JaipurVisitor: LOL. You're cheeky.

Ved smiled wider, enjoying the banter even though it was with a complete stranger. This guy got his humor. Pity, he'd probably never meet him in reality: Yes. I have nice cheeks. *Hint again*

Ved couldn't recognize himself. The last time he'd flirted with anyone like this had been four years ago. Why was he entertaining this guy anyway? What a waste of time. JaipurVisitor wasn't even looking to hook up. But when JaipurVisitor texted wow. Consider the hint noted, Ved texted him back. In fact, Ved texted JaipurVisitor back and forth during the entire car ride to Dolly's house in Worli.

CHAPTER 15

Dolly ran to meet Ved at his car right when he pulled up to her apartment. "Vedu, it's about time you came here to visit me!"

"I know, Mum." Ved reached out to hug her and kissed her cheek.

"Come let's sit, beta. I want to hear all about your date with the lovely Disha."

He knew that entertaining in her two-bedroom in the not-so-nouveau-riche part of Mumbai was a blow to Mum's pride. Having grown up middle class, it was only after her father had made a fortune in stock investments during the late seventies that her family was able to move from their modest apartment to an elite Delhi gated community, Maharani Bagh. Mum had never looked back after that and married higher, into the upper class. During her marriage, gaudy mansions and luxury cars were the norm, and she did everything to escape her days working part-time as a saleswoman in a fashion boutique. That is, until now. Now, after the divorce, she had returned, somewhat, to her middle-class life before marriage.

She led Ved inside to a sitting room and gestured to a hard-edged gray couch that only she could ever find comfortable. As soon as he sat down, she handed him a cup of steaming chai and a plate of freshly fried onion pakoras, still sizzling from the hot oil.

"Mum, you didn't have to make all this for me. Thank you."

She responded, "It's nice to see you've learned some respect," though the way she smiled with pride showed Ved how much she appreciated the compliment. "So," she continued, "how did you like her?"

Ved panicked and took a big gulp of chai. It scorched his throat and likely killed a few dozen taste buds; anything was better than having to talk right now. He then shoved a pakora into his mouth, further burning his tongue. "Wow. These are so delicious. You should open a restaurant."

"Ved." She reached out and tilted Ved's chin up so that he would meet her eyes. "How did you like her?"

"She is great." If Ved's hands had been free, he would've slapped his forehead. He was being so stupid. That was the absolute last thing he should've said!

"That's wonderful to hear! Remember what a great business opportunity this can be, beta. You could be heading Mehra Productions. *You*. Ved Mehra. Everyone in Bollywood would come knocking at your door; all the leading actors and actresses will want to be your friend . . . just imagine it! You know Disha's father, Dharmendra Kapoor, is one of the most influential Indians in the city. And Kapoor & Co. is the perfect partner for a prestigious technology company like Mehra Electronics. They own large fancy offices all over the world, Vedu. They have the biggest connections; all the politicians are in their pocket. That would be so helpful for you in setting up the Bollywood division . . . imagine, Priyanka Chopra coming over to your house for lunch. You better call me then, *haan*!"

Ved found it hard to take his mother seriously when she made such statements. He laughed and said, "*Dollyji*, we have enough of our own money, not to mention connections. Even if we don't start a new company, it's not like we're going to be paupers begging on the road. We *also* have offices in London and Dubai, in case you've forgotten. Don't make this out to be *such* a big deal. Please."

"So what, haan? You think that's enough? I want you to have the best. You should be CEO. It's about time, Vedu; you're so hardworking and more than qualified. I know you have the talent to take this company in a new direction, something to shake up the business world the way no other CEO has done before." Her tone remained sincere as she lightly tapped Ved on his hand. When Ved didn't respond, she continued, "Darling, why don't you take her out on a few more dates, see whether you think you two should get engaged."

None of his scenarios had predicted this. He knew of too many couples, even some of his own college buddies, whose marriages had been arranged by their parents after only a single date. It seemed absurd, but they had meekly gone along with their parents' wishes to keep them happy. With Dolly's enthusiasm about the business deal, Ved feared that Dharmendra Kapoor would walk into the room with his wife and Disha in tow, ready to get his daughter engaged.

Ved took a deep breath in, trying not to let too much hope into his voice. "Um, so you're not making me get engaged today?"

"Making you get engaged *today*? Honestly, Vedu, what century do you think this is?"

CHAPTER 16

So Ved continued going out on dates with Disha over the next several weeks, and it wasn't nearly as bad as he thought it would be. He actually had just as great of a time as he'd had on their first date. She was honest and ambitious. While she came from a traditional Indian background, there was nothing closed minded about her. Her years living abroad had clearly expanded her outlook, and she was knowledgeable enough to debate Ved on any topic, from politics to art, even though it was usually scandalous Bollywood gossip in the papers that they both laughed over, or her love of fashion, which she could go on for hours about. Ved really felt like he could talk to her about anything, because she was open and not judgmental. In that sense, Disha reminded him of Anaita.

Anaita was Ved's best friend growing up, his only friend, if he was being honest with himself. They used to do everything together—going to the movies, studying, drinking vodka for the first time. Now that Anaita had married that American guy, Steve, she lived in San Francisco, and Ved rarely spoke to her anymore. With Disha, Ved felt the same comfort, like he could hang out with her forever and never get bored.

He just wished he didn't have to lie to her.

———

JaipurVisitor: Wow! Can you believe it reached 80° today in Jaipur? It's February!

Ved: I believe it. India is known for her heat . . . and erratic weather.

JaipurVisitor: I didn't realize I would need to wear sunblock during the winter. I was the only idiot who didn't bring any.

JaipurVisitor: Has anyone told you that you look like George Clooney? The resemblance is uncanny!

Ved: You know, I do get that a lot.

Ved: I don't know whether it's to compliment my looks or point out how I'm getting older.

JaipurVisitor: Please. George Clooney is just as hot today as he was a decade ago.

CHAPTER 17

A couple of days later, Ved's phone rang while he was at the gym. For once, he was getting a phone call from someone other than his mother. It was Disha asking if he would join her for dinner that night. "My treat," she insisted. "I owe you for the lovely Indian dinner earlier this week."

They met at a trendy Asian fusion restaurant where all patrons were served from a tasting menu, curated specifically for the night by some celebrity chef. Apparently, the place had come highly recommended from Pamela aunty. Ved arrived thirty minutes early and was mortified to see Disha had beat him there. She stood when he found her table and reached out to hug him. Ved patted her on the back and moved away quickly, pulling out his chair with more force than strictly necessary. Disha looked confused, but she covered up her concern with a bright smile. "I felt so bad about keeping you waiting the other night that I knew I had to arrive early today." She had a habit of being late pretty much every time they had dinner together.

Ved refilled Disha's glass from the bottle of wine on the table. "Not at all. Just because I'm obsessively early everywhere doesn't mean you have to be."

She laughed. "You know, my father always says, 'If you're not five minutes early, you're late.'" The way she'd deepened her voice while quoting her father made Ved smile. "For some reason, I always end up being five minutes late everywhere I go, but maybe you'll be a good influence on me," Disha added with a wink.

As it turned out, the exorbitant prices did not reflect the quality of the food. The portions were so small that you would need a microscope to see them properly. When Disha signed the bill (despite Ved's many objections), her stomach gave a loud growl. She pressed her hand against it and snorted. "Sorry! I'm still starving. I feel like I didn't eat anything!"

Ved threw back his head and laughed. "Me too!"

She stood up. "Come on, then. I know a great kulfi stand around the corner, and I promise you that Pamela aunty wouldn't be caught dead there."

JaipurVisitor: You're so lucky to be in Mumbai.

Ved: Why's that?

JaipurVisitor: There is absolutely no nightlife here! No gay scene whatsoever.

Ved: Come on. I'm sure that's not true. I'm sure things will change if Section 377 gets scrapped. You know about that, right?

JaipurVisitor: Yeah, read about it online. That law is archaic for god's sake. There'll never be a gay club in India at that rate. No wonder poor me stuck at home. While you're probably living it up right now in the big city.

Ved: You'd be surprised.

CHAPTER 18

The next morning, Ved decided to call Disha. She answered on his second try. "Hi, Ved! What's up?"

"Hi, Disha. I'm just calling to thank you for dinner last night. It was very generous of you."

"Nonsense. I had a great time with you."

"I'm glad, so—"

Disha suddenly gasped, cutting Ved off. "Oh shit."

"What? What happened?"

He heard her typing quickly on her phone's keyboard. "Ugh, just give me a second."

After a minute she started speaking again, "Sorry, Ved. I just had a work emergency. You remember that photo shoot I had scheduled for the big bridal magazine today?"

"Yes, of course."

"Well, the male model I hired just canceled. The shoot is in four hours, and now I have no one to model the groom's clothing." All the chipperness had been sucked out of her tone.

Ved hated hearing Disha sound so deflated, so even though he knew he would regret it, he said, "Could I help?"

"What do you mean?"

"Could I model the groom's clothing?" he asked, conflicted between wanting to make her happy and knowing he had no idea what the hell to do. He had grown close to her and wanted to help her in whatever way he could. Even at the expense of making a fool out of himself.

"Do you really mean it, Ved?" Disha's enthusiasm was back in full force.

"Of course. I'd be happy to, just for you." Modeling clothes actually sounded like a nightmare, but this was such a big opportunity for Disha. She deserved to have a successful photo shoot. If it was in his power to help, he should.

"Thank you so, so, so much! I'll pick you up from the office at eleven a.m. Text me your address."

When Ved met Disha outside the building, she removed her sunglasses and waved him into the car. The back seat was filled with so many garment bags that Ved and Disha were pressed against each other. She turned as well as she could to look him in the eye. "Thank you, Ved." She then reached forward and kissed him gently on the cheek. "I really appreciate it."

Ved flinched uncontrollably and pressed himself against the garment bags to put some distance between himself and Disha. Though she looked troubled, Disha didn't say anything about how strangely Ved had reacted.

———

JaipurVisitor: I had the most amazing street food today! Here's a picture.

Ved: Ugh, I wish I could eat that. I haven't had proper pav bhaji in years.

JaipurVisitor sent another picture.

Ved: Yeah, rub it in. Here's a picture of my lunch.

JaipurVisitor: Is that a kale salad?

Ved: Yep.

JaipurVisitor: Color me envious.

Ved: Yeah, yeah.

CHAPTER 19

When Ved stepped back into his office after a board meeting the next afternoon, his phone rang. It was Disha. She sounded panicked, and he could barely hear her over all the commotion in the background.

"Ved! Quickly! Red or yellow? Which do you prefer?"

"What?"

She sighed. "Ved. Listen. I'm at Zara and picking up a halter! Which color do you prefer?"

"Umm . . ."

"I'm next in the checkout line!"

"But you look good in all the colors."

"Ved!"

———

JaipurVisitor: hey! I have the day off. Any sightseeing recommendations?

Ved: I've actually never been to Jaipur, so I can't help.

JaipurVisitor: you've NEVER been to Jaipur? Even though you live so close?

Ved: weren't you the one complaining to me about Jaipur the other day?

JaipurVisitor: oh, who cares about the nightlife? It is truly the most beautiful, peaceful place I've ever visited.

Ved: Oh BTW, I just added "model" to my resume.

JaipurVisitor: WHAT. A GQ shoot? Are you in the next issue?

Ved: I wish. Something more lowkey as a favor for a friend, though I was draped in equally fancy designer clothes. To be honest, I had no clue what I was doing but kept smiling at the photographer because he was cute. I even got his number *wink*

JaipurVisitor: LOLOL.

———

Ved and Disha saw each other every day the next week. Ved had even met Disha's parents when he went over to her house for Saturday-night dinner. On Sunday night, they met at Disha's favorite spot in the whole city, a restaurant dedicated entirely to chocolate desserts. While Ved dug into his lava cake, Disha cut her Nutella crepe into smaller and smaller pieces without taking a single bite. Ved set down his spoon. "Disha, what's wrong?"

She looked up and blinked, just coming back to the present moment. "No, nothing, Ved. Don't worry. This week has been great. Just great." She returned to her cutting.

Ved raised his eyebrows. He knew something was up. "Disha."

She looked up again, a desperate look in her eyes. "What?"

Ved tried to be gentle. "Tell me what's bothering you."

When she didn't respond, he added, "Please."

"It's just . . . everything is moving so fast." Her eyes turned misty. "We barely even know each other, and our parents expect us to get engaged. I know they do; otherwise we wouldn't even be going out so often."

"Disha, that's not true at all. I'm taking you out because I enjoy your company."

She scoffed and leaned forward. "Ved, what are you looking for in a life partner?"

The heaviness of the words pressed the guilt of lying farther down on Ved's chest, crushing his lungs. He paused to think. What *was* he looking for in a life partner? What could he say? Anything he said would make him sound like a fraud. Disha didn't meet the most basic qualification for being Ved's life partner: someone he was physically attracted to.

Disha leaned in closer. "Ved?" Her tone had turned hard.

Ved leaned back. "Trust and honesty, I guess . . . and love. Of course, love."

Disha shook her head, skepticism written all across her face. "Trust and honesty? Really, Ved?"

Now Ved was irritated too. "Yes, *really*, Disha."

"Well, if that is true, then explain to me why I get the sense that you're lying to me?"

"What?" How did she know? How much did she know?

She looked directly into his eyes. "Why do you get uncomfortable every time I try to hold your hand or hug you or kiss your cheek? Why am I the only one who speaks about marriage? Why do you look panicked every time our conversation shifts toward marriage? Why are you here if you don't want to marry me?"

Ved took her hand and squeezed it. She snatched it back. "Answer me, Ved."

He sighed. "Marriage is . . . a big step, and I never intended to let my parents have a role in choosing who I would marry. This is not what I expected. This is not what I wanted."

"So, what do you want, then?"

"I don't know." Ved felt his throat close around the words.

The silence dragged on and their desserts sat cold, long since forgotten. Finally, Disha took Ved's hand and returned the squeeze from earlier. "Sorry. I shouldn't have released my anxiety onto you. That wasn't fair. This relationship is so new and—"

"No," Ved cut in, "I'm the one who should be apologizing. I love spending time with you. Truly. I shouldn't be wasting your time when there are so many other guys who would marry you in a heartbeat. You deserve better."

She squeezed his hand again and only said, "I really love spending time with you too."

———

JaipurVisitor: So I ended up visiting the Hawa Mahal the other day. It was amazing!

JaipurVisitor sent a picture.

JaipurVisitor: Hello?

JaipurVisitor: You there?

CHAPTER 20

Ved trudged home Monday night and crawled onto the couch, still wearing his full suit. Fubu rested on top of his chest, fast asleep. This was the first night in a week back at his apartment after late nights at work followed by being out with Disha. The transition of having stone silence for company was jarring. Suddenly, Ved found himself staring at the park bench visible in the window again. Why wasn't he past a four-year-old relationship yet? Why was he feeling so deeply alone again? Why did he feel like running over to Akshay's house and shouting, "Screw it! Let's come out and run away together!" Akshay was married, for God's sake. He closed his eyes and tried to breathe. Fake marriage, lies, one-night stands, regrets— a lifetime of misery. That was the only outcome Ved could see from this whole situation. He would never be able to get out of this situation. *Never.* He didn't even want to think about what his wedding night would be like. How would he be expected to perform? How would he be expected to produce children?

Ved forced himself to breathe in deeper, straining until he felt his chest burn. In and out. In and out. He might've even had a chance at calming down if it weren't for the banging that started at the front door.

At first, Ved tried to ignore it, hoping Hari would come see who it was. It soon became clear that Hari was too preoccupied in the kitchen to do so. Ved pushed himself up, joints creaking, and slouched toward the door. He opened it to find his mother. Who else would it have been? Ved's posture straightened immediately. "Mum! What are you doing here?"

She ignored him and walked in, seating herself in the chair across from the couch. "Please sit, Ved." Her tone was devoid of emotion. That could only mean one thing—she was absolutely furious.

Ved walked slowly over to the couch. "Mum, whatever Disha's parents told you, I promise—"

"First explain to me how you knew I came here to discuss Disha." Her tone remained even.

"I just—"

"Didn't you promise me that you would make an effort with this girl?"

"Yes, but—"

"So, what is this I'm hearing about you not knowing what you want?"

"Mum—"

Her voice rose. "Tell me why I'm hearing this!"

Ved reached across the coffee table and took her hand. It was trembling. "Mum, please just let me speak."

She remained silent.

"Mum, please. Everything was moving so fast."

She slouched back and clutched Ved's hand tight. "What *do* you want, Ved?" Now she only sounded defeated.

Ved paused, unsure how to respond. Now was his chance. He should come out to Mum. He *wanted* to come out to her, but he held himself back, not willing to force her to endure the consequences of that truth. So all Ved said, his voice shaking, was, "I want what everyone in the world wants, Mum. I want to be happy."

"I want you to be happy too."

"I know."

She squeezed his hand tighter. "That's all I've ever wanted."

"I know."

"You are my only son. My only child."

Ved nodded, swallowing the words he wanted to say.

She continued, "I won't be around for much longer." When Ved opened his mouth to protest, she shook her head. "No, beta, I know I won't be. I just want to know that you're settled, that you're happy, while I still can. You deserve to be happy. So very happy."

Ved was shocked to see tears collecting in Dolly's eyes. She stood up and swiped a hasty hand over her eyes. "Sorry, beta. You must excuse me."

It was the first time Ved could ever remember seeing Mum get so emotional with him, and the only reason for it was because she wanted the best for *him*. That was all she had ever wanted, Ved realized, and look at how he had treated her for it. Like an annoyance. Ved stood up and hugged her, holding on for a few moments. "No, Mum, I'm sorry. Please sit back down. Let's finish talking about this."

CHAPTER 21

As was customary with Indian traditions, after consulting individual family astrologers to ensure that the "natal charts" or *kundlis* of both Ved and Disha matched perfectly, and that their charts were compatible with the Janam Rashi (moon sign) and Nakshatra (constellation) in alignment, both families were assured that theirs would be a happy union, and the Mehra and Kapoor families set the date for the engagement party. March first. Just three weeks from today. Ved had tried to tell Dolly he couldn't marry Disha. He'd really tried, but . . . he couldn't let her down. Not like that. There was still time. He could still find some way of postponing the engagement with Disha. At least that's what Ved told himself. And that's what Ved repeated to himself over and over and over again, whenever what he'd agreed to resurfaced in his mind. If he kept repeating this to himself, he was bound to believe it.

CHAPTER 22

Ved had stopped sleeping over the past several days. The last time he'd slept for a consecutive seven hours was before Dolly had come over unannounced. Since then, he had dozed in short spurts, jolted awake by stress dreams that left him trembling and drenched in sweat. The bags under his eyes had darkened, and not even Sheetal's fancy cucumber face masks could save his haggard appearance.

Disha said she was tired of going out on dates, that since they were as good as engaged, they might as well meet at each other's houses now. So, when she suggested that she bring dinner over tonight for him and his father, Ved agreed. After their engagement was announced, it was like Disha had forgotten completely about their conversation at the chocolate restaurant. She never showed any sort of anger or irritation again. She remained enthusiastic and funny. All the time.

Ved paced before the door, anxious for her to arrive. Prem sat on the couch, typing steadily on his laptop, the very picture of serenity. His calmness, his put-togetherness, made Ved pace even faster, back and forth across the foyer. Suddenly, Prem looked up, examining Ved through his glasses. It was weird enough as it was to see Prem out of his study. The staring wasn't helping. He cleared his throat and said, "How is everything, Ved?" His words were cursory, his tone casual.

Ved was in no mood to entertain a conversation right now. "Work is fine. All under control." He continued pacing.

"No, son. I mean with Disha. How is everything?" This time, his question sounded different. His voice didn't hold mere curiosity. It held concern.

"Fine. Fine," Ved said quickly. He wasn't remotely interested in having a heart-to-heart about Disha. It was what it was, and talking about how he felt so trapped he could hardly breathe wouldn't change his decision.

Prem closed his laptop. "Oh?"

"Yes. She's very excited to be meeting you," Ved said, making sure to keep his tone distant.

Prem grunted and reopened his laptop. "Okay, son."

Disha finally arrived five minutes late, her arms filled with bags of food. There had been a family *puja* at her place, a holy ceremony of prayers and blessings with their priest for the good news, and her forehead sported a traditional red dot. Her hands were covered with ornate gold bangles, and around her neck was a beautifully carved Indian gold necklace, something that her mother had made her wear after the puja. It was an heirloom that her mother's mother had passed down to her, or so Disha told him. Ved took the bags from her so that she could take off her shoes. Prem stood up and embraced her. "Disha, my darling. I didn't know to expect a feast tonight."

Disha laughed. "It's nothing, Mr. Mehra." She offered him some holy offerings of *prasad* that had been prayed over, and then did the same to Ved with a smile.

"Mr. Mehra? Disha, you needn't be so formal with me. You are like my daughter now."

What? Ved was so shaken by the ease of their conversation that he just stood still, even as Disha gently pulled the bags out of his hands. Even as she carried them into the kitchen, the door swinging shut behind her. Prem laid a hand on Ved's shoulder, startling him.

He waited until Ved stopped shaking before speaking. "What's wrong, Vedu?"

The last time Prem had asked Ved that question was after Akshay broke up with him.

Ved didn't come out to his family, but during those days, he wanted to more than anything. Despite the anxiety, the waves of nausea, that overtook him at the thought of coming out, he knew that once he spat it out, he could finally be free. No more constraints, no more hiding. Akshay was the only relationship he had ever had, a first love, even though it had come much later in his life than it had with others. Ved was convinced that Akshay was his future, that he was Akshay's future. He felt as if something had died within him, and as the days went on, it rotted, killing Ved from the inside. Slowly.

He became listless at work, spinning around his chair until he became dizzy, pausing to let the room come back into focus, and then beginning to spin again. Stacks of paper piled higher each day. His mind just couldn't focus. Prem was able to sense that something was deeply wrong. He approached Ved and came into his office, which he never did. He only ever ventured out of his office for board meetings. Until that day.

He stood there, silently observing Ved spin, before gently reaching forward to squeeze Ved's shoulder. He left his hand there. "What's wrong, Vedu? You look overworked," he said. "Why don't you take a holiday? Go clear your mind of its burdens somewhere abroad, like the Maldives or the Bahamas. It will do you good."

Ved looked up at him then, eyes ringed in dark circles, face unshaven, clothes wrinkled.

"Sometimes we all need some time, Vedu. To relax. To recharge ourselves."

Ved's voice was scratchy, barely a whisper. "It's not about work, Dad."

"I know, son. That's what worries me, because if it were work, I could fix it for you."

Ved mustered up his courage. "Dad . . . I have to tell you something . . ."

Prem nodded with encouragement.

"I . . ." Tears filled Ved's eyes. "I'm not the person . . . I'm not the person who you think I am."

Prem just continued looking at Ved. "I want you to be who you are." He smiled. "Your mother and I love you. No matter what. Remember that, Vedu. You are our greatest blessing."

When Ved reached out to hug his father, Prem hugged him back. That was when Ved realized that he could rely on Prem. Yes, their inter-actions were often distant, both at the office and at home, but Prem *did* love Ved. He did. And Ved could rely on him. Ved wasn't ready to tell his father everything yet. When he was ready, though, Prem would be supportive. Ved knew it.

They had stayed like that for a long time.

Just like after his breakup with Akshay, Ved longed to come out to his father, to finally find the strength to lift the massive weight off his chest, but right when he was opening his mouth to speak, Disha burst out of the kitchen, balancing several steaming plates, with Hari close behind. Ved continued looking his father in the eyes and forced a smile. "Nothing. Nothing is wrong at all."

CHAPTER 23

The truth was, Ved didn't particularly like the way Disha's cook made chicken biryani, swimming in oil. Every bite was laden with potatoes, and despite the copious amounts of cinnamon, it sorely lacked salt. However, this specific dish had become the staple "love" of Ved's life after he'd made the mistake of praising it at his dinner with Disha's parents. Since then, Disha's driver dropped off the biryani once every three days. Ved had hoped that, since Disha was bringing over the food, he could avoid the biryani tonight. No such luck.

As she laid out the food on the table, Disha provided Hari with dietary suggestions to improve Ved's health.

"Hari, remember to use water to thin out the *dal*, instead of oil, and make sure to serve it with quinoa."

"Hari, it's important that if you don't have quinoa, you use brown rice. Use white rice at a maximum of twice a week."

"Make sure to serve Ved multigrain toast in the mornings. It's more nutritious than whole wheat or white."

It was like Disha had transformed when she stepped into that kitchen, going into wife mode, with Hari as her comrade. And Hari had accepted her ascendance to the throne with a smile, eager to have a woman at home who could make Ved happy.

She looked up to see Ved and Prem watching her. "Come on, guys! The food's getting cold."

She made sure they'd sat down and then reached over to serve them both. Ved and Prem were so busy eating that Disha talked enough to fill the silence. "I know you've never had this chicken biryani, but I'm sure Ved has told you it's his favorite. It's Papa's favorite too. I had the cook make this batch specifically for Ved, and it was hard to keep Papa from eating it before I came over here."

Prem looked pointedly at Ved and responded, "It smells delicious, Disha."

Ved couldn't stomach more than a few bites.

CHAPTER 24

On Friday morning, for once, Ved didn't leap out of his bed when his alarm rang. Instead, he lay there, unable to force himself to move. He reached, instead, for his phone. The gym would have to wait.

Ved had never understood social media and had created an account simply because all his friends in college had one. It had helped him later on boast about his achievements with work and take solace in the requisite "likes," though he knew that feeling was short-lived. The more well known he got in business circles, the more friend requests came his way, and even though he had 1,750 Facebook friends, he only knew a handful of them in real life. Why should he care about their vacations? About their kids or their pets or their parties or their new iPhones? They all looked so happy. Smiles blurred across the screen as Ved stared blankly, scrolling up and down. Nothing was registering in his brain. Nothing until he saw that Disha had uploaded a photo album. One that celebrated the engagement. Ved sat up so fast that his head slammed against the headboard.

The album, "The Honeymoon Phase," featured pictures of them from the past two weeks. The night they went mini golfing. Them wearing 3D glasses at the IMAX movie theater. Eating avocado salads for lunch in Ved's office. All their dates were right there, for anyone to see. Both of their faces were smiling, their eyes sparkling. They looked like a real couple. They looked so happy.

Ved couldn't stand it anymore. He didn't really have a reason to be angry with Disha. He'd agreed to let her take the pictures. What did he think she would do with them? Keep them in her camera roll forever? Of course not. It made sense for her to share their joy with others. Ved just couldn't understand how he looked so happy in those pictures when he felt so miserable right now. When had this all happened? The promise he had made to himself, to take Disha out on a single date—what happened to that plan? When did Ved lose control?

He shut the Facebook app and noticed four unread messages from JaipurVisitor on Grindr. Not that it mattered anymore. Ved turned off his phone and tried to go back to sleep.

———

That same evening, Ved had plans to go out with Disha. It was Valentine's Day, after all. This time, they were dining at Olive, the famous Bandra café, crammed with its celebrity brigade. It was a Friday night, and the restaurant was packed with expats and party people. Disha had called in a favor with one of her wealthier clients to get them a reservation. Music thudded and excited chatter filled the room.

"How was your day, Disha?"

Disha groaned. "Oh, come on! You can do better than that?"

Ved furrowed his brows. "What do you mean? I thought that was a perfectly pleasant conversation topic to kick off the night."

"Sure, if there's nothing more interesting to talk about."

Ved put a hand up to his chest in mock shock. "And you think there are more interesting things to talk about than the quality of our days?"

Disha rolled her eyes. "Okay, I'm picking the conversation topic. Let me see . . ." She looked around the room. "Got it. What do you think of this music?"

"This club music?"

"Uh-huh." Disha nodded.

"I think it's god-awful."

"Right answer." Disha smiled. "I can't believe I never asked you what kind of music you *do* enjoy listening to."

Ved considered. "I don't have a specific genre that I prefer over others."

"That's impossible." Disha shook her head in disbelief. "You surely have one genre that you listen to more than others."

"Not that I can think of."

Disha narrowed her eyes. "Country?"

Ved shrugged. "Occasionally."

"K-pop?"

"When I'm in the mood."

"Opera?"

"Of course. No day is complete without it."

Disha threw back her head with her classically boisterous laughter, drawing the eyes of other patrons.

"Okay"—Ved leaned forward—"now your turn."

Disha leaned forward too. "I almost exclusively listen to heavy metal."

Ved gasped. "You do not."

Disha nodded. "There's something about the passion, the hyperbole of emotion, that makes heavy metal . . . exciting. Every song is a show, something that's performed for the listener."

Ved just stared at Disha, dumbstruck.

Disha's smile stretched into an outright grin. "Why so surprised?"

"Because you're—well, I guess—"

"I know it's the last thing people expect from me, considering that I spend my life making dresses for weddings."

"I guess I'm going to have to start listening to heavy metal. Any recommendations?"

By the time drinks arrived, Ved was thoroughly educated in the importance of heavy metal music as an art form and could name about twenty "turning point" songs in the genre.

"Okay," Disha said, "enough about heavy metal music. Let's pick a new conversation topic."

"Shoot."

"Well," Disha began, her voice playful, "you never told me what happened when my father called you into his study the other day?"

Ved laughed. "Don't remind me!"

Disha leaned forward. "Oh, now you've got to tell me what happened."

"Well, he sat me down in front of his desk."

"Uh-huh."

"He offered me a whiskey."

"He does that with everyone."

"Yes, and then . . ." Ved paused for dramatic effect.

"Ved!"

"*Then* . . ." Now Ved stretched the word even longer. "He pulled out a machine gun and described what he would do to me if I hurt you."

"That is not what he did!"

Ved laughed again. "You're right. It's not."

"Pray tell, then, what really *did* happen?"

Now Ved paused, the good humor vanished from his face.

As much fun as he had teasing Disha, his conversation with Disha's father was, to put it in the mildest terms, something he did not care to relive.

Ved had arrived at Disha's house that night dressed in a full suit with two bouquets of flowers: one for Disha and one for her mother, Alia. Despite the waves of nausea threatening to make him spew up his lunch from hours earlier, he did his best to emulate the casual, cool Ved he was with important business clients.

For all of Ved's anxiety, the dinner itself turned out to be unremarkable. In between bites of chicken biryani and an array of other dishes, Ved politely answered questions about his daily routine and work life. Sure, the conversation wasn't particularly interesting, but it was fine. No questions that Ved didn't anticipate, and Disha's enthusiasm for answering questions about wedding plans she was making with Dolly saved Ved from showing just how detached he was from the whole process. As the dessert plates were being cleared, Ved finally felt himself starting to relax. It seemed like he would be able to go home without any uncomfortable one-on-one conversations or deeper group conversation. But at that exact moment when Ved finally relaxed into his chair, Disha's father, Dharmendra, stood up and shot Alia a look—a look that made Alia immediately stand up and excuse both herself and her daughter. As she was being dragged out of the room, Disha turned back to Ved, mouthing "Good luck," while Ved slowly stood up, trying to delay the inevitable. He'd seen enough rom-coms to know what was coming. This was the infamous "You hurt my baby girl and you're *dead*" talk, straight out of a Hollywood film.

"Please follow me to my office, Ved," Dharmendra said, gesturing in front of him. Sure, it sounded like a polite request, but Dharmendra's tone held no warmth. Make no mistake, Ved had been *ordered* to go to Dharmendra's office.

Because he couldn't do anything else, Ved did follow Dharmendra into the office, all his previous nausea back with a vengeance. He really shouldn't have eaten the extra jalebi for dessert.

After walking through a long empty hallway, they entered a huge office, almost as big as the dining room they had just been in.

Without another word, Dharmendra pulled out one of the chairs in front of his desk for Ved and began fixing himself a whiskey. Dharmendra turned back to Ved, his tone still hard. "Joining me for a nightcap, Ved?"

Ved swallowed, trying to regain his composure. "Yes, thank you." He didn't think he could stand to drink anything, much less hard liquor, though Ved knew what he wanted wasn't really important at this moment.

With his back still turned to Ved, Dharmendra removed a tray of ice from a mini freezer in the corner. The silence in the dining room–size office was vast, and each clink of the ice cube hitting the glass reverberated like a clap of thunder: *clink, clink, clink.*

Naturally, this did nothing to ease the sense of doom rapidly rising in Ved.

After what felt like an eternity, Dharmendra turned to face Ved, handed him a drink, and took a seat behind his desk. Dharmendra's chair was so wide that it dwarfed his five-foot-ten frame. Ved clutched his glass tightly, waiting for Dharmendra to just ask his questions and get this whole ordeal over with.

Dharmendra, oblivious to Ved's renewed tension, lounged in his chair, taking time to savor his whiskey. When there were only a few sips left in his glass, he finally met Ved's gaze directly.

"Ved. There are a few . . . matters we need to address before you marry my daughter. Are you amenable to having this discussion?"

Ved swallowed again, his throat dry. "Of course."

"My daughter seems taken with you."

"Oh, I'm sure she—"

"Did I ask you a question?" Dharmendra cut in, his tone as hard and as even as ever.

Ved broke eye contact, looking down at his glass. So, this was how it was going to be. Dharmendra wanted to flex his dominance, fine.

Fine. Ved would let him. Still sitting up perfectly straight, Ved drank about half his whiskey in one go and then set his glass back on the desk with a soft thud.

"As I was saying." Dharmendra paused to clear his throat. "My daughter has expressed her strong desire to marry you. Why she chose you out of all her other prospects, I cannot say. As long as you accept your responsibilities as the man of this relationship, as long as you accept your role as a husband *fully*, I will be satisfied. For Disha, I would ask nothing less."

Dharmendra paused here, waiting to see whether Ved would fill the subsequent silence.

Ved remained silent.

"What I'm more interested in discussing is the business." Another long pause as Dharmendra finished off his whiskey. "It's no secret that this marriage would prove advantageous to both of our companies, so Ved, my *question* for you is, What exactly do you plan on doing with Mehra Electronics when your father retires? More importantly, what do you plan on doing with *my* company when I retire?"

For the next hour, that's exactly what Ved spoke about, and not once did Dharmendra make a sound. He just stared at Ved across the desk, never breaking eye contact. Even among the great Hollywood "You hurt my baby girl and you're *dead*" talks, this seemed extreme.

———

"He asked where I saw myself ten years from now. My business prospects. How I was going to support you. When I planned to start a family. The usual deal. Nothing special to note."

Disha sighed and shook her head in mock disappointment. "Honestly, with the way you milked that story, I expected something just a tad more dramatic."

Ved's shirt was soaked through with sweat. He reached forward to grab his glass of water, his hand trembling slightly. God, it was so hot today.

Disha looked at him, a crease forming between her eyebrows. "Ved, what's wrong? Is something bothering you?"

Ved shrugged, trying—and failing—to seem nonchalant. "Oh no. It's just been a long day."

Disha still looked skeptical. "It seems like something greater is bothering you. You've barely touched your risotto, and I know that it's your favorite."

God, it really was hot in here, and so overcrowded. The walls of the booth seemed to press against Ved's shoulders. He started breathing heavily. "Disha, I think I need to go home."

"What?"

"I'm going home. I don't feel well." Ved stood up and the room tilted. He reached forward to grab the table and threw a few bills down.

Disha moved quickly to support him, bringing his arm around her shoulders. "Okay, let's go."

She led him gently through the restaurant, her voice soft and soothing. "Come on, Ved. Let me take you home."

They sat in the back of Disha's car in silence, Ved with his head between his legs, breathing deeply, trying not to throw up, and Disha watching him, worry knotting her expression. About ten minutes into the car ride, Ved straightened and leaned back. The nausea had subsided. He felt steady again. Maybe Dad's breathing exercises weren't bullshit after all.

"Thank you, Disha. I'm sorry for the way I behaved back there."

She turned to look out the window. "Don't be sorry."

"I feel a lot better now."

She kept her gaze on the road. "I'm glad."

When they pulled up to Ved's apartment complex, she stepped out of the car with Ved. Ved turned in surprise. "You don't need to walk me to my door."

"I want to."

At the door to his apartment, Ved stood awkwardly, unsure whether it would be impolite to open the door without inviting her in. She saved him the trouble of offering when she said, "You know you can give me a good night kiss, right?"

She stepped closer and Ved stepped back, pressing his back flat against the door. He felt the tightness return to his chest, squeezing his heart. There was no way he could kiss her. This was not how an engagement should be. He shouldn't have to hurt or embarrass her to protect himself. "Um . . . I'm really tired."

Disha's eyes narrowed. "Fine." She turned and walked away, her high heels clicking down the hallway.

CHAPTER 25

When he got inside his apartment, Ved changed into his pajamas, turned out all the lights, and lay down on top of his covers, staring at the wall. He could hear Fubu scratching at the door to be let in, but Ved ignored him. His head was throbbing. The nausea had returned. It was killing him: the guilt, the lies. He had been so confident that he could find a way out of this situation. Maybe Disha would lose interest due to their lack of physical intimacy. Maybe Ved would run away under cover of night. Or maybe (just maybe) Ved would finally come out to his family. But that was before. Now, Ved wasn't so sure. Their engagement party was fast approaching, and he still had no plan, no idea what he could possibly do to save himself and Disha from lives of unhappiness. Ved grabbed the pillow next to him and screamed into it until his throat was raw.

He must've fallen asleep at some point because the next thing he remembered was his phone ringing. He opened his eyes as he groggily reached for his phone. Of course, it wasn't charging on his nightstand. Ved rolled out of bed and walked slowly over to his discarded suit jacket, all the way on the other side of the room. The ringing continued, loud, incessant. Why hadn't he remembered to put his phone on "Do not disturb"? When Ved found his phone, he saw that it was blank, on "Do not disturb," like it was every single night. What was causing the damned ringing, then? Ved forced himself out of the room, squinting from the dim lighting of the hall. The landline. He'd completely forgotten it existed. And still it rang. He picked up the phone, his voice gruff. "Hello?"

There was no sound on the other end. Ved's irritation spiked. "Hello?"

"Yes, sorry, Ved. It's Disha." Disha? At one in the morning? He could hear her hitched breathing.

"Disha? Is everything okay? What happened? Was there an accident?" There had been a series of robberies recently in her neighborhood. Now Ved was wide awake.

"Nothing. I just couldn't sleep. I felt so guilty about the way I lashed out at you earlier, and I know you put your phone on 'Do not disturb' before sleeping."

Ved rubbed a hand over his eyes. "It's one in the morning."

Her voice was shaky. "I know, I just—"

"Disha, we'll talk in the morning."

Ved hung up. And then stayed awake wondering if what he had done was right. He knew she was upset and wanted to console her in whatever way he could, but right now his mind was fuzzy, and all he needed was a good night's sleep. It would have to wait till tomorrow—he'd make sure things were fine between them.

CHAPTER 26

Several hours later, the landline rang again. At 6:00 a.m. on the dot, which could mean only one thing: it was Dolly. Ved made the trek out to the landline again, still groggy.

He picked up the phone. "Hello?"

"Hello, Ved! You sound so tired this morning, beta. I hope you're getting enough sleep."

If only. "Why are you calling on the landline?"

"I did try to call you on your phone, but you wouldn't answer."

"Mum. It's six in the morning."

"You think I don't know the time? I just wanted to check in with you before I left for my morning walk."

Something was up. "What did Disha tell you?" That was the only explanation. Why else would Mum call out of the blue?

Mum's voice became worried. "Disha? I haven't spoken to her since tea a week ago. What happened? What did you do?"

"What? I didn't do anything. Nothing happened. Nothing at all."

He could hear the alarm bells going off in Mum's head. "Ved Mehra, you had better be treating my future daughter-in-law like a princess, buying her nice designer things, reminding her how beautiful and talented she is."

Ved was about to respond, but Mum carried on: "Listen. Let me update you on the preparations for the engagement party."

So Ved stood there for half an hour with the phone to his ear, listening to Dolly's plans. He gave only the occasional "Mmm" or "That's nice." Dolly was happy to carry on the conversation herself, more excited than Ved had heard her in a long time. She had taken care of all the party preparations. A caterer had been contacted, a menu had been set, a flower decorator had been hired, and an astrologer had been enlisted to ward off any evil curses.

Invitations had been sent to all of India's most elite families: the Tatas, the Birlas, the Kirloskars. As for the clothes, Disha already had them handled. It was to be a production of epic proportions. The business union of the year, of the decade. The Mehras had managed to snag a billionaire bride for their son. The news was finally "official," and all Mumbai society was talking about was who had received one of the coveted engagement-party invitations—and who had been left off the list. People were marking their calendars and making new Indian outfits, complete with new sets of jewelry to show off. The engagement party was happening, whether Ved wanted it to happen or not.

But even while listening to Mum, Ved couldn't stop thinking about Disha. He'd been way out of line last night, both in the restaurant and later on the phone. She didn't deserve to be treated that way. Not by anyone, and certainly not by him. He was the one deceiving her every single day.

What was worse was that now, Ved didn't just have to worry about his and Disha's families. No. Ved also had to worry about all of elite Mumbai society, who kept Dolly on the phone all day with professions of their joy and excitement. There was no turning away, and even an inkling of that would turn Ved into the biggest joke of the year. No, that inkling would turn the Mehra *family* into the biggest joke of the year. Ved's panic rose, choking him. The engagement was already in all the papers. There was no way this high-profile marriage would stay out of the public eye, which meant Ved could forget about hooking up with anyone, especially on Grindr. Was he really ready to lead a sexless life? The panic was just about drowning him.

Ved still felt that guilt, a weight on his chest that grew heavier each minute he continued lying to everyone. The real question he should be asking himself, he knew, was, Could he live with that guilt? For every single second of every single minute of every single day until he died? Could he?

There was no choice: he had to make things right.

The minute he got off the phone with Mum, he called Disha.

———

"Hello?"

"Hi, Disha."

She sighed. "What do you want, Ved?"

"I need to apologize for last night. My reaction was inappropriate. You were only trying to be accommodating."

"I appreciate you calling, Ved. I've been . . ." Ved heard her take a deep breath. "I've been really worried about the way we left things. I'm sorry I pressured you."

"No, you have nothing to apologize for. I absolutely was in the wrong. I hope you know how sorry I am."

"I know." It really sounded like she believed him.

"I know you've been asking me to try on the engagement outfits you made, and today I'm all yours—"

"Aw, Ved! Thank you! I'll be over in half an hour."

CHAPTER 27

Disha burst through the front door. Ved couldn't even see her face with all the garment bags she was carrying. He reached forward to help, and she dumped the bags on him with a sigh of relief. Fubu came running toward her, barking loudly. Disha squealed and picked him up. "Hi, baby! Hi!" Fubu started licking her face. "Mr. Handsome, I'm so happy to see you too. Oh yes, I am!"

Ved set the bags down on the couch as carefully as he could and pretended to gasp. "To think that you would prefer my dog over me."

Disha laughed and put Fubu down. "Ved, don't worry, I was just kidding. You're the only Mr. Handsome in my life."

Seeing Ved struggle to entangle all the hangers from each other, she walked over to help. "The gray bags are for you, and the black ones are for me."

"We're both trying on clothes today?"

Disha grabbed her set of the bags. "Of course! Isn't it romantic?" She batted her eyelashes. "I'm going to go change in the guest room."

Ved went to change in his room. The outfit Disha had put together really was spectacular and fit him perfectly. How she was able to pull this off without once measuring him in person was beyond him. He turned to examine himself in the full-length mirror. There was a certain regality to her design, reminiscent of the classic designs new fashion designers were usually so eager to escape. The *sherwani*'s shoulders had some padding that made his posture look more intimidating than it actually was, and there were little red hand-embroidered paisleys on the cuffs of the arms and legs. When did she get the time to do that so quickly?

She pounded on the door. "Ved! Come on. If I'm dressed before you, we have a real problem."

Ved took a deep breath and opened the door. Disha rushed in. "You look fantastic, as expected."

"So do you." She really did. Even without makeup and with her hair tied back in a messy bun, she looked beautiful. Her outfit was the same white-gold color as his, made of the same fabric, though the hand-embroidered paisleys on hers were a deep salmon pink, and when she turned, the full skirt shimmered slightly in the light. "Disha, I don't know what to say. You've outdone yourself."

She took a bow. "Thank you, thank you." Then she stepped right next to Ved, facing the mirror. They looked like a couple. Disha smiled and tugged on Ved's arm. "Can you believe this? We've waited our whole lives to get married, and here we are wearing our engagement clothes. It's surreal."

What? Ved turned to look at her. "Disha, come on. You're better than that. You have not waited your whole life to get married. That's ridiculous. You have so much more to look forward to."

"Ved, it's just an expression. You know what I meant."

Ved wasn't going to let this go so easily. "No, I don't."

Disha rolled her eyes. "What I meant, if you really didn't understand, was that we've been told by our parents that we will get married one day. We got lucky."

"Really?" Ved shook his head, disbelieving.

Disha looked concerned. "Yes, of course. I'm marrying someone I enjoy spending time with, a man whom I became friends with before he became my husband. That means something to me." She turned back to the mirror. "I know my priorities in life. I want to work, and I want my freedom to live my life without having to dote on my husband day and night. Believe me, I didn't want an arranged marriage, but I'm getting one, and even finding a man who is willing to 'grant' that agency is rare."

Ved sat down on the bed. "That's not the point."

Disha sat down next to him. "Ved, look at me." She waited until he'd met her eyes before continuing. "What is the point, then?"

Ved looked away again, his chest constricting sharply. He knew he didn't want to hear the answer, but he had to ask. "Disha . . . do you love me?"

Disha laughed, obviously Ved was joking, but when she tilted her head down to look into his eyes, he knew she saw desperation. And then she hesitated. He was being serious. He really wanted to know the answer. "Not yet," she answered, her voice shaky. She closed her eyes. Her heart was beating so fast against his side.

Ved reached out and took her hands, clutching them in his own. With visible effort, he lifted his head up to look at her directly. He really needed to be honest with her, and here was the perfect opportunity. His voice hoarse, he whispered, "I don't love you." Fatigue was weighing Ved down, carved into every single line of his face. His eyes felt wild, his hands shook, his whole body was tense—tight with barely suppressed panic. He took a deep breath, his shoulders shuddering. The attempt to find calm was clearly ineffective. Tears welled up in his eyes. He was barely audible, even in the silence when he continued, "Not like I'm supposed to."

Disha just kept looking at him and squeezed his hands. It was a long time before she answered. "I think it's important to remember that we're going to get married either way."

"What?"

"Our parents are going to get us married off sooner or later. It's better to get married to a friend, and we're friends. I know you wouldn't break my heart. I can't say the same for the other guys my parents have, and would, set me up with."

Ved lay back on the bed with a huff. "Ugh. What a sorry couple we make. Crying in our engagement outfits about how we're only getting married to make our parents happy."

Laughing, Disha lay back next to Ved. "I'm pretty sure you were the only one crying."

Ved laughed, too, though it sounded more like he was choking. "No broken hearts here, that's for sure."

"Uh-huh." Disha nodded. "I'm definitely not thinking about that guy I broke up with in New York."

"And I'm definitely not thinking about the person who broke up with me four years ago."

"I don't even care that he used to let me light cake-batter candles, even though he hated the scent. Why should I care?"

"Exactly. Dating a person who knows exactly which parts of your favorite movie you like to skip is overrated."

"Who needs homemade banana bread every Sunday?"

"Not me. And what's up with romantic strolls in the park as the sun sets?"

"Boring. I can reach the highest cabinets of the kitchen all by myself. With the help of a stool."

"I can pop a bottle of champagne too. Sure, it always explodes everywhere, but that's all part of the fun."

"I wouldn't have it any other way."

"Me neither."

———

JaipurVisitor sent a picture.

JaipurVisitor: Can't believe how beautiful the Elephanta Caves are! Being there in person definitely beats the pictures.

CHAPTER 28

He had nothing to do the next day, so after a Sunday morning spent either lying around or pacing, he decided today was the day he'd text JaipurVisitor back. Ved couldn't exactly explain why, but all he could think about was the way he smiled when they texted. Their back-and-forth was flirty. Ved never acted that loosely anymore. Not with the company and the engagement constantly weighing on his mind. It had seemed easy to ignore JaipurVisitor at first, but if Ved was being honest, he wanted to be able to talk to someone he could relax with. Someone he could be himself with, without the pressures of "Ved Mehra" and all being that man entailed resting on his shoulders. After all, what harm could come out of some fun, noncommittal virtual banter?

Besides, Ved had been ghosted too many times on Grindr, which had hurt him and sowed insecurity. He'd been through the self-interrogation, trying desperately to figure out what was wrong with him, why he wasn't good enough. He'd already done that to enough guys, just because he didn't have the courage to come out to his parents or the world. JaipurVisitor was so sincere—he didn't deserve the "one night of sex and then avoidance for the rest of all time" treatment. They hadn't even slept together, and as far as Ved was concerned, they never would. Though he had laughed at the thought of finding a friend on Grindr, maybe it *was* possible. Maybe JaipurVisitor could be his friend.

Ved opened the Grindr app. There were now six unread messages from JaipurVisitor, along with the usual "Horny, let's meet" messages that had collected over the past week. Ved deleted all the other messages and opened up the ones from JaipurVisitor. Wait, he was at Elephanta Caves? That was in Mumbai! Ved smiled and typed out his response.

Ved: Wow, can't believe you finally made it here.

JaipurVisitor responded immediately: What I can't believe is that you're suddenly alive and texting me after all these days of silence.

Ved: The only possible explanation for my silence was that I was dead?!

JaipurVisitor: Of course. I can't imagine any other reason why you would neglect to enjoy my company.

Ved: So humble.

JaipurVisitor: I try.

Ved: What are you doing in Mumbai?

JaipurVisitor: I'm here for work. Curating fabrics for our summer collection.

Ved: One of my closest friends designs clothes for Indian weddings. Are you a fashion designer, too?

JaipurVisitor: Please. My job is to source fabrics for different internationally based fashion designers.

———

They texted for at least an hour, exchanging more personal information. Ved somehow trusted him enough to share his real name and a little about himself. He learned that JaipurVisitor's real name was Carlos Silva. He learned that Carlos's family was from São Paulo, Brazil, but that he was a born-and-bred American, having grown up in New York City. He learned that Carlos had a sister who was sixteen years younger than he was. He learned that Carlos's mother was an accountant, so

Carlos always knew exactly what he didn't want to be when he grew up. He learned that Carlos was "versatile," just like he was. He learned that during college, Carlos discovered his love for art and traveling, which was what had brought him to India. He learned that Carlos's job took him all over the world for a few months at a time and that Carlos absolutely loved it. That, and sugary cocktails.

———

Ved: Well, I would like to take you up on your offer to meet. In person. How long are you here?

Carlos: I leave on March 1st.

Ved: Fantastic. Today's still Feb 16. Are you free today?

Carlos sent a smiley face.

Carlos: Why so eager?

Ved: I feel bad for leaving you on unread. Let me make it up to you with coffee. My treat.

Carlos: I can't say no to free coffee. How's 4:00 PM?

Ved: I know the perfect place.

Ved sent an address.

Ved wasn't sure why that small action made that all too familiar guilt rise up again. It wasn't a date. It wasn't. Just some harmless non-committal fun, right?

CHAPTER 29

The café Ved chose had real hardwood floors that creaked when you stepped on them and matching bookshelves crammed tight with books. People lounged on the mismatched chairs and colorfully upholstered couches, reading the books, talking, sipping their drinks as if they had all the time in the world. The whole place smelled of deep dark espresso, and the sound of fresh coffee beans being ground underscored the light jazz music. No other café in Mumbai, or likely in India, could make americanos so dark or chocolate chip cookies so sweet. It loaded on the calories but was completely worth it.

Ved arrived thirty minutes early, which gave him enough time to prepare. Not that this was a date. Not at all. It was just polite to have conversation topics prepared, to fill the inevitable awkward silences. Ved typed out a list of talking points into his phone:

1. Favorite color
2. Do you like this cafe?
3. Pets
4.

He never got a chance to finish his list. The bell tinkled, signaling that someone had just walked in. He looked up to see Carlos, looking exactly like he did in his picture, except with a five-o'clock shadow and a tan. He took off his black Ray-Bans and looked around. Scratch that, he didn't look like his picture at all. He was so much better looking in person.

Ved stood up and waved. Carlos smiled and walked over. He had the same goofy smile as the one in his profile picture. Ved was suddenly really, really nervous, though he smiled and tried to remain professional as Carlos made it to the table. No such luck. When Carlos, still smiling, reached over to shake Ved's hand, Ved didn't just feel a few butterflies fluttering around in his stomach; he felt a whole horde of them lose their collective shit. He blushed. Blushed! Even Akshay hadn't been able to make Ved blush without saying a single word. Ved looked up to see Carlos looking at him. Oh crap. He must've said something.

"Sorry, what did you say?"

Carlos laughed. "I was just saying that you chose a really nice café. I love it."

Ved couldn't stop staring at Carlos's eyes. They were hazel—just like his, yet brighter. Ved tried to look away. Instead, he felt his mouth opening. Oh no. "You look so much better in person." Ved's whole face flushed red. Why had he said that?

Carlos laughed again.

His brain suddenly felt like putty, slowly trying to morph into a coherent thought. "Not that your profile picture isn't handsome," Ved continued, "but in person, you look like someone straight out of a big Hollywood movie."

"Thanks, Ved—"

"I mean like the kind of movie that wins Oscars." Smooth.

Carlos smiled even wider. "You're not too bad yourself."

Ved cleared his throat. Not awkward at all. "So, um, shall we order?"

Ved soon found out that Carlos loved sugar almost as much as Ved loved coffee. Carlos ordered an iced double-shot mocha latte with soy milk and a full-size chocolate chip cookie (warmed up), while Ved ordered a hot triple-shot americano and a mini chocolate chip cookie (room temperature). Ved was initially worried they wouldn't have anything to talk about. After all, how could a conversation survive without carefully prepared talking points? The only viable alternative would be sitting in silence.

He couldn't have been more wrong.

Ved had never seen someone talk as fast or as much as Carlos. He gesticulated wildly when he spoke, nearly knocking a cup of coffee off the neighboring table. Twice. Everything about him exuded enthusiasm, from his floral-patterned black shirt that Ved could never hope to pull off as a fashion statement, to his white jeans, to his conversational skills. Ved loved it.

Carlos downed the final sip of his coffee, the caffeine only animating him more. "So, that's the entire story of my time in Jaipur. Next month I'm off to Indonesia, and I should be there until July."

"That's amazing." Ved should really try to sound less like an awe-struck sixteen-year-old.

"The best part is all the posts I've been able to come up with for my travel blog. India has been a fantastic source of inspiration. It seems like I see something new to explore or try everywhere I turn."

"You have a travel blog?"

Carlos nodded. "Yeah. It's not serious or anything. More of a way for me to remember my travels, like a virtual scrapbook."

"What's the blog called?"

"Oh, you don't want to know."

"I do."

"You're going to laugh."

"I promise you I won't."

"Fine." Carlos took a deep breath. "It's called *Curious Carlos*."

Ved put a hand up to his mouth and coughed to cover up his laugh.

Smiling, Carlos said, "I knew you would laugh."

"I'm not laughing." Ved coughed again. "Not at all."

"Sure," Carlos laughed. "I'm tired of hearing myself talk." He leaned forward. "Now it's your turn."

Ved leaned forward, too, though the proximity made his heart palpitate. He struggled to keep his tone mysterious. "What do you want to know?"

Carlos raised a single eyebrow. God, that was hot. Ved hoped his sweat wasn't showing through his button-down shirt. Wait, what did Carlos just ask him? Damn it! Ved had spaced out again.

As if hearing what Ved was thinking, Carlos repeated the question, his tone playful, like he was building up to the punch line of a joke. "What do you want to tell me?"

Ved scrambled, saying the first thing that came to mind: "Be careful, because that smile is so bright it could blind someone." A pickup line? Seriously? Why had he just said that? He was being so stupid. At this point, his brain wasn't even putty; it was total mashed potatoes.

Carlos's whole body shook with laughter. "Do you normally use such cheesy pickup lines?"

Now Ved sat up straight, incredulous. "I'll have you know that I haven't used a pickup line in years."

"Mmm."

"Until just now."

"Right." Carlos was still smiling that goddamn goofy smile.

"It was involuntary!"

"What? My smile was just *that* dazzling?"

"Yes!" No! What was Ved saying?

Carlos leaned even closer, their noses mere inches apart. "What do you do for a living?"

Ved leaned back, his breath leaving his lungs all at once in a huff. He generally didn't reveal much about his family since it could come across as if he was showing off or, worse, lead to unnecessary gossip if things soured with the encounter. But with Carlos he felt safe, as if he'd known him for years. "Uh . . . um . . . I . . ." He tried clearing his throat. "I'm a vice president at Mehra Electronics. The technology company."

"That's impressive. How did you manage to pull that off? You can't be older than forty."

"I'm thirty-eight, and my dad is the CEO and chairman." Ved was surprised how comfortable he felt sharing such details about himself, something he had rarely done on a date except with Akshay.

"I see."

"No, it's not like that. Dad made me start from the absolute bottom, just like the other new recruits. I had to work my way up. The only way I managed it so fast was by working every weekend for the last four years."

"Now, *that* is commitment. I wish I had that kind of drive. I mean, I love my work, but more than anything, I want to be home by five, relaxing with a sugary cocktail in my hand."

"I can't remember what it's like to be home that early."

"Don't tell me you work on Sundays too?"

"Today was an exception."

Carlos put a hand on his heart, his voice teasing. "For me, Ved? I'm touched."

Ved bit his lip. He needed to stop smiling so much. "Where else have you traveled?"

"I thought we were talking about you right now?"

"Humor me." There. That made Ved sound a lot cooler than he felt.

"I've been to every continent except Antarctica, though I'm planning to go there on a cruise next year."

"Wow. I've hardly ever left India."

"I don't believe that!"

"It's true! Besides work trips, the last vacation I went on was with my parents to Goa when I was a child. We used to go there all the time, actually."

Carlos tilted his head to the side. "You don't go there anymore?"

Ved shook his head. "Not since my parents got divorced."

Carlos's tone turned grave. "I'm sorry to hear that."

"Don't be. It was a long time ago." Ved looked down at the last dregs of coffee in his mug.

"My parents are divorced too." Ved snapped his head up, meeting Carlos's eyes.

"My dad used to beat my mom," Carlos continued, "every night after downing nearly half a case of beer. Sometimes more. Always said she put too much pressure on him. That *she* was the reason why he was chronically unemployed. As if his total distaste for any hard work had no bearing on his job prospects. He was a fucking bastard."

"What happened?" Ved's voice was soft.

"When my dad found out my mom was pregnant again, he left the divorce papers on the counter and disappeared. I haven't seen him since. After he disappeared, I had to grow up fast, figure out a way to help support my family."

"I'm sorry."

"Oh, don't be." Carlos waved his hand. "It was a long time ago."

Ved waited. "Do you still miss him?"

Carlos shrugged. "I did once, especially when I saw other fathers teaching their kids how to drive or attending their graduations with tears in their eyes. I realized, much later on, that I could never reconcile what he did to my mom with my need for a father to love me."

Ved wished he could hug Carlos right now. Unfortunately, that simply wouldn't be possible in public.

Carlos looked at his watch. "Shit. Ved, I hate to cut this short, but I have to go."

"Wait! Listen . . . ," Ved began.

"I'm listening."

Ved released the words so quickly that they ran together, unintelligible from one another. "Carlos, I want to see you again."

"What?"

Ved took a deep breath in and let it out slowly. Before he could consider the implications of his words, he blurted out, "I want to see you again."

Carlos smiled. "Okay."

"As soon as possible."

Still smiling. "Okay."

"How's tomorrow? Same time. Same place."

Ved knew his Monday was relatively free since most in the office were out on some sort of team-bonding exercise. "I'll be here."

"Excellent. I'll be counting down the hours."

Carlos met Ved's eyes directly. "Only the hours? That's a shame because I'll be counting down the minutes."

Ved mustered all his bravado and stood up, then leaned down to whisper in Carlos's ear: "I'll be counting down the seconds." And then, he walked away before Carlos could respond.

———

Ved didn't even think about Disha until he stepped into the car waiting for him outside the café. And that made him feel like shit. Absolute shit.

What had he been thinking? Seriously? Asking Carlos out on another date? What happened to "harmless noncommittal fun"? What would Disha say? Ved closed his eyes. He could imagine so clearly the hurt that would be on her face if she ever found out. Trust and honesty—that's what he'd told her he valued in a relationship. What a load of bullshit. She would see right through him in seconds, know that something was up with him. The guilt that always lingered on top of his chest now pressed deeper in, intensifying the feeling of suffocation.

So why was it that, despite all that guilt, Ved still couldn't stop thinking about Carlos's stupid goofy smile? Why was it that the thought of that smile, the cause of the guilt, also managed to relieve some of the pressure on Ved's chest?

CHAPTER 30

Ved couldn't wait until the next day to speak to Carlos again, so he texted him that same night using his actual phone number, not his Grindr ID. The only other man Ved had texted with in a romantic way had been Akshay. Not that what Ved had with Carlos was romantic. It wasn't. Not in the slightest.

Ved: Hey Carlos, it's Ved.

Carlos: Wow. How did you know I was just about to text you?

Ved: Oh, I can read minds. Did I forget to mention that during coffee earlier?

Carlos: Seems to have slipped your mind.

Ved: Speaking of earlier, where did you get your shirt?

Carlos: Why ask?

Ved: It was really nice (though I don't think I could ever pull it off).

Carlos: I made it in fashion school (and you could totally pull it off).

Ved: I thought you studied digital arts at NYU?

Carlos: I did and then I got my master's degree in fashion design at Parsons.

Ved: Oh!

Carlos: Why "Oh"?

Ved: I actually just met someone else who graduated from Parsons. I know it's a really prestigious school. That's impressive.

Carlos: Aw, shucks, thanks. Where did you go to college?

Ved: I went to the Indian Institute of Technology Bombay.

Carlos: Ooh, fancy!

Ved: Don't be too impressed. I almost flunked out on several occasions.

Carlos: That's a shame. Where are you right now?

Ved: At home. In pajamas.

Carlos: At 8:00 PM? Sexy. Did you remember to take your dentures out, Grandpa?

Ved: Ha, ha. Where are you?

Carlos: Sitting in traffic on my way back to the company guesthouse. You wouldn't believe the noise. Where is the crossing guard to sort out all this madness?!

Ved: I believe it all right.

Carlos: Who honks when the cars are literally packed bumper to bumper? Where do they think the cars can move?

Ved: That's Mumbai for you. Everyone wants to come quickly.

Carlos: Ved! Was that a double entendre?

Ved: Maybe.

———

Disha: Hi Ved. I just tried calling. Call me back whenever you get a chance.

CHAPTER 31

Twelve days until the engagement party
Twelve days until Carlos's departure

It was only after a night of rest—ten hours of sleep without interruption—that Ved realized he hadn't thought once about shagging Carlos yet. Scratch that. Of course Ved had *thought* about shagging Carlos. He wasn't blind, but it wasn't what he was focusing on. He'd been so intent on talking to Carlos, on seeing him again, that sex was not the primary objective.

Carlos wasn't like the other guys Ved had met on Grindr. Ved didn't want to sleep with Carlos once and forget all about him, ignoring his texts and his calls for weeks after until, finally, all attempts at contact ceased. Ved wanted to get to know him. While Ved was tense and often stressed, Carlos was adventurous and relaxed. While Ved liked to plan things out meticulously, Carlos said, "Carpe diem!" It was that passion for life, that desire to always see and do more every day, that Ved had lost touch with in recent years. With Carlos, Ved felt inklings of that desire again, that love of living, feeling like there was more to live for than work and duty.

Besides, Ved could never shag Carlos, much less have a relationship with him. Ved was engaged and Carlos was leaving soon. It would be a doomed relationship from the start.

Nevertheless, Ved couldn't stop smiling. When he stepped out of his bedroom to head to the gym, he wasn't annoyed that the early rays of the sun burned his eyes. Instead, he stopped to bask in its warmth for a minute, ignoring a message from Disha that beeped on his phone, to watch people slowly beginning their daily routines through the window.

By the time Ved made it to the gym, it was a little past 7:30 a.m., but the heat outside made it seem like midafternoon. The glare of the sun was strong, maddeningly harsh in its blaze. For once, Ved wasn't complaining. He strode into the gym with a big smile, nodding to the trainers and calling out the occasional "Good morning!" Everyone's jaws dropped. After years of his silence, of sulking in and out of the gym, avoiding eye contact at all costs, these people had come to understand that they should stay out of Ved's way. Today, that all changed. Ved maintained a steady stream of chatter with the woman on the nearest treadmill and helped a man who couldn't figure out how to use the rower. And every time Ved thought of Carlos, his smile was renewed. No wonder the other gym patrons were now convinced he was a crazy person.

In the car, he saw Disha's message and called her immediately. "Good morning, Disha!"

"Hi, Ved. Wow, you sure sound energetic. Did you manage to sleep last night?"

"Yep. A full ten hours." Ved was still smiling. It was a good day. A really good day.

"That's fantastic. I'm on my way to a fitting, so I don't have much time."

"That's fine. What did you want to talk about?"

"Okay." She paused. "You won't believe this, but Hemant contacted me last night. He said he's in Mumbai."

"Your ex?"

"Yeah." She sounded worried.

"Is that a good thing or a bad thing?"

Disha released a breath. "I'm not sure yet, but I told him we could meet for coffee today. Is that okay with you?"

"Of course it is! You don't need to ask my permission. You should get closure."

"I know." She sounded relieved.

"Good luck."

"Thanks. I'm going to need it."

Ved knew the least he could do was afford Disha at least a shred of the transparency that she gave him. He wanted to, even opened his mouth to tell her, but the same fear that had stopped him from coming out to Prem all those years ago clamped down. So Ved didn't tell Disha about Carlos. He just let her hang up.

CHAPTER 32

By the time Ved made it to the office, Carlos had sent him several messages. All Ved had done all morning was think about Carlos, wondering whether Carlos was thinking of him too. It was gratifying to know that the interest wasn't one sided.

Apparently, Carlos was a morning person, and since he had the day off, he had already made his way through the sites of Mumbai, WhatsApping his journey for Ved with loads of images and captions.

Carlos at the Gateway of India with open arms and a wide grin. Captioned: I love Mumbai.

A rickety horse-drawn carriage moving on the pothole-riddled road right alongside a sleek navy-blue Mercedes. Captioned: Only in India.

A traditional South Indian breakfast with all the classic food from *dosa* to coconut chutney. Captioned: I'm never leaving.

And the stalls featuring handmade clothing lining Colaba Causeway. Captioned: Any idea how to bargain down the prices? I've only ever seen it done in movies.

Ved responded, Yeah, that's all great, but just try to beat my morning, and sent his own set of pictures: his cherry-red stapler, the view from his floor-to-ceiling windows, and a giant mug of black coffee.

Carlos: Color me envious.

Ved: What are you planning on doing next?

Carlos: I'm going to go see a movie at Regal Theatre.

Ved: Will you be able to understand it?

Carlos: The movie is called Court, so I think it'll be in English.

Ved: I hate to break it to you, Carlos, but the film is in Marathi.

Carlos: I guess I have two hours to learn the language, then.

Ved: Totally doable.

Carlos: Your faith in me is staggering.

Then, Sheetal knocked on the door, stepping in when she didn't hear an immediate reply. "Ved? Your next meeting with the New Delhi team is in five minutes. I just set up the PowerPoint and muffin assortment in Conference Room B."

CHAPTER 33

Traffic was murder, so, much to Ved's dismay, he only arrived at the coffee shop five minutes early. Carlos was already seated at a brown vinyl leather couch tucked away in the corner by the window. Today, he wore a bottle-green button-down shirt with the top few buttons undone and blue jeans that slightly flared at the bottom. He was reading a book, so he didn't notice Ved until he stood right in front of him.

"Ved!" he exclaimed, his face lighting up.

"Hi, Carlos." Ved offered his hand for a handshake, but Carlos pulled him in for a hug. Ved could smell his cologne. Definitely expensive. Ved quickly let go after realizing that he'd stood with his arms around Carlos's waist for a minute too long.

"So." Carlos sat back down, apparently unbothered. "Did you know that octopuses have no bones?"

Ved sat down next to him. "I thought the correct plural was 'octopi'?"

"Well, according to this book, the correct plural is 'octopuses.'"

"You've been reading a book on octopi?" Ved covered his mouth to try stopping his laughter.

"Oh, mock away. You'd be surprised how interesting some of this stuff is. Can you imagine moving without bones?"

"I don't have tentacles, so that's not a valid comparison."

"Smart-ass."

"Nerd."

Carlos flopped back against the pillows, clutching his heart. "You wound me, Ved."

"Yeah, sure. What can I get you to drink?"

Carlos straightened. "No, what can I get *you* to drink?"

"No way, I'm paying."

"You paid yesterday!"

Ved started walking toward the counter. "I invited you."

"So?" Carlos demanded, following him.

"So I have the right to pay."

"Not if I have anything to say about it."

Carlos ran the rest of the way to the counter. By the time Ved was able to dodge the people carrying trays of coffee and make it to the line, there were already four people between him and Carlos. Carlos stuck out his tongue and shouted back, "Hot triple-shot americano?" Ved gave him a thumbs-up.

But what he saw next made his stomach drop, and not in the fun roller-coaster way like when Carlos looked straight into his eyes. His stomach dropped in the horrifying way like when he realized someone was about to die a gruesome death in a horror movie.

Ved stumbled out of line and made his way back to the table, trying to hide behind bookshelves and tall potted plants. He sat down and craned his neck to look at the line. *Disha* was standing there with a tall man wearing a leather jacket who must have been Hemant—and they were chatting with Carlos, all three smiling, having a jolly good time. Holy hell. Ved lay down on the couch, his long legs spanning its length, and closed his eyes, trying to inhale deep breaths. It was okay. It was okay. He needed to calm the fuck down. Disha didn't even know he was here. So what if she was talking to Carlos? So what if Carlos told her he was on a date? Technically, he and Carlos weren't even on a date. They were just grabbing coffee together. Ved knew he was overreacting, getting paranoid because he had never in his wildest dreams expected this situation. But he wondered, Would Disha suddenly suspect he was gay just because he was with another man? Couldn't it be a business colleague?

Who was Ved kidding? Carlos wasn't dressed like a business colleague, and what was he doing with this young Brazilian chap at a coffee shop in the middle of the day when he was supposed to be at work? After all, wasn't that the reason he had been giving her so that he couldn't help more with all the arrangements—that he was swamped with work?

No way. He looked like he was totally on a date with Carlos, and here was his fiancée about to find out that he'd been cheating on her with another man. Ved squeezed his eyes even more tightly shut, his breaths coming out quicker and quicker.

Deep breath in—what if Disha saw him hiding here like an idiot? And out—what would he tell his parents? And in—Mum would be devastated. And out—could the Mehra name survive such a scandal? And in—what would *Carlos* think? And out—Ved would never see Carlos again if he knew the truth. And in—

"Ved, are you okay?"

Ved opened his eyes to find Carlos standing over him, looking concerned. Sitting up and rubbing his eyes, Ved said, "Yes, yes, completely fine."

Carlos didn't look like he believed him, but he dropped the subject. "I'm just waiting for them to call my name."

Ved swallowed. His throat was too dry. "Sounds good."

"You'll never believe what happened in line!"

Ved raised his eyebrows, praying that the panic he felt didn't show on his face. "I met a girl who graduated from Parsons! Small world, right? I think the guy she's with is her boyfriend. He went to Columbia. What lovely people."

"Yeah." Ved sighed in relief. "That is crazy."

A voice came from the counter. "Carllo? Carllo!"

Carlos laughed. "I guess that's me. Be back in a second."

Ved leaned back, hugging an overstuffed cushion to his stomach. Now he just had to make sure Disha and Hemant didn't see him and Carlos sitting here. It was time to prepare for all the possible scenarios.

Ved's attempt to plan was thwarted because just then, Carlos came back. He was carrying two coffees in to-go cups, one iced, one hot. "Okay, Ved, I have an idea."

"Okay." Ved gave a shaky smile.

"I got our coffee to go because I think we should walk around the city!"

Ved stared openmouthed at Carlos, who continued beaming like a fool. "Carlos, are you crazy? This is Mumbai!"

"Exactly!" Carlos set down the coffees and grabbed Ved's hand in both of his. "The best way to see any city is to walk its streets!"

"We'll be killed by a crazy driver. We'll die of sun poisoning."

Carlos squeezed Ved's hand. "What's life without a little adventure?"

Ved shook his head. "There aren't any sidewalks."

Carlos had a wild glint in his eyes. "That's never stopped me before."

Carlos dragged Ved out of the store and onto the street by his elbow. And so, they walked the streets of Mumbai. Just two guys with a death wish. There was barely any room for one person to walk, much less two side by side, so they moved in single file. Ved was so caught up in spending time with Carlos that his earlier paranoia about seeing Disha seemed long forgotten, thrown somewhere at the back of his mind. By 6:30 p.m., the sun was just beginning to set, so the heat was only mildly intolerable. They dodged rickshaws whose drivers looked back in shock at the two lunatics walking the streets, sipping coffee and chatting like they were on some sort of garden stroll. Every time that happened (and it happened more times than Ved cared to remember), Carlos gave a big wave and smiled his goofy smile. That only further convinced the drivers that they were crazy people.

Carlos talked the entire time, pointing out all the things he loved about the city. The way fresh produce was sold in small markets, the random cows being gently coaxed in certain directions, even the sky-scrapers. Craning his head back, Carlos stopped, causing Ved to bump into him. Carlos reached out a hand behind him to steady Ved without turning back and pointed to the largest skyscraper in the distance. "This city is remarkable. Look at how these roadside markets exist mere min-utes from a modern city with skyscrapers so tall you have to tilt your head back just to see their tops."

"I wouldn't call that remarkable," Ved said.

Carlos started walking again. "Why not? Isn't it nice that both ways of life can coexist?"

Ved followed. "You don't remember the city like I do. It was differ-ent when I was younger."

"Different how?" Carlos sounded genuinely curious.

Ved said emphatically, "Different in the style of urbanization, Carlos. Before, we urbanized to play catch-up with the rest of Asia—the rest of the world, really. Now, we continue urbanizing to turn our city into a playground of conveniences for the rich."

Carlos shook his head and reached out to squeeze Ved's hand, quickly pulling away when Ved stiffened. "You needn't be so pessimistic. Urbanization brings jobs and opportunities to those who need them the most. It isn't a bad thing. The city you remember is still there. It simply evolved." Ved must've looked skeptical, because Carlos continued, say-ing, "Just try to see the good in the city. It's so much more productive than pointing out its flaws. Try. For me."

And Ved really did try. During the rest of the walk, as the sun turned the sky pink and purple, when Carlos gasped and pointed out something he found beautiful, Ved tried to find what made it so special. When Carlos stopped in his tracks to get a better look at something, Ved examined it right along with him. Perhaps Carlos was onto something.

When the last streaks of pink in the sky blended with the purple, they stopped and stared at the sky, the honks of the traffic surrounding them. "I never take the time to look at the sunset," Ved realized.

"You should," Carlos said, eyes wide. "It's different every single day."

Then, Carlos raised an eyebrow. "Follow me," he commanded, and he pulled Ved into an alley that blocked out the dying light. He looked right and left to make sure no one else was around. Seeing that they were alone, he pushed Ved up against the steaming brick wall, kissing him. On the lips. In public. With tongue. Ved was so focused on Carlos that he couldn't be bothered by the possibility that someone could walk into the alleyway and catch them. Instead, Ved threw his arms around Carlos's neck, pressing their bodies closer together.

CHAPTER 34

When they finally broke apart, they stared at each other, trying to breathe, chests only an inch apart. Carlos's hair was ruffled, his cheeks flushed pink, and somehow an extra few of his shirt buttons had come undone, all of which made him look even hotter than before. Ved struggled to control himself. Where was the plastic, awkward sensation that normally came with kissing a stranger for the first time? How was it that kissing Carlos already felt so natural?

Ved struggled to form words. "What, um, what now?"

A slight smile formed at the corners of Carlos's mouth. "Let's go to your place. It's close by, right?"

Ved froze, caught off guard. He had never taken a guy home. Not once. It was too intimate.

Carlos stepped slightly away, frowning. "Unless you don't want to."

"No!" Ved reached for Carlos's shirt collar and pulled him back against him. He cleared his throat. "No. I want to. But . . . um . . ."

"Is there a problem with your house?" Carlos softly squeezed Ved's waist.

"I should have told you earlier." Ved tried to hide the sheepishness in his voice. "I live in an apartment with my father."

"Really?" Carlos looked taken aback, though he didn't move away this time. "You're doing so well for yourself that I thought you would have your own apartment for sure."

Ved leaned his head back against the brick. Now it felt cool. "It's more of an Indian thing than a money thing. A family responsibility as a son."

Carlos was clearly having a hard time hiding his smile. "Where do you hook up, then?"

Ved closed his eyes, mortified. "Hooking up is usually at the other person's place or a hotel room."

"Then . . ." Carlos waited for Ved to finish the sentence, leaning in to kiss Ved's collarbone.

Well, if he continued kissing Ved like that, Ved wouldn't have much of a choice. Ved pressed closer to Carlos, sucking air into his lungs. He opened his eyes. "Okay." His voice still sounded breathless. "My dad is always in his study or at work late anyway. He won't even know. Let's go to my place."

CHAPTER 35

Ved wished they could have teleported immediately to his apartment, where he would sweep Carlos into his arms fireman-style and kick down the door, kissing him the entire time, Carlos's hands desperately trying to unbutton Ved's shirt until he gave up and just ripped the whole damn thing off.

What really happened was far less dramatic and far more awkward. They stepped out of the alleyway after trying to make themselves look more presentable and then stood on the side of the road while Ved called his driver to come pick them up. They waited there, and for once, Carlos was silent. That only made Ved feel more nervous, so he stood there, ripping out hangnails. This was it: the first time he had ever brought another man home. It was something Ved had wanted to do for years, something he hadn't even felt comfortable doing with Akshay. And if Dad wasn't in his study . . . no. Ved couldn't worry about that. He would figure out an explanation if it came to that.

When the driver did arrive, Ved and Carlos had to sit next to each other in the back seat of the car, pretending that they weren't dying to tear each other's clothes off. Ved looked straight ahead at the back of the front seat, and Carlos gazed out the window. Ved could feel his body tensing up, but Carlos looked completely at ease, his breathing even, while Ved's hitched on every other breath.

When they finally arrived at the apartment, they stood with their sides pressed together in the crowded elevator, Carlos looking at Ved and smiling, Ved looking anywhere else and trying to frown. Then, they at last made it to the front door, only for Ved to remember that he'd left his keys at home that morning. He rang the doorbell, still trying to avoid meeting Carlos's eyes, and Hari answered the door.

Ved had been so focused on avoiding Prem that he'd completely forgotten about Hari. What would Hari think about Ved bringing Carlos into the apartment? Into his bedroom? Thankfully, Ved's fears proved to be unfounded. Hari didn't point his finger at Ved and shame him for bringing Carlos home, threatening to tear down the entire Mehra family and exposing Ved as a cheating liar.

Instead, Hari looked panicked, likely worried that he would have to figure out something special to cook for Ved's guest. Ved told him not to worry and ushered Carlos into his bedroom, stopping only to pick up Fubu on the way before he could start barking.

Ved leaned against the closed door, and Carlos leaned down, tentatively reaching out to pat Fubu on his head. "Ved, this is quite possibly the cutest dog I've ever seen in my life. I hope he doesn't bite."

"Don't worry. Fubu is the friendliest little furball you'll ever meet." Then, Ved locked the door and reached for Carlos's waist, leaning down to kiss him. Carlos stopped Ved by putting a hand on his chest, blushing. *Carlos* was blushing. Carlos lowered his voice to a whisper: "Not in front of the dog, Ved!"

Ved laughed. "He sleeps with me, Carlos. Don't worry. He's not going to tell anyone."

Carlos still looked doubtful.

"Okay, hold on." Ved kissed Carlos on the cheek. "I'll go put him away in the kitchen." On his way, Ved checked to see if his father was home. He wasn't, probably out for dinner with the clients visiting from New Delhi.

Ved returned to the room and latched the door, immediately drawing Carlos close to him. This time, he kissed Carlos first. First, on his neck, then on his lips. He'd meant to be gentle, though he couldn't resist biting Carlos's lip. Carlos moaned when Ved started unbuttoning his shirt. What a turn-on. Most men Ved had been with were silent, too afraid that someone would hear them. All Ved wanted to do was find ways to make Carlos moan louder.

He flipped Carlos around to push him against the wall and kissed him, pinning his arms above him. Ved loved the tautness of his body, soft yet firm—not overworked. He licked his way down Carlos's body and bit the side of his stomach. Carlos only grunted, now running his hands through Ved's hair and along the back of his neck. He seemed more than happy to hand over the reins.

Ved had never enjoyed pleasing another man so much.

CHAPTER 36

Afterward, they both lay naked, side by side on Ved's bed. What a wonderful feeling it was. Normally, now would have been the time for Ved to put on his clothes, mutter a hasty goodbye, and walk out the door, never to see the man lying in the bed again. Carlos, however, seemed happy to simply lie there, together. Ved reached for Carlos's hand, and that's how they rested, enjoying the silence, only interrupted by the hum of the air conditioner. Bliss.

Of course, it didn't last.

Just as Carlos was turning to face Ved, Ved's stomach grumbled in the loudest display of hunger possible. Carlos just laughed and, seeing him turn bright red, leaned in to plant a soft kiss on his lips. He stayed leaning over Ved's chest. "I can't believe that after all of that, your hunger is what finally makes you feel embarrassed."

Ved's stomach rumbled again, and Carlos wouldn't stop laughing. Ved pushed himself up, still red but smiling. "Do you want to eat something?"

Carlos stayed lying back down. "Yes, please. I would like to formally request some grapes for you to feed to me."

Ved got up and shrugged on a T-shirt and lounge shorts, hating how he now felt the chill in the air. "Why, of course." He gave a mock bow and left the room.

He returned with a tray, holding an open bottle of champagne and two platefuls of piping-hot mutton kebabs. "Sorry, Carlos. No grapes."

Carlos pretended to frown but brightened after noticing the champagne. "What are we celebrating tonight?"

Ved poured him a glass. "Do we need to have an occasion?"

"Of course!"

"What do you suggest?" Ved slipped back into bed, trying to balance the tray on his legs.

Carlos reached over to help balance the other half of the tray on his own legs. "How about to . . . holding someone's hand in bed!"

Ved clinked his glass against Carlos's. "Hear, hear."

After downing half his glass of champagne in a single gulp, Ved took a deep breath. "I don't generally do this, you know. Hold someone's hand in bed after sex."

"Me neither. It's pretty great, right?"

"Yeah, it is." Ved reached for Carlos's hand and squeezed it. Carlos burst out laughing.

Ved quickly let go of Carlos's hand and turned to the door. "What? What is it?"

"No, no, it's nothing." Carlos took Ved's hand back in his own. "It's just that you have really large hands."

"Oh." Ved leaned back into the pillows, his posture relaxing. "I always thought my hands were of average size."

"Yeah, maybe for a person who's six feet tall."

"Six one, actually." Ved held up their hands, pressing their palms flat against each other to see how they compared. "How tall are you?"

"Five five."

Ved smiled.

"Ved, don't you dare smile. It is not funny."

Now, Ved started laughing.

"Ved!"

Ved tried covering his mouth, but that only made him laugh harder. "Sorry!"

Carlos shoved his shoulder, the goofy smile back across his face.

After minutes doubled over, laughing so hard he thought he would throw up, Ved straightened to see Carlos looking at him, his expression serious.

"Carlos, what's wrong?"

He looked down. "Nothing's wrong, per se; I just realized I never asked if you were seeing anyone."

"What?"

"Well, are you?"

Ved was taken aback. "No! Of course not." This was not technically a lie, but neither was it the absolute truth. At least that's what he told himself. Now was not the time to get into details about Disha and the engagement; after all, Carlos was leaving the city in a few days.

"Why 'of course not'? I'm familiar with how Grindr works, Ved. I know people don't go on the app to find monogamy and a life partner."

Ved looked down, too, staring at his lap. "But I thought we aren't like the other people that meet on Grindr." His voice sounded pitifully small.

Carlos reached over to put his arm around Ved's shoulders. "We aren't like those other people. I just had to be sure. Forget I said anything."

Ved was quiet. Here was Carlos being loving and caring, and all he was doing was lying to his face. He wished he could just tell him the truth—what a mess he was in, his foolishness in agreeing to get married to make his parents happy, how all he wanted now was to be with Carlos, have him in his life—but he knew that it would change everything between them. He couldn't risk that.

"Listen, Ved, I was being an idiot. I shouldn't have accused you of anything. I can't even imagine how hard it must be for you to be out in a conservative country like India."

Ved stiffened.

"Ved, you are out, right?"

He moved to get out of bed, but Carlos pulled him back, his voice concerned. "Talk to me."

Leaning against the headboard, Ved brought his knees up to his chest, curling himself into a ball. "I . . . no. I'm not out."

Carlos rubbed Ved's arm, making soothing circles. "Not even to your parents?"

"Especially not to my parents!" Seeing Carlos shrink back slightly made Ved instantly regret raising his voice. "I'm sorry for yelling. I . . . I think they suspect, or at least my dad does, but Mum . . ." Ved was shaking. He knew how much Dolly wanted him to be married, to experience the kind of lasting comfort and happiness that she hadn't had in her own marriage. Ved tried steadying his voice. "Carlos, for years growing up, I always questioned myself if something was wrong with me for being attracted to other boys, for playing with those kitchen sets instead of cricket with the other boys in the neighborhood. Even my relatives used to tease me about it . . . it's really taken a lot for me to fully understand my gayness. Many years of pain and unhappiness and solitude."

Now Carlos leaned up against Ved's side, hugging his waist. "Hey, it's okay. It's okay."

"I wish I could tell you I was out, Carlos. I really do."

"I know." Carlos's voice turned steady, calming.

"It's just that my parents have all these expectations for me, like with most Indian business families. I'm their only son—I'll someday run the company, take over the reins from my father and look after them in their old age, and—"

"You don't have to explain yourself to me."

"You deserve better."

Carlos smiled. "I do, don't I? It's just my luck that I got stuck with you."

Ved smiled too.

"You know, the last guy I dated was in the closet too. This was back in Jaipur, by the way. I met him at work. He was one of the lawyers that my boss hired on retainer. It was only after we slept together that I found out he was married. Three dates and not one word about his wife." At Ved's stricken expression, he softened. "Of course, I know that you're different. The only reason I even brought it up is because I don't want to be humiliated like that again. I want both of us to be honest with each other."

Ved wanted so badly to be completely honest with Carlos at this moment, but he knew it could easily backfire. "Me too, but you have to realize that some people are trapped in situations they can't control. They might not know how to escape or who they can ask for help. They feel trapped and hopeless and live their entire lives filled with guilt."

"Don't defend him. He was a bastard."

"I'm not trying to defend him." If only Ved sounded less defensive.

Carlos held up his hands in surrender. "Can we at least agree the whole situation was *chootya*?"

Ved couldn't help but start laughing at Carlos's pronunciation of *chutiya*. Carlos smiled, too, though he seemed confused at the sudden shift in Ved's demeanor. "What's so funny?"

"Who the hell taught you Hindi curse words?"

"It was pretty much the first thing my coworkers taught me when I moved to the Jaipur office. Am I pronouncing it correctly?"

"Absolutely not."

Carlos raised an eyebrow. "Care to enlighten me?"

It took Ved a minute to compose himself. Every time he opened his mouth to speak, he started laughing again.

"Laugh it up."

"Sorry, Carlos." Ved smiled. "It's pronounced *chutiya*."

"Okay, I've got it: *chootya*."

"Listen to me." Ved made sure to exaggerate the syllables this time: "Chu-ti-ya."

Carlos sounded hesitant. "Chu—chutiya."

"There you go! I think that deserves another glass of champagne."

"Yes, please. Let's get drunk and have sex again!"

Ved, much to his later embarrassment, snorted. "As long as you promise to moan softer," he teased.

Carlos held out his glass. "Oh, please. You loved it."

Ved poured champagne for the two of them, willing himself not to blush. "Mmm. I'm sure the neighbors really loved it too."

"Ved!"

So they lay there like that, teasing each other back and forth, eventually finishing the entire bottle of champagne. As much fun as Ved was having, he felt more anxious as time passed. He knew that asking Carlos to stay the night was absolutely out of the question. They'd already spent enough time in Ved's room to arouse suspicion. Whether Ved wanted Carlos to stay or not didn't matter. Carlos *could not* be here when Ved's alarm rang in the morning. How could Ved make him leave without hurting his feelings?

Ved was saved the trouble when Carlos leaned in, cupping both sides of his face and kissing him so deeply that Ved instantly forgot what had been worrying him moments before. "Ved, I wish I could stay the night, but I really should get back to the company guesthouse. I have to be up by eight for work tomorrow." He stood and began pulling on his clothes. They were scattered all over the room. Grabbing his pants off the lampshade, he said, "I want to see you again."

Ved stood up too. "Was that ever a question?"

"I should hope not."

Ved couldn't resist it; he grabbed Carlos's waist and kissed him again. Carlos protested halfheartedly, eventually giving in. "Ved . . . Ved! I really have to go."

"I know, I know." Ved buttoned up Carlos's shirt and kissed him on the cheek. "I'll call you in the morning."

"You'd better." Carlos unlocked the door. Before leaving, he turned back to Ved. "I had a really great time."

"Me too."

Ved had had a really good time. He felt warm and loved all over, like he hadn't in a really long time. This was something special: he could feel it deep inside as sleep slowly enveloped him.

CHAPTER 37

When Ved woke up the next morning, his entire body felt like it had slept for an eternity. He had the deep, comforting feeling of being awake yet content to rest in bed a little while longer. Like every morning, Ved woke to feeling that crushing weight of guilt on his chest, but rather than wallowing in it like he normally did, agonizing over what he would do to ensure that everyone (maybe even himself) would be happy, Ved took in a deep breath, enjoying the scent of Carlos's cologne that had managed to sink into the sheets. He would agonize over his plans later. Now, Ved pressed his cheek into the pillow, where the scent of Carlos's cologne was even stronger. Ved smiled, allowing himself to focus on the moment, and could already feel his cheeks heating up as he remembered what had happened the evening before. He really couldn't stop thinking about Carlos, and not just because of the sex.

The sex had been great, electric, really; there was just something more about Carlos. Maybe it was his never-fading curiosity or his wanderlust or the way he raised a single eyebrow. Maybe it was the way he listened. Oh, he could talk about himself all day, that was for sure, but he could listen well, too, in a way that made Ved feel like the single most important person in the world, like every little detail of his life was interesting.

During his time with Akshay, Ved had never spoken much about himself or what he was feeling. In hindsight, he could see that most of their conversations had revolved around Akshay: *his* anxieties, what *his* parents expected, *his* day at work. And Ved never used to mind. He'd loved hearing about Akshay. Akshay's life was what Ved lived for. Of course, he should've taken the time to listen to Akshay's opinions, what Akshay had to say. Ved had been so grateful that anyone could love him at all. Therefore, he rationalized that the person who loved him deserved all his attention. Ved had made no effort to resist the way of things.

With Carlos, the way of things was different. Ved's infatuation didn't mean that Carlos took preeminence. Ved didn't need to prove how much he liked him by making him the center of attention. They could both be important—*equally* important.

Ved was so glad they'd met.

He picked up his phone and saw that Carlos had already sent him a "Good morning" text, saying he'd woken up early to do some sightseeing before work. He was crazy, voluntarily waking up before six in the morning. Ved's smile widened. This truly wasn't a one-night-stand situation. Carlos meant what he had said last night. They *were* different. This relationship wasn't like any of the others they had endured through Grindr. There would be no pining, no shamefully shed tears, and certainly no booty call several months down the line.

Ved responded with his own "Good morning" and went to grab a cup of black coffee. Hari, seeing Ved smiling at the breakfast table, was immediately concerned and asked what was bothering him. Ved shook his head, dismissing the question. "Nothing at all. I'm just looking forward to this beautiful day." Hari had returned to the kitchen looking even more concerned than before.

After his quick cup of coffee, Ved ruffled through his closet looking for something nice to wear. Usually, Ved just threw on a suit, with little consideration for how he looked. As long as he met the office's formal dress code, he was fine. Today was different. Carlos clearly put effort into his appearance every day, and it paid off. He always looked fantastic. Ved wanted to make a similar effort, hopefully with similar results.

Ved's search yielded four new shirts and three new pairs of jeans, all with the tags still on, pushed to the back of his closet. They were more daring than anything Ved normally wore, bought on a whim after a pint of ice cream late at night. He'd always vaguely planned on wearing them "someday." Today was that day. He wanted to look his best.

In the bathroom, Ved examined his appearance critically, turning his head from side to side. His stubble didn't look bad, but he knew he would look better clean shaven. There was no way he could pull off a five-o'clock shadow the way Carlos could. He then pressed his nose with two fingers to check for blackheads. He needed to ask Sheetal which brand of face wash she would recommend for him. That odd hair growing upward from his eyebrows really needed to be plucked. He patted his belly. It could still use some trimming down. He stretched his back sideways to the left, then to the right, and jumped down to do ten sets of push-ups and crunches.

He showered and sprayed on some Dolce & Gabbana Light Blue cologne. He never wore cologne, so how the unopened package had appeared in his vanity was a mystery. Likely, it had been a birthday gift from a well-meaning aunty years ago. He also tried gelling his hair back in a way he knew would be attractive to Carlos. The change was nothing short of transformative—Ved looked at least five years younger.

CHAPTER 38

Carlos filled Ved's mind in the car on the way to work. Ved couldn't wait to see him again. Going to work, for the first time in years, would be a chore, not a necessary distraction. He finally had someone to be with after work. No more nightly pints of Honey Nut Crunch. No more lonely cry fests during romantic comedies.

The only question was where he should meet Carlos in the evening. Having coffee again was out of the question. They were way past such a formal setting. They needed to go somewhere more fun with plenty of drinks, and a place where Ved would surely not bump into anyone he knew. After a few minutes of scrolling through Zomato, he realized that he already knew the perfect place: Toto's, the legendary Bandra garage pub. Ved, having spent many drunken nights there in his college days, knew that anyone his age had long outgrown the place, opting instead for small courses at expensive restaurants or starvation at trendy health food cafés. Most importantly, he was sure Carlos would love its grungy vibe with the loud rock music and even louder conversation. The greasy food and gargantuan pitchers of ice-cold beer would be absolutely perfect.

Ved suddenly received a calendar notification. Shit. He'd already agreed to go out to dinner with Disha tonight to discuss what he would be wearing at the preengagement cocktail party with her friends at her home. She had promised her fashion expertise in seeing to it that he would look über-stylish on that night. Ved had left it in her able hands, and she had seemed more than happy to help him out. How could he cancel now without making her suspicious? The coffee turned around Ved's stomach, making him feel sick. As if reading his mind, Disha called him.

"Hey, Ved!"

Ved tried, with considerable effort, to match her light tone. "Hey, since when did you read minds? I was just about to call you."

Disha laughed. "Since always, silly. Please don't be mad."

"About what?"

"Well, I'm actually calling because I can't make it tonight. I know I had promised to sort out your clothing for the cocktails, and I promise I will. I'll see to it that you make every other guy in the room eat his heart out." She laughed. "You don't have to worry about anything. I'll take care of all your fittings. It's just that tonight I have other dinner plans with someone else. I know it's last minute and probably a big inconvenience. I'm sorry."

Ved tried not to sound too upbeat, though he was now smiling. "That's totally fine, Disha. We can discuss it any other day. Just text me whenever you want to reschedule."

"I will. See you soon."

"Bye."

Ved couldn't believe his luck. Now all he had to do was text Carlos. Looking at his messages, he saw that Carlos had already been to the Haji Ali Mosque. There were seven pictures of Carlos posing outside, and the caption I can't believe this shrine is on the SEA! He'd covered his head with a bandanna to comply with the dress code, which made him look hopelessly adorable.

Ved: I've heard it's beautiful.

Carlos: what? You've never been to see it yourself?

Ved: nope.

Carlos: I don't think we can be friends anymore.

Ved: ha ha. Are we still on for tonight?

Carlos: you know it. Same coffee shop?

Ved: I want to do something more special.

Carlos: do tell.

Ved: meet me at Toto's, Pali Road in Bandra. It's a cool garage pub. I think you're going to love it.

Carlos: sounds good. What time?

Ved: how's 8:00 PM?

Carlos: perfect. See you soon.

Ved: not soon enough.

CHAPTER 39

When Ved stepped into the pub with its thick smoky air and dim strobe lighting, "Another Brick in the Wall" was blasting from the stereo. The place hadn't changed at all in the last sixteen years. He and his oldest friend, Anaita, along with their circle of college buddies, used to get drunk here every Saturday night, acting like idiots, standing on the tables singing along to music they didn't know the lyrics to. Ved couldn't even remember the last time he'd eaten greasy pub food or been in a place with such loud music. This beat the stuffy fine-dining restaurants he frequented with Disha and his clients any day.

Carlos hadn't arrived yet, so Ved took a seat at the bar, waiting for a table to open up. There were some single men sitting next to Ved, wearing disheveled shirts, sleeves rolled up, nursing jugs of beer, looking lonely and tired. The tables were mainly filled with college students, laughing loudly, their arms around each other. In a corner, a screaming group of women surrounded a woman wearing a plastic tiara and a hot-pink sash reading "Bride to be." Waiters were careful to balance the trays of beer and cocktail peanuts as they dodged drunk people trying to dance. Finally, a corner table with two barstools freed up. Ved quickly made his way over, noticing some of the women at the bachelorette party check him out. One of them, slim with frizzy hair and a zebra-print body-hugging dress, followed him to the table.

Her words were slurred when she said, "Is this seat taken?"

Ved backed into the corner wall. "Um . . . yes, it is."

She deepened her voice, trying to sound sexy. "What's a handsome man like you doing at a bar all alone?" She stumbled over to Ved and put a hand on his chest.

Ved pushed away, walking around her. "I'm not here alone. Just waiting for someone."

She pouted. "Come on, baby, let's get out of here." Baby? What?

"I think you're confused, er, ma'am."

"Ma'am?" She started giggling and grabbed onto the table to keep herself from falling. "You don't need to be so formal with me, hot stuff."

"Hot stuff, huh?"

Ved turned, horrified, to see Carlos standing behind him. Worse still, Carlos was smiling. "Ved, care to introduce me to this lovely woman?"

She was staring moon eyed at Carlos. "Now, tell me, who the hell are *you*?" She reached out a hand and ran it along his bicep. "Ooh, yeah. Come on, baby, let's get out of here."

Carlos burst out laughing and nudged Ved. Well, at least someone was enjoying this. "Lighten up, Ved."

Ved frowned and turned to the woman. "Please leave."

"I . . . am *not*"—she paused to burp—"going to let some . . . some . . . *man* try to tell *me* what to do."

Carlos took her hand. "Are you here with anyone?" She pointed to the table with her friends. "Okay," Carlos said, and he led her over there, gently murmuring about how she should try to get a good night's sleep.

When Carlos returned, he met Ved's anger with his goofy smile. Ved tried to stay frowning, but that proved to be impossible.

"Ved, you chose a fantastic place. I love it."

Ved gave in to his smile. "I knew you would. It's quite the landmark in Bandra. One of the first pubs that opened here."

"We Are the Champions" began playing, and some of the men wearing cricket jerseys on the other side of the bar stood up on their table, singing along, hopelessly butchering the chorus.

"See!" Carlos gestured over to the men. "That's what I like to see. How about it, Ved? You in the mood to sing?"

"I would rather die."

"Okay, I'll take that as a maybe."

"No."

Carlos winked. "We'll revisit the matter later."

"No." Damn it. Maybe he would sound sterner if he weren't smiling.

A waiter approached the table and shouted over the music and drunken singing. "What can I get for you two?"

Carlos turned to Ved. "Can you order for us? You know what's good here."

"Sure. We'll take the largest pitcher of cold beer you have and a plate of chicken *tikka*."

"Make it two plates," Carlos added.

Ved looked at him, eyebrows raised. "You've had chicken tikka before?"

"No, Ved," Carlos said, his voice filled with sarcasm. "I've lived in India for the past two months, but I've never once eaten chicken tikka."

Ved laughed. "I'm assuming you like it, then?"

"Like it? Ved, I'm convinced that chicken tikka is the best food that man has ever created. I honestly don't know how I managed to survive for twenty-seven years without ever trying it. I first had it at this great open-air barbecue stall in Jaipur late at night after work. It's a hole in the wall but gets jam packed on weekends. I used to go there with my coworkers all the time."

"I have a feeling that the chicken tikka here will beat Jaipur's."

Their waiter brought over the pitcher of beer and two large chilled jugs. Ved poured until both were filled to the brim. They clinked their jugs together and shouted "Cheers!"

Carlos sighed in content. "After the heat today, this is exactly what I needed. I swear, Mumbai is hotter than hell itself."

"You know," Ved said, setting down his jug, "I think the last time I had this much beer was in college."

"Okay, old man," Carlos teased. "You know, it's amazing how Bandra is crammed with so many different places to eat. In that way, it reminds me of New York, though the street food here is much better."

Ved leaned in. "So, besides chicken tikka, what's your favorite Indian street food?"

Carlos leaned in too. "Man, that's a difficult question. Let me think . . . okay, so you remember when I went to see *Court*?"

"You actually attended a film in a language you can't understand?"

"Of course I did—it's a visual experience, too, but that's not the point. After the movie, I stopped at this street-food stall and must have had five of these crispy potato cutlets stuffed in soft white bread. My mouth is watering just remembering it right now."

"Oh yeah, I love *vada pav* too. It's the Indian version of the burger." Ved chugged more of his beer. "How was the street food in Jaipur? Was there a lot of variety?"

"Besides one meat stall, there wasn't much. Compared to Mumbai, Jaipur is a village. Sometimes, I used to find a little activity by hanging out with the expat crowd. They all used to go out on Wednesday and Friday nights, getting drunk on wine until the restaurants closed and had to kick them out. There were two gay men, from Britain actually, so the group wasn't bad company."

Ved felt a tinge of jealousy, though he knew he had no right to. "What's the gay scene like there?"

"Ved, trust me, you have nothing to worry about. Jaipur is such a conservative place. The one gay bar is only open on Saturday nights, and it's filled with guys anxiously staring at each other under a disco ball, waiting for someone to make a move."

"Mumbai is pretty conservative too. All of India, really. Being gay is still considered unnatural." He hated that word—"unnatural." It was used to alienate others, and everyone knew that. By using the word "unnatural," people could easily dismiss ideas they weren't comfortable with. Rather than putting the burden on themselves to confront what they weren't familiar with, it became easier to blame the topic that was causing discomfort. That way, those who did the alienating felt the most justified in their opinions. Ved had spent years feeling like an outsider, feeling like he wasn't worthy of the most basic love or respect, just because of who he was. Since meeting Carlos, he'd started challenging that belief. Because, honestly, who were they to say who was worthy of anything? He could tell Carlos never for a second thought he deserved less than the utmost happiness.

Carlos squeezed Ved's hand under the table. "I wish I could show you what the gay scene is like in New York. You wouldn't believe how open and proud people are, entirely at ease with themselves. Of course, there are still those that curse at us and try to pretend we don't exist, but I can say that if I leaned across this table and kissed you, which I really want to do, by the way, I could. Without any hesitation."

Ved returned the squeeze. "I really want to kiss you too."

"They do say that patience is a virtue."

"Patience is overrated."

Carlos emptied the bowl of cocktail peanuts, then licked the salt off his fingers. "I couldn't agree more."

CHAPTER 40

The chicken tikka finally arrived, piled high on steaming plates. Carlos dug in, unafraid to cover his piece in the mint chutney. Ved waited, blowing on his own piece.

Carlos closed his eyes after taking a bite. "Ved, I think I'm in love."

Ved snapped his head up to meet Carlos's eyes. "What?"

"You were right. This *is* the best chicken tikka I've ever had."

Of course he was talking about the food. What else would he have been referring to?

"I'm glad you like it." Ved took a bite and immediately started coughing. He reached for his beer, struggling to breathe, his face now bright red.

Carlos stood up and walked over to rub Ved's back. "Ved? Are you okay?"

"Yeah, yeah." Ved cleared his throat. "I'm fine. I just don't remember the chicken tikka here being so spicy."

Carlos's eyes widened. "Ved, you're not seriously telling me that this chicken is too spicy for you!"

Ved's brows furrowed. "That is exactly what I'm saying."

"But I don't find it to be spicy at all, and I'm American and you're Indian."

"So?"

"*So* I'm supposed to be the one coughing right now. You're supposed to have some sort of supernatural spice tolerance."

Ved laughed. "I hate to be the one to break it to you, Carlos. Not all Indians have high spice tolerances. Much to my mother's disappointment, my nose starts running when I eat anything above a medium spice level."

Carlos smiled. "Should I break out the Kleenex, then?"

———

Before Ved knew it, they were on their third pitcher of beer. Carlos could hold his alcohol well. While everything seemed slightly fuzzy to Ved, Carlos seemed more alert than he'd been before all the jugs of beer.

"I heard something strange at work the other day," Carlos said.

"Do tell."

"I heard that the local trains are apparently where people go to have sex in Mumbai. Is that true?"

"Oh yeah. My last boyfriend was groped a few times riding the rush-hour train, though I don't think it's necessarily a gay thing. The men who grope others and do have sex there are likely married and frustrated with their lives. They believe the trains are their only option."

Carlos tilted his head to one side, eating another piece of chicken. "Do you think all those men are in the closet?"

"I honestly don't know. In the villages here, it's common for men to sleep with other men who they call their 'brothers,' only to later marry women. It's accepted as part of being a teenage boy."

"Maybe things would be better if queer love weren't criminalized in India. These men could see that there are more options, that they don't have to feel pressured to marry women." That bit in a way Ved hadn't been expecting. Ved was one of those men Carlos had described: a man unaware that there were other options beyond what society told him was acceptable. For years, and even now, if Ved was being honest, he had let himself believe that he had no control over the path he took. Carlos, on the other hand, believed in the control everyone had over their lives if only they could open their eyes to see it.

Ved thought back to the articles he'd read in the newspapers a few weeks ago. "It seems likely we will have our freedom soon enough."

Carlos raised his jug. "Then, I propose a toast."

Ved raised his own. "To what?"

"To gay sex! May India soon see what it's missing out on!"

Ved laughed. "Salud!"

Carlos's smile suddenly became slyer. "That reminds me. I have something to show you." He reached into his satchel and pulled out a book.

"Is that a book?" Ved squinted in the dim lighting, trying to make out the words on the cover.

"Not just any book. This is the *Kama Sutra: The Collector's Edition*."

"*Collector's Edition?*" Ved laughed. "Oh my God. I can't believe you bought a copy of that."

"Here is ample proof that queer men have existed in India forever. I mean, look at some of this stuff." He turned the book toward Ved and flipped through a few pages. "It's like sexual gymnastics in here."

Ved was glad the lighting was dim because were it not, Carlos would have seen him flush bright pink. He tried to remain composed. "So . . ."

Carlos looked into Ved's eyes. "So . . . why don't we go back to your apartment and study this rich educational text?"

———

The rest of the evening was a dream. Empowered by all the beer, Ved started kissing Carlos in the rickshaw ride on the way to his apartment, ignoring the driver's look of horror. Ved didn't care who saw them. They couldn't keep their hands off each other. This time, there wasn't any awkwardness about where they should go. Ved's apartment was no longer unfamiliar. After unlocking the door, Ved burst in, still kissing Carlos. It wasn't carrying Carlos in his arms fireman-style, but it was pretty darn close.

The sex that night was filled with kisses and playful bites along each other's necks that melted Ved's brain. They fumbled to remove each other's clothes, eventually just ripping them off out of impatience. They rolled on top of each other, laughing, during the drawn-out foreplay.

This time, Carlos wasn't the only one who moaned.

That's when it hit Ved: he would be crazy to give up Carlos for a sham marriage that would only guarantee future unhappiness for all parties. Maybe it was finally time to end this engagement once and for all. Why did it *really* matter what Mumbai socialites and the business community would think? Maybe it really was time . . . the existence of a gay son had never toppled a business. How silly! Ved smiled and closed his eyes, envisioning the life he could have with Carlos, someone who would stand firmly by his side. Someone who wouldn't be pressured into marriage by his parents. Someone who wouldn't dump him for a woman he didn't love. And that was the difference. Carlos would be by his side. Regardless of the inevitable scandal, humiliation, and shame, Ved would have him.

———

Dolly: sent a photo.

Dolly: let me know what you think of the catering menu for the engagement party.

Dolly: while we're still young, Vedu!

CHAPTER 41

Ved woke up smiling ten minutes before his alarm rang and turned over on his side, snuggling deeper under the comforter. Last night had been . . . well, fantastic, to say the least. With Carlos, things weren't awkward. Ved, who was normally reserved and habitually alone, could relax and tell jokes. With Carlos, Ved had transformed into a new version of himself. No, not a new version, the old version that he thought had ceased to exist after Akshay had broken up with him. This Ved was looser, more willing to relinquish control—someone who could see each new day as an opportunity, not an obligation. After all, how could the day be a chore when he was dating someone so wonderful? Ved reached out to turn off the alarm on his phone before it rang. He wouldn't want it to wake up Carlos.

Carlos?

Ved quickly sat up and turned to see Carlos sleeping on his stomach. Right next to him.

In his bed.

How did this happen? How drunk did Ved have to be to allow Carlos to spend the night? To *ask* Carlos to spend the night? Carlos let out a soft snore. It was adorable, but Ved was no longer in the mood. He stood up to go change and brush his teeth. Dad would be out on his morning walk right now. Ved needed to either get Carlos out of the house before Dad got back or somehow force Carlos to stay in this room until Dad left for work. How he could do that without making Carlos feel uncomfortable was a mystery.

It had been four years since Ved had woken up next to another man. He rubbed his toothbrush harder against his teeth. He should have known better. He, of all people, should have known that the happiness of the night must remain relegated to the night. He did love the feeling of having Carlos next to him, of knowing that Carlos had wanted to stay the night. However, that feeling wasn't worth the risk. All it would take was someone stepping into Ved's room for his relationship with Carlos to end. Just one door opening. That would be it.

What the hell had Ved been thinking?

Ved stopped brushing furiously to stare at himself in the mirror. He knew exactly what the hell he'd been thinking. He had wanted to be with Carlos so much, to have some semblance of a normal relationship, that he hadn't cared about the cost of such normalcy. You couldn't attach a cost to it at all—normalcy was impossible in this situation. Ved knew that now, even if he didn't know it a few hours ago. He would find a way to get himself and Carlos out of this unscathed. There was no other option.

Ved spit out his toothpaste, put on a suit, and marched back to the room. Then . . . he sat down on the bed. What had he been planning on doing? Waking up Carlos and telling him to get out? That certainly wouldn't work. All that would do was make Carlos feel confused and hurt. No, he had to come up with a plan, a *concrete* plan.

Caught up in his rapidly rising panic, Ved hadn't noticed Carlos crawl over to his side of the bed until he was wrapping his arms around him. Ved's whole body tensed and he turned. Carlos, sleepy and unaware, leaned forward to kiss Ved. "Good morning," he whispered, and then began unbuttoning Ved's shirt.

Ved broke off the kiss, hands fumbling to rebutton his shirt. He opened his mouth, preparing to speak, not knowing what to say. "Err . . . love—"

"I love it when you call me 'love.'" Carlos smiled. "Please do it more often."

Why couldn't he just understand what Ved was trying to say without Ved needing to tell him? He was making this more difficult than it needed to be. Usually, Ved had no problem telling other men to get out of bed. Granted, all those other men had been in a hotel bed, but still, this shouldn't be that different.

Ved's breaths were shallow. He tried to breathe in slowly for four counts, following Dad's exercises. Nothing happened. Maybe they were bullshit, after all.

"Carlos," Ved began, trying to sound firm, "listen—"

Carlos looked down at his watch. "Sorry to cut you off, Ved; I need to get to work. You mind if I shower before I leave?"

Without waiting for an answer, Carlos stepped into Ved's attached bathroom and started showering with the door open. Was this how couples acted when they lived together? Showering with the door open? Not bothering to grab an extra towel from the linen cupboard? Akshay had always been anal about personal space. He and Ved had never even shared a bathroom. Akshay had used the one attached to his bedroom, and Ved had used the one in the hall. Akshay would have found the thought of using Ved's towel revolting.

Ved started pacing the room. Dad would be back any minute (if he wasn't already). How could Ved sneak Carlos out of the room? Somehow distracting Carlos to get him to stay in the bedroom was out of the question now that Carlos had to get to work. Maybe he could say Carlos was a business associate who missed his flight and needed a place to spend the night? No, that wouldn't make any sense. Why would a business associate ever spend the night at a client's apartment and not a hotel? And why would this associate sleep in Ved's room when his apartment had three separate guest rooms?

Ved paced faster, making sure his eyes stayed away from the open bathroom door. Think. There was surely an obvious solution that he was overlooking. Minutes passed and Ved still didn't have a single idea. He felt sick, the onion-laden chicken tikka and jugs of beer and gallon of mint chutney sloshing together in his stomach. Finally, he couldn't stand it anymore. Ved opened the door a crack to look outside. Sure enough, he could hear Dad chatting with Hari about the benefits of french press coffee over drip. In a matter of five minutes, Dad would be dressed and eating at the breakfast table. Ved slammed the door shut. Think. He just needed to think.

Carlos stepped out of the bathroom, toweling off his hair. If only the way it curled against the nape of his neck wasn't so sexy. Ved decided the best way to handle this was to avoid making direct eye contact with him.

Ved started buttoning up Carlos's shirt. "You need to leave. My dad just got back from his morning walk, so you have five minutes to get out of the apartment before he sits down at the breakfast table." Ved hated how he sounded, harsh and distant. He could see Carlos's whole demeanor change in response, his back stiffening, his eyes hardening. The air felt awkward, strained.

Carlos furrowed his brows. "Ved, I know you're not out to your father—that it's still criminal to be gay in India. I get it. Just relax, okay."

"We'll meet later."

Carlos's voice turned cold. "Fine."

Ved tried to soften his tone. "I promise."

"I've never had to leave someone's place the next morning like this, without even a cup of coffee or some breakfast."

"I'll make it up to you. I promise." Ved moved closer to kiss Carlos goodbye, but Carlos turned away. He grabbed his bag and walked out. He didn't look back.

CHAPTER 42

Ved leaned his head against the wall, trying to reassure himself. Everything was going to be fine. He would take Carlos out to dinner that night and apologize. He would just explain that he had panicked. It was out of fear, he would confess, not because of anything Carlos had done. Hurting Carlos was the one thing Ved had been trying to avoid, yet here he was dealing with the aftermath of doing exactly that. A lump formed in his throat, constricting when Ved tried to breathe. Hot tears collected in the corners of his eyes.

The doorbell rang.

Ved snapped his head up, quickly rubbed away the tears, and ran to answer the door. It had to be Carlos! What other lunatic would be up and about ringing doorbells at 6:45 in the morning?

Hari had beat him to the door, and Carlos wasn't standing there on his knees with two dozen roses, begging Ved to make up: it was Disha, dressed head to toe in Lululemon, holding two plastic cups filled with pale-pink goop.

She walked in and kissed Ved's cheek. Before Ved could overcome his shock, she said, "Ved, call Sheetal. Tell her you're coming in late today."

Ved blinked. "I am?"

"Yes, you are. This is the only time I've got to take your measurements for the cocktail outfit." Disha nodded. "Both our schedules have gotten so hectic lately that I never get to see you anymore."

"We *do* text nearly every day."

"Come on. *I* text you every day, and you respond whenever you feel like it."

Ved knew she was right. But every time he had contact with Disha, that all too familiar guilt returned. It was far easier to carry on with Carlos when he could pretend that Disha and Dolly and Mehra Electronics didn't exist.

"So, now is the best time for us to catch up? Right as I'm leaving for work?"

Disha rolled her eyes. "I have fittings for clients all day and dinner plans tonight. This is literally the only time I have to see you, so yes, now is the best time." She held up the two cups, smiling. "And I brought strawberry smoothies."

Ved remained unmoved. He wasn't ready to relinquish his previous frustration. Not yet. "You know that I don't like smoothies."

"You'll like this one, I promise. It has—"

"I doubt it."

"You're being impossible!"

Ved shrugged.

"Just drink the goddamn smoothie, Ved! And then raise your arms so I can take your measurements. I've seen the most luxurious gray-striped material made of Pashmina threads for a suit. You'll love it, I promise." She held out the cup in one hand with a measuring tape dangling in the other, waiting for him to take it. Naturally, it had one of those gross, mushy cardboard straws.

Ved didn't move to take it. What she was saying sounded all fuzzy in his head.

Disha huffed and shoved it into his hand. "You look as if you're hungover. Was it another late-night business meeting? You need the antioxidants."

Ved grudgingly took a sip. It actually wasn't nearly as bad as he'd expected, though there was no way he could ever tell Disha that. "Now you sound like Sheetal."

"I'll take that as a compliment."

CHAPTER 43

"So, are you going to tell me why you were so sullen earlier?"

Ved and Disha were sprawled on the L-shaped couch, Disha with her legs stretched out straight.

"I don't want to talk about it." His voice no longer held any irritation. He just felt tired; his head felt heavy.

"Oh, really?" Disha raised her eyebrows. "Because you were being a real dick."

"I'm sorry."

"No, no," she laughed, "don't apologize. Why should you? Your lovely fiancée was just considerate enough to wake up early and bring you breakfast. And then painstakingly take all your measurements. She deserved to be treated like trash, of course."

Ved closed his eyes. "I really am sorry." He felt like a louse, seeing how caring Disha was being, looking after his every need, while he was repaying her by cheating on her.

Disha frowned when she seemed to realize Ved wasn't going to tease her back. "Hey, are you okay? You seemed so happy just the other day."

"I'm just . . . I'm okay. Don't worry about me."

Disha mimicked Ved's voice: "Don't worry about me." Her impression was eerily accurate. Ved started laughing and began feeling better. Just slightly better—but still, better.

"Hey." He looked up at Disha.

"Mmm?"

"I never asked how your coffee meeting with Hemant went." He was curious to see if she would bring up meeting Carlos, if she had anything to say about him.

Disha beamed, her eyes bright, and she opened her mouth to respond, only to be interrupted by Ved's phone ringing. They both sat up and turned to see "Dolly Mehra" flash across the screen. Ved made no move to answer the call.

"Ved? Aren't you going to answer that?"

"No."

"Ved, come on. Why wouldn't you want to talk to her? She's so sweet. Talking to her always makes my day."

Ved scoffed and lay back down. "I'm not in the mood."

"She's your mother! You don't get to decide whether or not you're in the mood." Disha answered the call and put it on speakerphone. Before Disha could get a word out, Dolly was already speaking.

"Ved! Thank goodness you answered!"

Disha looked to Ved, who looked to the ceiling. Disha answered for him. "Is everything okay?"

"Disha?"

"Yes, it's me." It was remarkable how she could look so angry at Ved yet sound so sweet with Dolly at the same time.

"Beta, what a nice surprise. How are you?"

"I'm doing well. What's wrong?"

"Is Vedu there?"

"Yes." Disha shoved the phone toward him. "He's right here."

Ved groaned. "I'm here, Mum."

"Great, just great. Disha, I'm glad that you're here too. There's been a terrible emergency."

Ved sat up again, now feeling concerned. "What happened?"

"My cocks have been left in the lurch."

Ved and Disha turned to each other, speechless. Thankfully, Disha answered for them both. "What did you say? The reception in this room is really bad."

"My cocks! My beautiful golden peacocks! The ones I had Kiran Khosla design specifically for the backdrop of your engagement party. It's tragic, I tell you. They were meant to be painted in real liquid gold, their tails entwining to form a lotus in the center. I simply don't know how we can have the engagement party without them."

Ved and Disha burst out laughing.

Dolly was indignant. "Well, I'm glad that you two think this is funny. If you knew what I had to go through to make this happen, maybe you wouldn't be laughing so much."

Ved doubled over, clutching his stomach, while Disha gasped for air.

"You two," Dolly huffed, "my goodness, such jokers. You know my cocks were almost ready just yesterday. If only that main worker hadn't suddenly left to go back to his village, claiming that his wife was not feeling well and that he needed to tend to her."

Ved tried to compose himself. "Mum, please don't refer to the peacocks as 'cocks.'" He couldn't even make it through the sentence without starting to laugh again.

"Do you know how high my blood pressure is spiking over this? Disha, you surely understand the importance of these *pea*cocks. What do you have to say?"

Disha took a deep breath and mouthed "Stop smiling" at Ved, which, of course, only made him smile more. Biting her lip, Disha said, "I understand that you went through a lot to make this happen for us, but can't we do without them? The party already sounds great."

Dolly made a sound of exasperation. "We will be the laughingstock of Mumbai!"

Seeing Disha's desperate look, Ved tried to come up with his own solution. "So why don't we shift the date of the party?" Disha gave him a thumbs-up.

Dolly's voice rose. "Ved, are you crazy! It's already far too late to do such a thing. Nearly two hundred people have already confirmed. The Taj ballroom has been booked; the food has been ordered; the florist from Paris has started arranging bouquets. I've even already had Disha's jewelry set made!"

Ved looked to Disha to help him out. She shook her head and shrugged.

Dolly gasped. "I know what to do. I will send the family doctor to quickly rush to the village and treat the main worker's wife, all expenses paid, of course. We can also send a few saris and a *mithai* box from the two of you as a get-well gesture."

Ved smiled. "See? You didn't need our help. You've already got everything under control."

Disha smiled too. "We really do appreciate all the preparations you've put into this one party."

"Uff, you're too much. I'm doing nothing compared to your father."

Ved furrowed his brows. "What's Disha's father doing to prepare for the engagement party?"

Disha looked panicked. "You don't have to—"

Dolly carried on, her voice proud: "Disha's father is gifting you two a house in Kemps Corner in the very building he grew up in. It's also where Disha was born, no?"

"Yes, I was born there, but—"

"Then it will certainly be the perfect place for you both to raise my grandchildren."

Ved stiffened. "Mum, my apartment is big enough. There's no need for us to move anywhere." This conversation was making Ved very uncomfortable. Decisions were being made on their behalf even *before* they had married. The thought that he could call off the marriage now seemed further and further away, as if one leg was caught in quicksand and the other one was quickly being grabbed too.

"Nonsense. You would be stupid not to accept such a generous gift. I'm sure Disha would love to live in Kemps Corner again."

Disha shook her head. She looked just as worried as Ved felt. Though she tried to keep her voice light, it sounded strained when she said, "I think Papa actually wanted that to be a surprise."

Dolly carried on as if Disha hadn't said anything. "And don't get me started on what he has planned for your honeymoon."

The room tilted sharply to the left. "Honeymoon?" Ved choked.

"Gstaad for twenty days!" Dolly couldn't have sounded happier. "All expenses paid. So romantic, don't you think? It will be just like those Yash Chopra films. And the romance can continue here when you drive Disha around in that fancy new Jaguar her father is buying for you!"

Ved couldn't take it anymore. "Okay, Mum, we need to go."

"Yeah . . ." Disha seemed to hesitate for a moment before adding, "Thanks for calling, Mom." She disconnected the call.

Yes, of course Dolly would expect her future daughter-in-law to call her "Mom," just like any future mother-in-law, but Ved still looked at Disha, stricken. *"Mom?"*

"What else am I supposed to call her? She is going to be my second mother, after all."

CHAPTER 44

Another unproductive day at work. Now, Ved stared at the 108 unread emails in his inbox, hoping that if he looked at them long enough, he could magically will himself to answer them. No luck. Yet.

He really didn't like how Carlos had left in the morning. Again and again Ved replayed the way Carlos's face had changed when Ved had asked him to leave. He had been surprised—that Ved could even consider kicking him out, that Ved could treat him like just another Grindr hookup. Nothing seemed more important than making up with Carlos. Nothing. Dinner, coffee, even another walk through the streets of Mumbai—Ved would do anything with him, would drop anything to be with him. Work could be completed anytime. He and Carlos didn't have many days left together. By March 1, Carlos would be off to Indonesia, and Ved would be making his engagement official to the world.

When he'd first met Carlos for coffee, that expiration date on their relationship had been a comfort, something to reassure Ved that he had nothing to feel guilty about. Except over these past few days, Ved had felt sicker with guilt than ever. Not only was he lying to his family and Disha and to the world, but now he was also lying to Carlos—one of the only people who had completely accepted Ved for everything he was. He would have to make a decision by March 1. Fulfill his own happiness with Carlos, or sacrifice his and Disha's happiness to fulfill his family's and society's happiness. The anxiety made Ved's head spin and the world around him blur into the background.

What made Ved even more anxious was how Carlos hadn't texted him all day. No pictures of him sightseeing, no "How's your day going?" no "I miss you." Ved wasn't going to just sit around here waiting for Carlos to text. He clearly had no intention to if he hadn't already. And who said that Carlos had to be the one to text him first?

Ved: Hey! What's going on with you?

Carlos didn't respond. Ved stared at the screen of his phone, waiting to see the message immediately marked as read.

Ved: Are we still planning on meeting later?

What else would Carlos be doing? Wait, what kind of question was that? Carlos wasn't staring at *his* phone screen waiting for Ved to text. Carlos could be doing literally anything else: working, watching a new movie at Regal Theatre, taking a nap, hooking up with another guy from Grindr . . . no, not the last one. Definitely not the last one. Ved didn't always respond to Carlos's messages immediately, and he was sure that Carlos would never accuse him of cheating because of it. He himself had left Carlos on unread for days! And Ved knew he really wasn't in a position to be getting mad at Carlos about infidelity.

Ved shouldn't delude himself into believing that he and Carlos had any semblance of a normal relationship. They both believed in finding a life partner, sure, but they also knew that there was a time limit on their relationship. They would have fun for a couple of days and then move on with happy memories to remember their time together. That was it. That was all their relationship ever could be.

And that was *horrible* to imagine, because out of all the things Ved was unsure about, he was sure that he would never meet someone like Carlos ever again. No one else would be as funny or smart or levelheaded or passionate. How could Ved go back to being alone? After getting married, where would Ved ever get the chance to be his true, unfiltered self?

Ved: Our usual coffee shop? 5:00 PM?

Still no response.

CHAPTER 45

Ved showed up at the coffee shop anyway. On the way there, he'd stopped at home to change, donning a fitted black Armani T-shirt with black jeans and gelling his hair back. He'd even applied a generous splash of Tom Ford Black Orchid perfume that was so sexy it would have made mosquitos swoon. Sitting at a table, he looked down at his phone. His messages were marked as read, which meant that Carlos had seen them, which meant that there was still a chance he would show up. He had said he wanted to discuss what had happened in the morning, after all. He would show up. He wouldn't leave Ved on read.

Then it was 5:15 p.m., and Ved's excitement turned into worry.

And then it was 5:30 p.m., and Ved's worry turned into panic.

And then it was 5:45 p.m., and Ved was on his third cup of coffee.

And then it was 6:00 p.m., and—

The bell at the front door jangled, and Ved turned to see Carlos walk through. Ved was so relieved that he entirely forgot why he'd been so worried in the first place. Carlos didn't smile when Ved waved him over, though Ved couldn't have cared less. Carlos was here, and that was all that mattered.

Carlos sat down and looked at Ved. His cheeks were flushed and his hair unruly. "Sorry I'm late, Ved."

"Don't worry about it." Ved smiled as wide as he could. "What happened?"

"I don't want to talk about it." His voice sounded flat, his tone cursory.

Ved tried to raise a single eyebrow but ended up raising both. "Oh?"

"Fine." Carlos slouched back in his chair. "A bird shat on me."

"Wait. What?"

"A bird shat on me, okay! I had to go back to the company guesthouse and change."

Ved moved his hand to his face, trying to cover up his smile. "Well, you should consider yourself lucky. Bird shit is a sign of good luck."

"Lucky?" Carlos scoffed. "What the hell are you talking about?"

"It's an old wives' tale."

"It was gross."

They sat in silence after that. The air seemed tense and unfamiliar. Ved had never seen Carlos like this. Carlos was the one who steered the conversation forward, who always had something more to say. Now, he just sulked in his chair and avoided making eye contact with Ved. Worst of all, he wasn't smiling.

Ved smiled enough for the both of them, desperately trying to get the conversation going again. "Carlos, it's okay. Don't get worked up about something as small as this. It's happened to everyone in Mumbai at some point, even tourists. One time, I stepped out of the car about to—"

"Ved, that's not what I'm upset about!" Carlos's voice was sharp. "What happened to you this morning?" Now he looked at Ved directly. "You kicked me out of your house like what we shared was nothing, like you never wanted to see me again! I'm honestly surprised that you even bothered to text me after that."

Ved opened his mouth and then closed it, trying to come up with a response.

"You seriously don't have anything to say for yourself?" Carlos waited and shook his head in disbelief when Ved remained silent.

"You treated me like I was a nobody—you do realize that, right? I'm not some guy you can just sleep with and expect to leave the next morning, according to your convenience. I shouldn't have even come here today." Carlos stood up and grabbed his bag.

"Wait!" Ved reached out and took Carlos's hand. "Please, wait, Carlos."

Carlos didn't sit back down. "What, Ved? Why should I wait?"

Ved's voice rose. "Carlos, it's one thing for my dad to suspect I'm gay and *entirely* another thing for him to see a *man* walking out of my bedroom in the morning."

Carlos stayed silent, waiting for Ved to calm down.

When Ved spoke again, his voice was shaky. "You are *not* a nobody. You mean so much to me. I know I hurt you, and I truly am sorry for that. As soon as I realized you'd stayed over, I . . . I panicked. I don't know what else to tell you. I just panicked."

Carlos released a deep breath and sat back down. "Look, Ved. I understand that you're in a difficult position. That still doesn't excuse the way you treated me."

"I will never treat you that way again. *Never.* I promise."

Carlos looked skeptical.

Ved reached for his hand under the table. "Please, Carlos. I'm sorry."

A minute passed.

Carlos squeezed Ved's hand back.

Ved smiled. "Don't worry. I'll be much nicer tomorrow morning."

Carlos started laughing in full force, causing the customers at the surrounding tables to turn. "Very forward of you to assume that there even will be a tomorrow morning."

That was the Carlos Ved had been waiting for all day.

Ved leaned across the table, his voice teasing. "Do you not want there to be a tomorrow morning?"

"Whoa, don't be crazy." Carlos held up his hands in surrender, goofy smile wide across his face. "I didn't say that."

CHAPTER 46

Carlos and Ved ended up walking outside in the sunset. For once, the air didn't feel thick with humidity. Rather, a soft breeze cut through the otherwise searing heat. This time, they walked side by side, pressing themselves against each other to remain on the narrow strip of sidewalk before the road. The silence felt comfortable. The tension in the air was gone. Ved could finally relax. Well, as much as one could relax in the midst of the rush-hour traffic.

Carlos brushed his knuckles against Ved's. "I'm sorry if I was rude back at the coffee shop." His voice was soft. "I was just feeling hurt. I spent all day with this pent-up anger about what happened this morning, and it had nowhere to go except out."

Ved shook his head. "No, no. It was my fault. I was the one who lashed out at you first. I'm sorry."

They fell silent again, walking toward the promenade, where there were other people walking, some with their dogs, others in groups, and lots of college students. Dim streetlights lined the path, but most of the benches were shrouded in darkness. Just like on the benches outside his apartment, Ved could see the faint outline of couples holding hands and cuddling. At the edge of the path, they came across an empty bench overlooking the ocean. The gentle waves lapped the sand with steady, soft whooshes, returning in and out, in and out. Carlos and Ved sat down. By then, the sky had darkened to a deep plum purple, and if Ved squinted hard enough, he was sure that he could see the faint twinkle of stars. Probably just wishful thinking.

Although Ved hated to break the silence, he had something he needed to say to Carlos. He reached for Carlos's hand. Carlos turned, his mouth agape at seeing Ved acting so boldly in public. Ved continued staring at the ocean. Without turning, he said, "My last serious relationship lasted for four years. It was with a guy who was eleven years older than me. I was head over heels in love with him. I used to do whatever he said. I used to stay over at his house every weekend, and I believed I was the happiest I could ever be, that I had the true happiness people live their lives trying to find. It didn't matter that he hogged the bed or that he made me use a different bathroom or that he had a quick temper." Ved stopped and tried to swallow the lump in his throat. It only grew bigger.

His voice sounded choked when he continued. "He broke up with me by telling me that he was engaged and that we could continue our relationship on the side. He thought that after four years, I would settle for being his mistress. I said no, and I haven't had a relationship since . . . well, until now, I hope."

Ved paused, trying to ignore the awful realization that he was doing to Carlos exactly what Akshay had done to him. His relationship with Carlos *had* to be different. Even though he was engaged to Disha, he would find some way to . . . well, Ved didn't even know what he *could* do. What he did know was that he would do everything he could possibly do to avoid hurting Carlos. He and Carlos wouldn't end after an ugly fight and deep betrayal. They wouldn't.

"I know that we've only known each other for a few weeks," Ved continued, "but I haven't felt the way I do right now in a long time."

Carlos squeezed his hand. "I haven't felt this way in a long time either. I wish we had more time together, to see where this relationship can go."

Ved leaned his head on Carlos's shoulder. "Me too. I never thought that I would like you so much, especially since we met on Grindr." All of that self-consciousness and discomfort he'd felt from showing affection in public with Akshay was gone. With Carlos, Ved felt as if he was part of any other couple. Like there was nothing he'd needed to feel self-conscious about in the first place.

Carlos laughed. "I thought you were a horny old man looking for sex."

Ved laughed too. "That I was." He turned to look at Carlos. "Carlos, you make me very happy; you know that, right?"

"Of course I know that. But one day, I'm sure you'll find someone who can make you happy for longer than a few weeks."

Ved sighed. "I don't want to have to find someone else."

"I said the same thing to my boyfriend in New York City before I moved to South Africa two years ago."

"Why did you break up with him if you loved him so much?"

"I didn't break up with him. He broke up with me. He'd cheated on me for months before with several other guys, and I knew, and he knew I knew. I was an idiot, still hopelessly in love with the bastard, and when I told him about how my new job would take me all over the world, he said he didn't want a long-distance relationship, and that was it. We were over."

Ved leaned closer to Carlos, enjoying the ability to be comforted by someone he trusted. After so many years of approaching intimacy with a "no strings attached" policy, Ved had forgotten what it meant to be in a relationship with someone who wanted to be there day after day. More than that, Ved had forgotten what it meant for *him* to want someone to be there day after day. Carlos was that "someone," and the thought of anyone else filling that role was just as unimaginable as finding Carlos in the first place. Turning his head up to Carlos, Ved asked, "How are you so sure that there are other people who can make us happy? What if we break up, only to be unhappy for the rest of our lives?"

Carlos gave him a wistful smile. "Well, at least we'll be able to remember the happiness we feel right now."

Carlos and Ved sat there like that until their peace was suddenly shattered by the loud ringing of a bell. A caretaker was riding up and down on a bicycle, shining a flashlight at the benches as he went along, signaling that it was time for everyone to go home. Ved looked at his watch. It was well past midnight, yet it also felt like he'd just left the office to meet Carlos mere minutes ago.

After they got up, Carlos looked down at his phone. His face fell. "Shit, Ved, I'm sorry. Just realized my boss needs me to get to the office early tomorrow morning for a product presentation, so I can't stay over at your apartment."

Ved tried not to let his disappointment show. "No problem."

Carlos checked to make sure no one was around. Seeing that they were alone, he pulled Ved close and kissed him. When Carlos broke away, he smiled. "See you tomorrow."

Ved stood there with a hand over his lips, trying to remember how to think.

———

At home, Ved mulled over his earlier conversation with Carlos. Carlos was sure that their relationship had to end, and Ved knew that too. He knew that there was no way he and Carlos could last, but even knowing that, Ved still felt his heart constrict every time he thought about saying goodbye, because he also knew that no one could ever make him happy the way Carlos made him happy. Carlos was special, worth fighting for, even if the odds were stacked against them.

Ved stretched his arms over to the empty side of the bed where Carlos had slept just the night before, trying to feel for some sign that he was there. How was Ved supposed to let Carlos just walk away without putting up a fight? How was Ved willing to sacrifice away his future happiness—and by extension, Disha's future happiness—to make his parents happy? To make Disha's parents happy? Why didn't his own happiness matter just as much as theirs?

———

Dolly: Ved, why are you ignoring my calls?

Dolly: Here I am losing years of my life planning your engagement party. The least you could do is call me!

CHAPTER 47

Ved woke up once again ready to leap out of bed and begin his day. He went to the gym, thinking about Carlos and wondering what he was doing, trying to plan the perfect evening for tonight. That is, until he checked his calendar on his phone during breakfast.

Being that Ved could never remember his schedule, he and Sheetal had devised a color-coding system. Green was for minor events that Ved could neglect to attend. Red was for major events that, if forgotten, would end Ved's entire career. That night, Sheetal had blocked off 7:00 p.m. through 11:00 p.m. in red with the label "annual office party."

Ved really didn't know how he'd managed to forget the annual Mehra Electronics party celebrating the company's founding. Especially this year, considering the party was celebrating the company's fiftieth anniversary. It was all anyone at the office had been talking about for weeks, speculating how the normally lavish party would be elevated for the extra-special occasion. Ved himself had no idea what to expect. His father had made sure to keep him out of the party-planning group emails.

Ved knew he would have to make sure to block off time dedicated to Carlos tomorrow. They had to spend as much of Carlos's remaining time in India together as possible. Ved started planning the next day right away and texted Carlos to let him know that, much to his disappointment, they wouldn't be able to meet later that day.

Ved: Good morning! Hope the product presentation went well.

Carlos: It did go well, thanks for asking. What's the plan for tonight?

Ved: That's what I wanted to text you about. I'm actually not free tonight.

Carlos: Ved! I'm leaving in nine days!

Ved: You don't need to remind me. I set up a notification on my phone.

Carlos: You did not.

Ved: Of course I did, but that's not the point. The point is that I have a work party to attend tonight that I completely forgot about. It will not look good if I miss it.

Carlos: You had better make this up to me tomorrow.

Ved: Don't worry I will. Meet me at 3:00 PM tomorrow. I'll text you the address.

Carlos: I'm looking forward to it.

Ved: Miss you.

Carlos: Miss you more.

———

Dolly: The peacocks have arrived, just as beautiful as the designer promised.

Dolly: Call me! The idiot cutlery supplier doesn't have enough gold forks, so we need to pick a different design.

Dolly: Also, call Disha! You can't expect her to figure out your future life as a family on her own.

CHAPTER 48

After work, Ved rushed back to his apartment to change into his best black Zegna suit with a silk tie. He even took the trouble to gel back his hair. Though he wasn't meeting Carlos for a date, Ved couldn't deny that gelling his hair did wonders for his appearance. He snapped a picture of himself in the mirror and sent it to Carlos, who responded immediately.

Carlos: Wow. Remind me, are you going to a work party or a red-carpet movie premiere?

Ved smiled. And just like that, his confidence went through the roof. One text from Carlos managed to make him feel good—no, not just good—like the best version of himself. For once, Ved didn't feel like he was going to a work party. He'd never enjoyed work parties and especially not this one, with all the social interaction it entailed. He dreaded it. Usually, Ved would find a corner to hide in where he could nurse a single glass of champagne. Ved would wait out the clock and return home exhausted from having to pretend to smile during his father's speech. Ved didn't feel like acting that way this year. Not again. Only now could he see what a drag he'd been. The party was meant to celebrate the founding of the company that would one day belong to him, as well as a night of festivities for all the company's top executives and important clients. Ved should want to celebrate its future, and that's exactly what he planned to do.

Ved stopped at Disha's house on the way to the party to pick her up. Apparently, Dad had told her about the party right after the engagement and had invited her to attend on Ved's behalf. Of course, Ved didn't know anything about this until Disha had texted him that afternoon asking him what she should wear.

She got in the car wearing a finely embroidered black-and-gold salwar kameez with her hair in a loose chignon. *Jadau* diamond earrings drooped from her ears, and she'd completed the look with dull gold *jootis* on her feet.

"Oh my, Disha, you look great. Miss India better watch out."

She rolled her eyes. "Look who's talking, Mr. Handsome. Did you actually gel your hair?"

Ved smiled. "Is it that obvious?"

———

The car pulled up to the St. Regis hotel about thirty minutes later. It was 7:00 p.m. on the dot.

While Ved got out of the car, Disha stayed sitting. "Ved, there's no way anyone is going to be here this early. We should go grab a drink somewhere and come back in an hour."

"Nonsense. The invitation said seven p.m."

"I guarantee you that not even your father would have arrived yet."

Ved raised his eyebrows. "Do you want to make a bet?"

As it turned out, the ballroom was packed with people. Disha gasped and turned to Ved. "What sort of party is this? Why is everyone here on time? I thought this was India, for God's sake."

Ved laughed. "This is *my father's* party. Anyone who arrives late is not welcome."

Disha shook her head. "Unbelievable."

They both looked around the room, eyes wide. "Your father has outdone himself," Disha said.

Prem really had outdone himself this year. The ballroom ceiling had so many crystal chandeliers that it was a wonder it didn't collapse in on itself. The live orchestra played Vivaldi, and everyone was dressed in their finest clothes. A seemingly unlimited amount of champagne flowed from aged bottles, while an army of servers circled the large room, offering hors d'oeuvres: fresh oysters, bone-marrow crostini, truffle pâté.

Ved intended to outdo himself this year too. Every year, Dad would pull him aside at some point during the party and ask Ved to speak to important clients. Dad believed the best way to get a client interested in their products was to treat them to whatever luxury the company could afford. This party, being the company's biggest annual expense, was a prime opportunity to forge new and stronger client relationships. Ved always mumbled something about getting to the clients later, but he never followed through, and while Dad had never commented on it, Ved knew that his negligence disappointed him. The company could always use a few more multimillion-dollar contracts, and tonight, Ved had the confidence to approach the most important clients with ease. Tonight, those interactions that had once made him so uneasy no longer felt painful or awkward. Ved was able to move between clients with Disha by his side, shaking hands, hugging, offering pats on the back. What was weirder was that Ved found himself *enjoying* the dealmaking.

"Mr. Gupta, how are your beautiful wife and children doing?"

"Ms. Gopalan, we have to grab lunch soon so I can tell you about all the amazing new products we're releasing this year."

"Mr. Sarf, I would love to play golf with you sometime at the country club, though I should warn you, I'm only a beginner!"

When they stopped to eat a few hors d'oeuvres, Disha stared at Ved, her eyes just as wide as when they'd entered the ballroom. After half a minute of this, Ved finally asked, "What?"

Disha shook her head in disbelief. "I've just never seen you act that way. Like you owned the party."

Ved smiled, still feeling that confidence he'd felt texting Carlos earlier in the evening. "To be honest, I've never seen myself act that way either."

"What changed tonight?"

Ved considered. What had *really* changed? Yes, Carlos had certainly made a difference, making him even more comfortable in his skin as a gay man, as if the striking down of Section 377 was being planned just for the two of them to be happy. But that wasn't all of it. Even when Ved had been with Akshay, when he thought he couldn't be happier, he had never felt so sure of himself. That surety couldn't come from another person, and Akshay was proof enough of that. But then, what could it be?

Shaking his head, Ved responded, "I'm not sure. I definitely feel . . . happier. You know me. Coming to this party would be the last thing I'd normally want to do, yet tonight . . . it just feels so great. With you by my side . . . you know, it's something I've never done before. Tonight I feel like I belong here."

"That's because you do."

"You don't need to flatter me, Disha. It's okay."

"Ved, I'm serious." Disha set down her plate and waited for Ved to meet her gaze. "*This* is why your dad wants you to take over the company; *this* is why my dad wants you to take over his company. They were able to see your talent for talking to these other people and getting the tough work done."

Ved wished he could believe that. "You should've seen me at this party in past years. I would sulk in the corner and avoid conversation at all costs. The person you saw tonight is different."

"No, he's not, Ved. He's not." Disha's voice became firm. "That person is still you. That person was *always* you. Maybe you didn't see it, but other people clearly did."

"Disha . . . I never signed up to work at Mehra Electronics. It was always just an expectation. The situation with your father's company is no different."

Disha raised an eyebrow. "Isn't it?"

"How so?"

"Listen. After our fathers retire, both of the companies will be yours. I'll be honest, I have no interest in running my father's business whatsoever. Yes, I agree with them that you could run them both spectacularly, and I hope you know that too. But if you don't want to run the companies, no one will force you."

Ved's eyes went wide. "What?"

Disha nudged his shoulder lightly. "Hey, when you're the big boss, all those expectations go out the window. I wouldn't mind if you sold your stock and cut ties completely to figure out which career you *do* want to have."

"I know how much your father's company means to your family—"

Disha held up a hand, cutting Ved off. "No. After we get married, *you* will also be my family, and I refuse to be another person making you feel pressured to live a life you don't want to live. Those skills you demonstrated tonight would be something any company would die to have in an employee."

Ved stayed quiet for a while. "What would our fathers think?"

"That they want us to be happy."

CHAPTER 49

Ved continued speaking to clients for the better part of an hour before deciding it was well past time for Disha and him to have some fun. With a renewed bounce in his step, Ved walked to the bar to grab them both some glasses of champagne. On his way there, he saw Sheetal was already at the bar. She waved and Ved waved back, smiling. She stood next to a nervous-looking young man, probably around Carlos's height. As Ved approached them, the look of panic grew in his eyes, and he tugged on Sheetal's hand, urging her to leave. Ved was close enough to hear her respond, "He's just my boss—don't be silly."

Ved arrived at the bar and leaned his back against the counter. "How are you, Sheetal?"

"Hello, stranger. I'm looking for this tall, kind of stiff, guy. Have you seen him? His name is Ved Mehra."

Ved laughed, and Sheetal lightly punched his shoulder. "What happened to you? Why are you so smiley?"

"I guess I'm just feeling good today." Ved shrugged.

Sheetal smiled wider. "It's not just today. You've changed recently. For some reason, you don't need my cucumber face masks anymore."

The man next to Sheetal coughed. Sheetal and Ved both turned to face him. Sheetal grabbed the man's hand. "Sorry! Ved, you remember my boyfriend, Rahul? You met him at last year's party."

Ved held out his hand. "It's nice to see you again, Rahul. You'll have to forgive my earlier rudeness."

Rahul looked at Ved's hand like he didn't know what to do with it, perspiration beading along his brow line. It was only after Sheetal nudged him that he moved forward to shake Ved's hand.

Ved reached across the bar and grabbed two glasses of champagne. He handed them to Sheetal and Rahul before grabbing two of his own. "Well, cheers, you two. I hope you enjoy the rest of the party." He didn't miss Sheetal's raised eyebrows as he walked away.

When Ved returned to Disha, carrying a glass of champagne for her, he saw that she was talking to Prem. Prem was actually laughing, which was a minor miracle. How did Disha manage to get along with everyone she met so easily?

Ved smiled. "Congratulations, Dad. This party is beautiful."

Disha nodded. "I knew it would be elegant, but this exceeds even my highest expectations. No wonder you kept Ved out of the planning."

Prem laughed again. "You both don't need to flatter me. I'm just happy that you're here."

"Well," Disha laughed, "if you don't want me to flatter you, I think I should at least flatter Ved. You should have seen the way he spoke to some of the high-profile clients. I swear they were practically swooning after Ved was done with them."

Prem smiled and clapped Ved on the shoulder. "I wouldn't expect anything less from my son. Disha, would you mind if I spoke to Ved in private for a few minutes."

"Not at all."

Prem led Ved out of the banquet hall. The sound of the music and chatter was muffled once the large wooden doors shut, leaving a heavy silence. They continued walking down the hallway, carpeted in plush red damask. Ved wasn't sure if he should be the one to speak first. He just looked down and fiddled with the bottom button on his suit jacket. After a few more minutes, the ballroom was far in the distance and the silence became deeper. The threads around the button were now frayed. The silence was too much. "Dad," Ved began, "what did you want to talk to me about?"

Prem stopped and leaned against the wall. "I just wanted to say that I am proud of you."

"We walked for five minutes so you could tell me that? You already said that in the ballroom."

"That's not the main reason why I'm proud of you, son. I am also proud to finally see you happy."

Like the bubbles in his glass of champagne, memories of his time with Carlos rose in Ved's mind. "I am! I've finally found a person who makes me feel good about myself."

"Well, I can't say that I'm surprised. Disha truly is a lovely girl."

Right. Of course, Prem hadn't been talking about Carlos. Carlos would be out of the picture soon enough, and Ved would be alone. Again. He would go back to being that lonely, depressed, awkward man he'd been until that moment when he'd decided to text JaipurVisitor back. All of Ved's previous confidence and bravado deflated, leaving him feeling hollow.

CHAPTER 50

Ved stepped out of the elevator, making the walk down to his office while whistling a Billy Joel tune. Employees turned, their eyes wide in shock, but Ved couldn't care less. In fact, he stopped at several cubicles to wish his team members a good morning. Today was Friday, which meant that he was about to spend an entire weekend with Carlos. Ved was going to do everything in his power to make sure the time they had together was special. After breezing through all the emails that had collected over the past few days and reviewing a PowerPoint his team had set up for their presentation on Monday, Ved checked his calendar. No meetings scheduled for the rest of the day. Perfect. He took out his phone to text Carlos.

Ved: I'm leaving work early. Meet me in Colaba at 2:00 PM in front of the Regal Theatre.

Carlos: Leaving work early for me? I'm honored.

Ved: Be prepared. I have a surprise planned.

Carlos: Can't wait.

Ved packed his briefcase and bounced outside to Sheetal's desk. He knocked on the wall next to her. "Hey, Sheetal. Since I don't have any meetings for the rest of the day, I'm going to leave right now. Please feel free to leave early too."

Sheetal laughed. "I wish. There are still board papers that need filing and contracts that need photocopying. Remember, Ved, *some* of us still have work to do."

"You're telling me that it can't wait until Monday?"

"Of course it can, if it really needs to."

"In that case, I think you should leave early."

Sheetal still looked skeptical.

"Come on!" Ved urged. "We're always the ones staying late anyway."

"Well, if you insist."

Ved beamed. "See you Monday." He wanted to spend every moment he could with Carlos before he left, and that meant that there could not be any distractions to draw them apart—certainly no engagement-party planning. Ved quickly took out his phone to let Disha know he'd be too busy this weekend to help out.

———

Ved: Thanks for accompanying me to the office party last night. Hope you had a good time. Seeing you certainly made my dad's night.

Disha: You give me too much credit.

Disha: What's the plan for this weekend? Do you want to go clubbing? Some of my friends from Parsons are in town and they invited me.

Ved: Clubbing isn't really my thing, but you go ahead. I'm sure you'll have a great time.

Disha: Okay. Do you maybe want to grab brunch on Sunday? I hear Veranda is good.

Ved: Sorry, Disha. I have other plans this weekend.

Disha: Wow, you've been busy lately.

Ved: Why don't you go with some of your Parsons friends? Are they still in town on Sunday?

Disha: You know, most fiancés help plan the engagement party. So far, it's just been me and Dollyji planning the whole thing.

Ved: I promise I'll help next week. Let me take you out for lunch. What does your schedule look like?

CHAPTER 51

On the way to Colaba, Ved passed the South Mumbai promenade. Teenagers fooled around while eating freshly roasted peanuts; couples stood with their arms wrapped around each other, staring out at the sea; senior citizens dressed in sporting caps and white shorts walked briskly with their arms outstretched; street vendors sold cups of chai and fresh jalebis; stray dogs ambled around, sticking close to allies. Usually, Ved would've glanced over all the city's activity without a second thought. Carlos really had him seeing Mumbai differently.

By the time Ved reached the entrance of the Regal Theatre, Carlos was already waiting on the steps. Today, he was wearing a fitted yellow short-sleeved polo with light-blue ripped jeans. How he managed to travel with such an extensive wardrobe was beyond Ved. Carlos smiled and waved. Ved rolled down the car window and shouted, "Hey, Carlos! Jump in."

As Carlos settled beside him in the back seat, Ved reached over and pecked him on the cheek. The driver's eyes flashed in the rearview mirror, though today, Ved wasn't bothered by what his company driver would think or the gossip that would spread among all the other drivers subsequently. Carlos was shocked too. "Since when did you get so bold?"

Ved smiled. "Since I met you, of course."

"Right answer."

Really, seeing Carlos had brought the butterflies right back to Ved's stomach. And they were in full meltdown mode. Even separated by only a few feet, Ved couldn't wait to get Carlos in the car with him. It felt like he hadn't seen Carlos in ages, which was ridiculous, of course, because they'd only been apart for one day.

"So, Ved"—Carlos turned from the window to look at Ved—"this mysterious place we're going to better have air-conditioning. The humidity today has been insane."

"If you think this is bad, just be thankful that you're not here during the summer, but yes, there will be air-conditioning."

"Care to provide any more details?"

"Nope."

"Like, for example, the name of the place we're going to?"

Ved turned to look out the window, smiling. "I'm not telling you anything."

"Come on! The anticipation is killing me."

"Okay." Ved met Carlos's eyes. "We're going to the Taj Hotel for coffee."

"That's some surprise. I pass it every day on my walk around the Gateway of India, although I've never been inside. It seems really fancy."

"Trust me, the inside is even better than the outside."

When they stepped into the hotel, Carlos stopped and craned his neck to stare at the high, ornately carved ceiling with expansive chandeliers. "Ved, this place is gorgeous. No wonder all the guidebooks rave about it." Carlos continued walking, only to stop again, this time in front of a wide red painting, encompassing almost an entire wall. "I can't believe it! They even have an M. F. Hussain painting."

"Yes, isn't it amazing," said Ved, admiring the painting.

"He is one of the most legendary cubist painters in the world! I've never seen one of his works in person. Wow. A computer screen can't do justice to that kind of vibrant coloring."

"You haven't even seen the best part yet. Come on." Ved led Carlos past the corridor of luxury boutiques up the wide, curving staircase to the Sea Lounge restaurant. The sunlight from the floor-to-ceiling french windows flooded the place in light, making the pale-blue walls seem almost like they were glowing. As usual, the place was packed. The maître d', Arjun, immediately recognized Ved and greeted him.

"How do you do, Mr. Mehra?" He quickly led them to one of the sea-facing side tables. "Your usual table."

"Thank you, Arjun. We'll order in a bit."

Arjun nodded. "If you need anything, you know where to find me."

Carlos turned to look out the window, and his jaw literally dropped. The window featured a sweeping view of the Gateway of India set against the sparkling turquoise-blue sea, with rows of bobbing boats that didn't look larger than specks along the horizon.

Ved looked at Carlos. He had already seen the view out the window countless times during client meetings. What he'd really wanted to see was Carlos's reaction. For once, Carlos was speechless, just gazing out the window, his eyes far away. It even seemed like he was holding his breath.

"Ved . . . I don't know what to say. Thank you so much for bringing me here."

"I knew you would love it."

"I really do. If there weren't so many people around us, I would definitely be kissing you right now."

Ved laughed. "Are you in the mood for something to drink? The cold coffee is excellent here, and it's bound to cool you off."

"Yes, please. I can't wait to write about this place on my travel blog." Carlos turned back to the window. "I could stare at this view all day."

Ved continued looking at Carlos. "Me too." When he was with Carlos, it was like everything else in his life faded away. As if it was just the two of them in an alternate dream world, and reality for the moment would have to wait. He wasn't sure if it was love, but he definitely loved being with Carlos. That he was very sure about. Every single moment of it.

The cold coffees arrived in tall, narrow glasses, topped with a thick layer of foam and a sprinkle of cinnamon. As a bonus, the waiter brought out a selection of fresh butter biscuits, still warm from the oven. Though Ved had only planned on eating one or two and Carlos insisted he needed to cut back on sugar, somehow the whole plate ended up getting eaten.

Carlos ran his finger around the rim of his glass with his spoon to collect the excess foam. "Ved, I hope you're not missing too much at work to be here with me. Of course I'm touched, but I know you have an important job, and I don't want to disturb your schedule." He tilted his head to the side. "Wait, let me rephrase that. I don't want to disturb your schedule *too much*."

"Don't worry about it. I technically own the company, remember?"

"You know, I actually didn't remember that. Thank you for reminding me."

Ved laughed. "In all seriousness, I didn't have much to do today. There were no meetings to attend, and I completed most of the hard work two weeks in advance."

"When did you have the time to do that?"

"I used to spend my weekends at home, and to distract myself, I would continue working, sometimes getting more done than I would get done on a weekday, even. This always put me well ahead of the work that needed to be completed for the next week."

"I can't imagine doing that. You didn't laze around watching Netflix or go out with any friends?"

"Honestly, Carlos, I don't really have a group of friends."

"Ved—"

"I mean, I did have a wide circle of friends in college, but as the years got on with work and the long hours I kept, it slowly dwindled. Everyone settled into their own lives—marriage, babies, in-laws to deal with—priorities changed for everyone. But enough about me. I want to hear about your day! What have you been doing?"

A crease of concern formed between Carlos's eyes. "Um, earlier today I went to the Jehangir Art Gallery. My Mumbai guidebook rated it as a must-see."

"You are not still using a guidebook."

"Of course I am! It's such a great source of information."

"What about Google?"

"Hey, I thought you wanted to hear about my day, not attack my sightseeing preferences."

"Okay, okay."

"So I arrived at the art gallery, really excited to see some Indian art. What I ended up seeing were a bunch of cameras and overdressed people that all blocked the art. I think some TV show was filming. I guess it was just bad timing on my part."

"I guess you're just going to have to come back to Mumbai to see the art gallery properly."

Carlos held Ved's gaze. "I guess that's my only option."

Then, a person walked up to them, his tall frame casting a shadow down the length of their table. "Ved! How have you been?"

CHAPTER 52

Ved knew without looking who it was. He would have recognized that voice anywhere—Akshay. What was going on? How was it that the only two times he'd run into Akshay in years happened when he was on dates? Ved couldn't open his mouth. Ved couldn't bring himself to meet Akshay's eyes. Ved's whole body felt frozen.

Akshay cleared his throat. "It's been a really long time."

Ved continued staring straight forward, unmoving.

Carlos nudged Ved with his foot.

Ved shook his head, trying to focus. He turned to look at Akshay but still avoided meeting his eyes. Akshay, dressed in a dark-blue suit with a shiny red tie, smiled tightly with his lips closed. He looked every bit the dapper corporate executive his parents had always dreamed of. His face, however, was carved with worry lines, and faint dark bags hung from his eyes. His voice seemed natural when he said, "I saw you when I walked in, and I knew I had to come over to say hello to such a dear old friend." He was acting like they were on friendly terms, like they had casual conversations in restaurants all the time.

Ved opened his mouth and said, "That's nice," though his voice sounded distant and dead. Ved really wished he had more to say. His mind felt like it was caught in molasses, being rendered more and more useless with every effort to function.

Carlos looked at Ved, his brows furrowed. Seeing that Ved was done speaking, Carlos stepped in. He held out his hand toward Akshay and smiled like everything was fine—like this conversation was *normal*. "My name is Carlos, by the way. I'm one of Ved's friends, visiting from Jaipur for work."

Akshay's smile became more strained, his lips thinner. He didn't shake Carlos's hand. "I hope I'm not disturbing you two; I just thought that after all these years, it might be nice to catch up with Ved, and my wife is out of town for the next month, so—"

"What was your name again?" Carlos leaned back in his chair, his posture relaxed. He wasn't smiling anymore.

Akshay clenched his jaw. "Akshay."

"Well, actually, Akshay, you are disturbing us." Carlos turned to Ved, who was now ripping down his hangnails.

Akshay still didn't leave. "Ved, I really think we should—"

"You should leave." Carlos looked Akshay straight in his eyes.

Akshay's eyes went wide. "But—"

Carlos returned to the remaining foam in his glass. "Thanks for stopping by."

Without another word, Akshay turned and walked swiftly away.

Ved tried to take deep breaths, but every time he tried, his breaths only became shallower, so he gave up and chugged the remains of his cold coffee instead. His face was flushed and his mind seethed. He felt like he was going to throw up. What the hell had Akshay been thinking? How dare he show up at Ved's table expecting some sort of reconciliation? How *dare* he? And what was he implying by saying his wife would be out of town? Did he really think Ved would slink back to him without question? That after four years, Ved was still waiting for him?

Ved leaned back against the plush chair, closing his eyes, and tried to massage the migraine out of his temples. He could feel Carlos looking at him and could also feel the pity in his gaze. Without opening his eyes, Ved said, "Stop looking at me like that." His voice still sounded devoid of all life, cold in a way that wasn't like him.

Carlos's expression didn't change. If anything, he only looked more concerned. "Ved, was that your ex?"

Ved gave a single tight nod.

"Are you okay?" Carlos's voice was soft, trying to keep Ved calm.

Ved opened his eyes and tried to sit up straighter. "Of course. We broke up a long time ago."

Carlos shook his head. "Ved?"

Ved snapped. "No! No, I'm not *okay*. A guy who dumped me four years ago to marry a woman still has the power to make me feel like nothing! Is that what you wanted to hear, Carlos?"

"Absolutely not." Carlos squeezed Ved's hand under the table.

Ved snatched his hand back.

Carlos remained maddeningly calm. "You're wrong, you know."

Ved huffed, not even sure who he was mad at anymore—Akshay, Carlos, himself? "What are you talking about?"

Carlos leaned across the table. "You're wrong to think that Akshay still has the power to make you feel like nothing."

Ved shook his head, feeling tears collect in the back of his throat. "Then why do I feel like nothing right now? Why did I act like a complete idiot when he tried to have a civil conversation?"

"He wasn't trying to have a civil conversation. He wanted something from you—he wanted you to be his mistress, just like you said. *You're* the one who has moved on into a new relationship. *He's* the one still clinging to the past. You shouldn't feel less than what you are based on what someone like him thinks. He's a dick."

Ved wiped his eyes. "You know this guy used to be my whole world, right?"

Carlos laughed. "He's still a dick."

Ved laughed too. "Yeah, he is."

"You know you're so much better than him, right? In literally every possible way?" Carlos smiled at Ved, his whole face lighting up.

Carlos clearly believed Ved was different, but Ved wasn't so sure. Ved had once been the one to smile at Akshay like that, with his whole face open, with such trust. Ved had done that from this very seat at this very table. Now, the roles were reversed. In this scenario, Ved was Akshay.

And that terrified him.

Ved didn't want Akshay's life, to be married to a woman he could never love the way one is supposed to love their spouse. Akshay had sacrificed the potential of their life together, and for what? What had he gained that Ved now stood to gain? The way Ved saw it, Akshay hadn't gained *anything*. He'd lost his chance to embrace his identity forever. Ved wasn't willing to make the same mistake. He *couldn't* make the same mistake. Give up the chance to be with someone he had finally found who cared so deeply about him. Who had come into his life unexpectedly and removed the weight of loneliness he had been carrying around all these years. No, there was no way he ever wanted such a miserable, loveless existence.

CHAPTER 53

Ved returned home, planning to pick up Carlos later for drinks at an Irish pub and dinner at a small Chinese bistro. That all changed when he saw that a package had been hand delivered for him. It had a big red bow. It was from Disha. It contained his new finished engagement outfit. The attached note read, "Let me know if it fits, Mr. Handsome." The walls started closing in on Ved, and he sank to the floor, right there in the middle of the entrance hallway, his hand crushing the note. He sat there, ripping the note into tinier and tinier pieces, and eventually stood up and brushed the paper off his suit. All he needed was a change in plans.

———

Ved: Can you actually meet me at the Gateway of India in an hour?

Carlos: Sure. Why the change in plans?

Ved: Bring a suitcase. Pack for two days. We're getting away this weekend.

Carlos: Ved! Where are we going?

Ved: My speedboat is waiting to take us to my Alibaug house. It's like the Hamptons of Mumbai. You're going to love it.

Carlos: What!?

Ved: We did say that we wanted the last few days we had together to be special, right?

———

Dolly: The seating cards just arrived at the venue.

Dolly: Gilded with silver on cream cardstock, exactly as requested.

Ved: Thanks, Mum.

Dolly: Oh, so you're still alive?

Ved: Sorry I haven't been in touch, Mum.

Dolly: You'd better be sorry. You know how much work Disha and I have been doing to prepare for this party over the past few days?

Ved: I know. I've just been busy.

Dolly: We're all busy, Ved. I still found the time to worry about table-cloths and napkins.

Ved: Sorry, Mum.

Dolly: AND the shape of the ice cubes AND how many bottles of champagne to buy.

———

Disha: Ved, did you get your engagement suit? I dropped it off the other day.

Disha: Let me know soon. I'll need a few days to finish any necessary alterations.

Ved: No alterations necessary. It fit perfectly (as expected).

Disha: That's a relief. I still need to go down to the venue and make sure the seating cards are in the correct order.

Ved: Does it need to be done this weekend?

Disha: Unfortunately, yes.

Ved: Sorry I won't be able to help you.

Disha: What did you say you were doing this weekend?

Ved: Just some work stuff.

CHAPTER 54

Ved and Carlos were soon on the family speedboat, whirring across the Arabian Sea with champagne glasses in hand, the city skyline quickly fading behind them. The cool ocean breeze ruffled their hair, and the clean scent of saltwater surrounded them. Ved felt giddy with excitement. He couldn't wait to show Carlos Alibaug, to spend an entire weekend alone with him. No Mum, no Dad, no work, no flight to Indonesia, no Akshay, no engagement party, no Disha. No distractions whatsoever.

A waiter dressed in a white tuxedo hovered on the other side of the boat holding a plate of canapes, though neither Ved nor Carlos was interested in eating. Ved was busy trying to mentally plan for the last-minute vacation while Carlos stood at the helm, clearly trying to take in as much of the world as possible, not caring that the water was soaking through his shirt.

At the pier, there was a silver Mercedes waiting to take them to Mehra Manor. The manor had an imposing edifice, with whitewashed walls covered in thick bougainvillea and a giant wooden gate. At the gate a security guard ushered them in, and as the car made its way up to the mansion, they drove through miles and miles of carefully manicured grass. To their right, trees lined the sides of the road, laden with fresh fruit and bright flowers. Carlos said he'd never seen such a large expanse of greenery in India. To their left was a sprawling golf course.

"It's the largest privately owned golf course in the city," Ved said, seeing Carlos's shocked expression. "My dad often invites clients here for a game or two during weekends. This weekend, we have the whole compound to ourselves."

The car pulled up to the front door, and Ved and Carlos stepped inside. The mansion actually wasn't a mansion originally. It had been a country club before Prem had purchased it years ago and converted it into a mansion. While Prem had maintained the building's original structure on the outside, he'd hired one of his friends from Oxford, a French architect, to redo the inside. Consequently, the inside was entirely modern, with large glass windows overlooking the sea, art in an exclusively blue-and-green color palette, abstract metal sculptures, and an indoor infinity pool attached to a Jacuzzi.

Carlos leaned in to smell a vase of exotically colored flowers. "What a beautiful house, Ved."

Ved smiled. "This is our paradise for the next two days, so make the most of it."

"Well, if you say so." With that, Carlos undressed and jumped into the pool wearing only his underwear. "Come on in! The water is perfect."

Ved stripped down, too, and jumped in. Normally, he would have been horrified at the thought of swimming in his underwear, but he had given the servants the weekend off, and with Carlos being so carefree, Ved didn't mind.

They swam side by side, and when they were out of breath, they lay floating on their backs, allowing the natural current to take them. Ved swam over to the stocked wine cooler and pulled out two ice-cold beers. He handed one to Carlos and was about to take a sip when Carlos stopped him.

"Wait! We can't drink without making a toast."

"To what?"

"How about to Grindr? The app that brought us together!"

"I'll drink to that."

They clinked their bottles together: "Cheers!" For about an hour, they stayed in the pool, gently treading water and sipping their drinks. Carlos wrapped his arms around Ved's neck and kissed him, entwining their legs together underwater. Ved leaned his forehead against Carlos's. "You know," he whispered, his voice breathless, "I could really use a warm bath right now, and . . . the tub is big enough for two."

Carlos pulled his head back and raised a single eyebrow. "You don't say?"

After long and languid lovemaking that began in the shower and ended in the large, claw-footed marble tub, Ved and Carlos lay naked, side by side, on the four-poster wooden bed in complete bliss, their legs tangled together. Ved gently ran his hand through Carlos's hair. The fan spun slowly above them, and they could hear the cicadas clicking outside. Carlos turned his head to look out the window and stood up before walking over and placing his hands flat on the glass. Ved joined him and wrapped his arms around his waist, pressing their bodies close together.

The sun had almost set. Currently, it cast a bright-orange glow that made the sea shimmer. The clear water formed light, frothy waves that splashed against the dark sand beach lined with tall, leafy palm trees.

Carlos let out a sigh.

Ved rubbed his back. "What's wrong?"

Carlos shook his head. "Nothing is wrong. Everything is absolutely perfect." He tilted his head back to kiss Ved's collarbone. "I just can't believe I'm going to leave India without seeing some of her most iconic sites. I mean, look at how beautiful this place is, and I didn't know it existed until a few hours ago. Imagine all the things I'm going to miss. I haven't even seen the Taj Mahal yet."

Ved nipped Carlos's ear lightly. "I haven't seen the Taj Mahal yet either."

"That's not possible."

"It's true. I've never been to Agra."

"But you live in India!"

Ved shrugged.

"Ved, foreigners travel from halfway across the world just to see it."

"It's always like that. You've been in Mumbai for two weeks, and you've already seen more of it than I have in my entire lifetime."

Carlos laughed. "I don't think that's the only reason why you haven't seen more of India."

"That's true. I'm not a big fan of traveling. The last vacation I took was to Goa when I was a kid, remember?"

"Why is that?"

"I have everything I need right in Mumbai, and really, I'm a homebody. I'd much rather watch a movie in bed eating ice cream wearing my pajamas than have dinner outside at some restaurant in a foreign country wearing jeans."

Carlos shook his head. "I don't believe that, Ved. Being at home can be relaxing, sure, but it's boring. There's so much to see in the world, so many new people to meet, so many different kinds of food to try. There is unlimited potential, if you open yourself up to it. Everyone has wanderlust. Some people just trick themselves into believing that it can be satisfied at home."

Ved suddenly turned to look at Carlos.

"What?" he asked.

"You are the most amazing person I've ever met." Carlos's unquenching thirst for seeing the world made him wish he could travel more with Carlos by his side. It seemed so much fun, such an adventure, a kind of feeling he had never had before.

CHAPTER 55

Ved and Carlos stood next to each other at the window until the sun had completely set and the sky had darkened to a deep indigo. Here, on the beach, the stars shone brightly. Thousands, millions of them filled the sky, winking in and out of sight. In typical fashion, Ved's stomach had to spoil the moment by growling loudly. Carlos laughed, completely unbothered. "Do you want to eat some dinner? I can try cooking with whatever's in the fridge."

"That won't be necessary. I had a meal prepared."

"You're spoiling me."

Ved kissed Carlos lightly on the lips. "Is that such a bad thing?"

They went down the curling gold-and-white staircase to find the long dinner table decorated with candles and scattered marigold petals. An array of ten dishes on traditional Indian silverware awaited them to give Carlos a true taste of India.

Carlos was awed. "Ved, when did you get the time to set this all up?"

"If I told you, that would spoil the fun."

Really, Ved had called the house's cook before they left the city to instruct him on what to prepare. To maintain the surprise, Ved had also told the cook to lay out the dishes at seven and to come back to clean up at half past eleven. That would also ensure that he and Carlos would have the maximum amount of privacy.

Ved and Carlos gorged themselves on plates of Mysore *masala dosa*, tender lamb kebabs, shrimp biryani, brown-gravy fish, soft garlic naan, and much more. And even though their stomachs were bursting, they still found room for dessert: juicy, piping hot *gulab jamuns*. Ved broke off a piece of the spongy dessert, his hands dripping with the sugar syrup, and fed it to Carlos, who licked the excess sugar off Ved's fingers. Carlos fed Ved another piece, and soon enough, there was syrup all over their hands, mouths, and the table.

Ved frowned. "They make feeding people gulab jamuns seem much cleaner in the movies."

Carlos licked the syrup off another one of Ved's fingers. "Yeah, but I'd still say it's pretty romantic. No one has ever fed me food before, much less food as enchanting as this."

"Me neither."

Carlos looked at the skylight spanning the entire length of the dining table meant to seat twenty. "What a gorgeous night. Isn't it fitting that there's a full moon?"

"Yes. I doubt we'd be able to fully appreciate it in the city."

"You're right. The sky is so clear here. It almost reminds me of Jaipur."

"Was Jaipur more or less polluted than here?"

"More. It's rural compared to Mumbai but cosmopolitan compared to the beach here."

"Mmm." Ved ate another piece of gulab jamun.

Carlos still looked upward. His eyes had that same faraway look as before, from when they were looking out the bedroom window. "Did you know that I wanted to be an astronomer when I was a kid?"

Ved nearly choked on his bite. "Really?"

Carlos laughed. "You don't need to act so surprised."

Ved gulped down some water. "No, it's just . . . not what I would have expected from you. It would've been an entirely different career path."

"I know. I didn't consider fashion as a viable career option until college. Before, I was focused on charting the stars, tracking moon phases, all of that stuff."

"You used to track moon phases?"

"You'd better believe it. Every night, I updated a moon-phase chart that hung on my bedroom wall. I had a really cheap telescope that I bought with the money I made working as a delivery boy at a Chinese restaurant, and I would use it every night, even though I couldn't see much in the New York City skies. It was almost as polluted as Mumbai."

"Then how did you manage to chart stars?"

Carlos snorted. "I read books that showed me the star charts, so I knew their relative position. However, I'm pretty sure that most of what I saw was actually imagined."

Ved leaned back and stretched his legs onto Carlos's lap. "What were you like as a child?"

"You really want to know?"

Ved nodded.

"I was apparently very naughty, like sometimes, I used to tie my grandmother's hair to the bedpost while she was sleeping, and I used to shake the soda bottles in the fridge. You wouldn't believe how mad all the constant pranks made my mom. Her face would practically turn purple. My grandmother, on the other hand, used to laugh."

"Your grandmother lived with you?"

"Yeah. I was really close to her. My mom was always working to make the rent, and my dad was always out getting drunk at some bar, so she raised me. She died when I was eighteen, and after that, I was on my own."

Ved squeezed Carlos's hand. "You're lucky that you had the chance to meet your grandmother. I never met any of my grandparents."

Carlos returned the squeeze gently. "You're right. I don't know how I would have made it through high school without her."

"You've never told me about your high school experience."

"There's a reason for that." Carlos smiled. "Does anyone really want to relive their high school years?"

Ved nudged Carlos with his foot. "Come on."

"Okay. Well, in high school, I was campy, and my voice hadn't broken yet and my face was covered in acne, so my classmates would make fun of me, push me up against the lockers, stuff like that."

"I'm sorry to hear that. That must have been awful."

Carlos shook his head. "It was okay, honestly. Without that experience, I don't know if I ever would have learned how to stand up for myself."

"You stood up to your bullies?"

"Oh yeah. I started working out, and by the end of high school, they didn't bother me anymore. I just had to show them that they couldn't get away with pushing me around. My grandmother taught me that."

"I was bullied, too, all throughout school. For my weight."

"Ved, that sucks."

"It did, and what made it worse is that I wasn't ever as brave as you were. I wish I'd had the courage to stand up for myself. I'm hoping things will change in India with Section 377 getting wiped out. It will do a world of good for all the young gay guys growing up. They won't have to put up with any of this sort of crap. Feeling like they're less than normal. It will make them so much surer of their own identity at a younger age, to stand up for who they are . . . something I wish had been the case with me."

"It will change things for sure. For them, and even for you." Carlos took Ved's hand. "Here's hoping for a better future."

Carlos was always so self-assured, so confident. Everything for him was a choice, and looking back at his life, Ved had never believed he had the power to make any choices, at least not the choices that mattered. He didn't choose his career or when he would come out when he was dating Akshay or whom he would marry. And Ved knew that Carlos wouldn't have let *anyone* make those kinds of choices for him. Why did Ved have to be any different?

CHAPTER 56

Later, Ved and Carlos moved outside to sit at the patio. It was overrun with lush greenery. Emerald-green leaves framed fuchsia bougainvillea bushes bursting with full blooms. Gray stones paved the path, cool with the nighttime sea air. That air penetrated the whole area, the salt mixing with the sweetness of the slightly damp grass. Two brass lanterns glowed softly in either corner. The only other light came from the occasional firefly and the moon.

Dolly had stocked the house with the finest tableware from Italy, including two ornate crystal glasses from which they drank crème de menthe. For a while, they sat in silence, soaking in the fresh air, a sharp contrast to the smog perpetually hanging over Mumbai.

Ved turned to look at Carlos, and Carlos turned to meet Ved's gaze.

"Carlos," Ved began, unsure of how exactly he should phrase his question. "How . . . how did you manage to come out?"

"Why do you ask?" Carlos looked worried.

"Because I want to come out, to my parents, to my coworkers, to everyone. I just don't know how. I know that revealing the truth will change how people view me forever. No one in traditional business families like mine ever comes out and admits that they're gay. Their parents probably know, their wives probably know, but everyone pretends otherwise. People can't accept homosexuality so easily. Instead, you end up getting treated like an abnormality. Still . . . I . . . I think it's time. For me. To come out."

Carlos paused for a minute before responding. "The first person I came out to was my grandmother. I must've been fifteen or sixteen. She was understanding and told me that she wanted me to be myself, no matter what. At school, it seemed like all the kids knew I was gay before I could even accept it myself, so I didn't need to tell anyone there. Telling my mom was the hardest for me. She started to cry, though I think she's come to accept it now. She doesn't want any more unhappiness in our family."

"Mum will be shattered for sure. All she's ever wanted was for me to have a family with a beautiful wife and lots of children. My team at work will never take me seriously again, and I know that will be a blow to Dad. A big part of the reason why he's worked so hard for all these years was to make sure he had a successful company to pass on to me, to help me have a prosperous future."

"Why do you feel so strongly about coming out, then? Why now, after all these years?"

Ved looked up at the stars. "Because of you."

Carlos looked shocked. "Me? What did I do?"

"You're confident, entirely comfortable in your own skin. I didn't believe it was possible to feel that way, not really, not until I met you."

Carlos put his arm around Ved, squeezing his shoulder. "What's holding you back?"

"All my parents ever wanted was a son they could be proud of. Someone who they could brag about to their friends and coworkers. I did my best, graduating from college, working my way up Dad's company. The next step is getting married to a beautiful, wealthy woman and having children, which I can't do. It's not like the other things I've done for them. I can't force myself to do it. I just can't." Ved sighed. "I don't want to disappoint them, and I know that I will, no matter what I do."

"What made you think that you had to do all those things?"

"Carlos, it's not like anyone gave me a list of things I had to do to be a good son. Everything I did was expected. I never explored different classes in college. Why would I, when I already knew I would be majoring in electrical engineering? I never thought about finding a job that would make me happy. Why would I, when I stood to inherit a multimillion-dollar company? And now, I'll never get the chance to marry someone that I love."

Carlos squeezed Ved's shoulder harder. "What's the point of trying to please everyone? You deserve to be happy."

Maybe Carlos was right. Maybe Ved did deserve to be happy.

Dolly: Hello?

Dolly: Ved, why aren't you responding to any of my texts?

Dolly: Where the hell are you?

CHAPTER 57

When Ved woke up, lying on his stomach, the sun was already high in the sky, flooding the room in bright-yellow light. Looking at the clock on the wall, Ved saw that it was ten a.m. Ten a.m.! Ved hadn't slept past six a.m. since he'd started his job at Mehra Electronics. Carlos really did put him through some workout the night before. Ved planned on staying in bed a little longer, just because he finally could, but then he turned and realized Carlos was already up. Ved pulled on a pair of striped pajama pants and headed downstairs to the kitchen. Carlos was standing there, fully dressed, chopping up an array of vegetables into neat cubes.

"Good morning, sleepyhead!" Carlos put down his knife and walked over to kiss Ved on the cheek. "Someone had a long rest."

"You're telling me. For once, I feel well rested."

Carlos laughed and returned to chopping. Ved hugged him from behind. "Why are you cooking? We could have picked up something from one of the local restaurants."

"No, I wanted to cook for you at least once before I left. I've been told by many that my cooking skills are one of my best qualities." Carlos winked.

"Well, I feel bad letting you do all the work. Can I help?"

"Sure." Carlos went to the fridge and pulled out a carton of eggs. "Crack four of these in that bowl." He gestured across the counter to a deep glass bowl.

"Okay." Ved stood in front of the bowl and stared at it. Sure, he'd never cracked eggs before, but how hard could it be? Ved carefully grabbed an egg from the carton and slammed it against the side of the bowl, which sent pieces of shell flying everywhere.

"Ved!" Carlos ran over. "Are you okay?"

Ved blushed. "Yeah, I'm fine. I'm sure I'll get the next one right." He picked up another egg from the carton.

Carlos laughed. "Oh no, you don't. Watch me." Carlos took the egg from Ved's hand and gently tapped it a few times on the rim of the bowl. When a crack appeared down the middle of the egg, he slowly pried it apart with his fingers, taking care that the shell didn't mix with the yolk. "See? You have to be gentle with it."

"Got it." Or at least Ved thought he had it. As it turned out, Ved's second, third, and fourth attempts were all just as catastrophic as the first. Carlos didn't seem to mind, though. He replicated the motion for Ved each time with patience.

Somehow, Carlos managed to prepare a full breakfast despite Ved's attempts to help, which brought disaster to whatever he touched. They were soon sitting at the patio table, sipping freshly squeezed orange juice and eating fluffy vegetable omelets with Canadian bacon and buttered white toast. While Carlos had added jalapeños to his omelet, he made sure to exclude the chilis in Ved's. And of course, there was also lots of ketchup for the both of them.

In the sun, Carlos's skin was already turning a faint pink. He slid his Ray-Bans up his forehead and looked at Ved, his expression suddenly serious. Ved sat up straighter. "What's wrong?"

Carlos narrowed his eyes, as if trying to puzzle something out. "Ved." He paused. "You know you can tell me anything, right?"

"Yes, I do. You already know that." Ved reached for Carlos's hand. "Why are you asking?"

Carlos still looked confused. "I just get the weird feeling that you're not telling me something."

Ved took both of Carlos's hands in his and held them against his chest. "Carlos. I'm not hiding anything. You already know everything about me. I promise."

And Ved didn't believe he was hiding anything from Carlos either. Yes, he was well aware of the fact that he was engaged to a woman and that his engagement would be made official in a matter of seven days, but there was also no way Ved would let the engagement go through. He would find a way to stop it, he reassured himself. He would come out to his parents and his coworkers and Disha—facing the consequences. *All* of the consequences. But, for some reason, even though he wanted to come out, Ved still felt that all too familiar weight of guilt press deeper into his chest.

Mum and Dad would come around. Ved knew they loved him enough for that. Mehra Electronics would be fine even without Mehra Productions. There were many other executives who had faced scandals of their own without taking down their companies for good. Ved would be ostracized, but that was something he could handle. The guilt . . . that guilt was for Disha. Because in order to be with Carlos, he would have to tell her how he'd betrayed her. And lose her friendship. Forever.

That guilt was also for Carlos. Ved had never considered what Carlos would say once he found out that Ved had been engaged. What would he say? Would he even want to be with Ved after—

"Come on," Ved said, pushing away the double load of guilt with all the will he could muster. "Let's forget this serious talk and enjoy the rest of the day."

Though Carlos still looked uncertain, he nodded. "Okay. You're right. Let's not waste the little time we have left together."

They spent the rest of the afternoon and the next day alternating between lying flat on their stomachs in the grass, dozing over a picnic blanket, and enjoying the warm, bubbly flow of the Jacuzzi. Even though it was hot outside, a steady breeze blew. At one point, both of them dozed on the couch, Ved with his head against Carlos's shoulder.

Neither of them was ready to leave anytime soon when Sunday afternoon arrived, but unfortunately, the latest the company speedboat could depart was 6:00 p.m. On the ride back, Ved stood at the helm of the boat with Carlos, holding hands.

Ved couldn't stop smiling. That anxiety about what the future held was still there. It was always there. The only difference was that now he had Carlos by his side, and with Carlos, he could handle anything.

———

Disha: Answer your phone!

Disha: Ved, I swear to God!

Disha: This engagement party is your responsibility too. I don't see why I had to be the one who spent her entire night in an empty ballroom anxiously rearranging seating cards!

Disha: What have you been doing this weekend?

CHAPTER 58

Five days until the engagement party
Five days until Carlos's departure

Ved decided to skip going to the gym on Monday morning and got to work early. He knew that after not working through the weekend for the first time in years, there was bound to be more work than usual waiting on his desk and in his inbox. Boy, was he right. "More work" was a massive understatement.

Sheetal had left a stack of at least thirty contracts on his desk, except Ved didn't just have to sign them; he also had to revise them wherever there was a yellow Post-it tab. The documents were so thoroughly covered in Post-it tabs that Ved would practically have to revise everything. Plus, he had to present the fall line of products with his team to the rest of the board, and he had to get back to all the clients who had emailed him over the weekend.

Seeing that Ved was frazzled, Sheetal periodically came in to refill his mug of black coffee and to provide encouragement. By 2:00 p.m., Ved was finally ready to take a break for lunch. He leaned back in his chair with a Mexican quinoa bowl and was about to put on some headphones to listen to music when the door to his office burst open. It was Disha, and she looked furious.

Her face was flushed bright red, and her eyes held the fires of hell. As if by instinct, Ved pushed his chair back against the wall. "Disha? What are you doing here? I—"

"Save it, Ved." She put her hands on his desk and leaned forward. "Why the hell haven't you been responding to your messages?"

Ved glanced down to his phone. Shit. What had he been thinking? Of course she was upset; she had every right to be. He had to—

"Ved. Look at me right now." Her voice had gone from furious to deadly calm. That couldn't be good.

Ved looked up.

Disha narrowed her eyes. "Who do you think you are?"

"What?"

"Don't make me repeat myself."

"I'm sorry, Disha."

"Oh, you're sorry?"

Ved nodded quickly.

"Well, that makes me feel all better. Consider yourself forgiven."

"Really?"

"No, you idiot! You don't just not respond to someone's texts for three days! And I'm not just some random person, Ved! In case you need reminding, I'm your fiancée."

"Disha, of course I know that you're my fiancée. I told you I had back-to-back meetings; it's been hectic with product presentations and monthly reports to complete. I didn't even have time to look at my phone. That's all."

Disha scoffed. "You're going to need a much better excuse than that. I'm tired of hearing how busy you are with work all of a sudden. I'm not so dense that I can't see when I'm being pushed away. In case you didn't realize, Ved, I have a hectic work schedule too. Do you see me slacking on engagement preparations whenever I feel like it? Absolutely not, because *I* committed to this engagement. *I* don't make excuses when it comes to that commitment. You could stand to help out more often! I really shouldn't have to hold a gun up to my fiancé's head to get him to help out with the planning of *our* engagement party!"

"Disha, I don't know what to say besides I'm sorry. What else do you want me to say?"

"Just show me some respect, Ved. That's all I ask." She walked away and slammed the office door shut. The thud reverberated through the metal doorframe.

Ved knew Disha was right. No, he didn't think of her romantically, but she was his friend, and she deserved respect from him. More than that, she deserved the truth. He *should* tell her the truth, do everything he could to reduce the pain she would feel when she found out what Ved had been doing behind her back. He really should.

CHAPTER 59

The second the clock hit 5:00 p.m., Ved left work, went home to grab his workout bag, and headed for the gym. If the state of his fingers with their ravaged hangnails was any indication, he had a lot of nervous energy he needed to release. The best way for Ved to clear his head was to take a run. He arrived, dressed in a new set of workout clothes, downed a glass of strawberry-infused water, and hit the treadmill. Today, he not only increased the speed, but he also increased the incline. The steepness made his legs burn, which was exactly what he needed to distract himself. Music blared in Ved's ears, though he wasn't really listening to it. He just focused on putting one foot in front of the other. Over and over again. The repeated action helped soothe his nerves. Soon, Ved was drenched in sweat and feeling a whole lot better.

After an hour, Ved stepped off the treadmill, his legs weak like Jell-O, and felt a pair of eyes on him. He turned to see a balding middle-aged guy with a goatee, a thick beer belly, and hairy armpits staring unabashedly at his crotch, as if inspecting it. The moment he noticed Ved noticing him, he quickly stepped off his treadmill and made to follow Ved, shouting "Please wait!" Ved stiffened and speed walked toward the locker room, pretending that the headphones in his ears blocked out any noise. No straight guy would look at him like that, and Ved certainly wasn't interested in whatever the man wanted. From the corner of his eye, Ved could see the man was still following him. Shit. At the locker room, Ved busied himself packing up his towel and protein shaker, acting like he was in a hurry. The man didn't take the hint and instead leaned against the set of lockers closest to Ved.

"Hey," he said, smiling with a full set of yellowing teeth.

Ved acknowledged him with a short nod.

"I think I've seen you around before." He winked and nudged Ved's shoulder. "*Outside* the gym."

What was he implying? "Really?" Ved tried to keep his voice cool. "Maybe it's when I've been out shopping with my wife." That should throw him.

The man smiled even wider. "Don't worry, man. I'm married too."

Ved realized with a jolt that this could very well be him in the years to come, one more closeted married man hitting on some random guy in the gym in desperation. Was that the sort of life he wanted? Just to make his parents happy? He felt sick in the pit of his stomach as he rushed out, knowing that first he had to make things right with Disha and then muster up the courage to come clean to her. Or else he would end up destroying both their lives.

CHAPTER 60

Ved: I'm sorry.

Disha: the only reason I'm forgiving you is because our engagement party is coming up so soon, but don't think I'll forget what you did.

Ved: I'll make it up to you.

Disha: fine.

Disha: good night.

Ved: good night.

———

Carlos: night, Ved.

Ved: good night.

———

That night in bed, Ved tossed and turned, shifting his body into every possible position, yet he was still unable to fall asleep. He kept thinking about what the man at the gym had said to him. Was that what Ved was going to be like two years from now? Five years from now? The creepy old man who hit on younger guys at a members-only gym?

How was what Ved was doing with Carlos any different from what the man had proposed? Ved was cheating on Disha, just as that man had intended to cheat on his wife. What right did Ved have to look down on someone like that? They were in the same situation. The only difference was that Ved still had time to change his future. He didn't *have* to end up like that man, or even like Akshay, for that matter.

His engagement was five days away, and he, the man who always had a plan for everything, had absolutely no idea how he was going to get out of marrying Disha. No idea at all. He was in too deep.

A part of Ved had hoped that somehow Carlos, or his relationship with Carlos, would be what stopped the engagement. That the scrapping of Section 377 could not have been better timed just so the two of them could be together. That being with someone would finally give him the courage to stand up for himself. But Carlos was leaving. Their relationship was almost over. Forever. Carlos wasn't going to save him from his choices. Ved was going to have to face them. He was about to doom himself and Disha to a future of unhappiness—unless he stopped things right now. Disha should be the wife of someone who would love and respect her. Not someone who would date another man behind her back. Ved should be with a man. Disha deserved much better, and so did he.

It was about time Ved faced reality head-on.

No more excuses.

CHAPTER 61

Being that it didn't seem appropriate for Ved to wake Disha up at two in the morning to tell her the truth, Ved waited until later in the morning. He hadn't slept well that night, or really at all. He mostly dozed in and out of dreams, jolting awake whenever he seemed to sink into a deeper sleep. At 5:59 a.m., he turned off his alarm before it could ring and pushed himself upright against the headboard, rubbing the grime from his eyes. He was still groggy and could already feel a migraine developing at his temples. He clutched his phone tighter in his hands, trying to stop their shaking. He inhaled deeply and pressed Disha's contact card.

The phone rang and rang and rang.

And rang and rang and rang.

No response.

Ved left a message, his voice shaky. "Um, Disha . . . please call me back as soon as possible. Please. I really need to talk to you."

CHAPTER 62

While Ved was fraying the threads on the bottom of his button-down shirt in the car on the way to work, Carlos called.

"Hi, Ved!"

"Hi, Carlos."

"Where are you? There's so much noise in the background."

"I'm just in the car on the way to work. Where are you?"

"My boss took the entire team to an old part of Bandra. We ate at a restaurant that you would have loved. The tablecloths were adorable! They were made of red gingham cloth. And don't get me started on the food. We were served these delicious hot buttered buns and tiny cups of"—he hesitated—"chay?"

"Chai," Ved corrected. "It's actually called 'cutting chai' when they serve it in half, in small glass cups. As a single order that is shared by friends, mostly in small old-time cafés."

"Good to know."

Ved waited for Carlos to continue, anxious to get back to fraying his shirt's threads.

Carlos cleared his throat. "The reason I'm actually calling is to check what time you want to meet for the Salvation Star party tonight?"

Shit. Ved had completely forgotten that he'd agreed to go to that. Salvation Star was a private gay party, known for its classy, modern vibe and high-profile attendees. Ved, of course, had never attended, but Carlos had been counting down the days until the event ever since he'd arrived in India.

Ved scrambled. "Oh, um, how about nine p.m.?"

"Sure. Do you want to meet there?"

"I can pick you up. Just text me your location at the time."

"Sounds good. I'm really excited! Listen, I was also thinking we could—"

"Carlos, I'm almost at work; I really have to go." Ved was still at least thirty minutes away from the office, maybe more with all the traffic. He just couldn't handle the spasms of guilt he felt while talking to Carlos.

"Okay, see you—"

Ved hung up.

———

Ved was back to spinning around in his office chair, and when that made him too dizzy, he stood up to start pacing. Unfortunately, his fingers were already ravaged and bandaged, so he didn't have any more hangnails to pull down. He quickened his pacing, going from the door to the window and back again, trying not to throw up.

He knew he should wait for Disha to call him back before he took any further action. She should be the first one to know. Of course she should be. She had to be.

But after an hour of going back and forth, back and forth, across the room, Ved was about ready to collapse in on himself. He had to do something. He couldn't just *wait*. He had no idea when Disha would call. No. He had to take action now.

Ved burst out of his office door, ignoring Sheetal's look of concern. His heart thudded against his chest so hard that Ved was later surprised it didn't leave bruises across his chest. He hadn't eaten anything all day, and the mugs upon mugs of black coffee he'd drunk to compensate now burned holes in his stomach. Nevertheless, Ved was feeling reckless, his face flushed bright red, his fingers tingling. He marched to the other end of the office until he arrived at a tall wooden door. The secretary outside tried to stop him, but Ved continued walking, barging straight into the office—his dad's office.

Prem was clearly deep in thought, mulling over a stack of contracts. Seeing Ved, he pushed his spectacles up his forehead, bushy brows furrowed together.

Ved took a deep breath, trying to slow his pounding heart. "Dad. I need to talk to you."

Prem opened his mouth to speak. Ved cut him off.

"Right now."

CHAPTER 63

Prem looked at Ved, and for a moment—just for a moment—his eyes widened in shock. The moment quickly passed. Ved continued looking at Prem, forcing himself to maintain eye contact. Prem pressed the intercom button on his telephone and told his secretary to hold his calls. His eyes softened. "What is it, Vedu?"

Ved felt the defiance leave his body. He suddenly just felt very tired and sank into one of the chairs across from his father's desk. Prem stood up slowly, as if trying not to startle Ved, and sat in the chair next to him. He turned, his posture relaxed, his face back in its default neutral setting.

They stayed silent for a while. Ved was breathing heavily, mentally yelling at himself to get a grip. Prem, on the other hand, looked so serene that it was impossible to tell what he was thinking.

Finally, Ved took one deep breath and slowly released it. Waiting wasn't going to make this any easier.

"Dad, I'm sorry. I can't marry Disha or . . . or, any girl. I'm . . . I'm gay."

CHAPTER 64

Ved's whole body tensed involuntarily as he braced himself for Prem's reaction, the scenarios quickly running through his head, each more painful than the last.

Scenario #1

Prem opened his mouth and yelled at Ved: for being selfish, for being a deficient son, for being an utter disappointment. It was the first time Prem had ever raised his voice with Ved.

Scenario #2

Prem's shoulders began to shake as tears ran silently down his face. It was the first time Ved had ever seen his father cry.

Scenario #3

Prem looked at Ved, his face twisted in complete disgust. He leaned over the side of the chair and spit onto the floor.

Scenario #4

Prem said only one thing—"You are not my son"—before getting up and leaving the room. That was the last time Ved ever saw his father.

———

As much as Ved dreaded seeing his father's reaction, *any* reaction would have been better than no reaction. And what did Prem do? He didn't react. His face remained neutral, impassive. His posture was as relaxed as ever. The silence in the room became suffocating, like the smoke in the thick of a wildfire. When Prem finally did speak, all he said was, "Okay, Ved. Thank you for telling me."

Ved's posture remained rigid. He stared at his father, openmouthed, speechless. And suddenly, Ved reached forward and hugged Prem tightly, unable to control the tears streaming down his face.

"Thank you, Dad."

Prem squeezed Ved tighter against him. "All I want is for you to be happy, son. That is all I want."

Ved sniffled, but it was no use. He was now sobbing like a child, clinging to his father's back for support.

Prem, in turn, rubbed Ved's back, making small, soothing circles. "I would never want you to do something that you do not want to do. I will be happy whenever you choose to marry, and I will support and love whomever you choose to marry like my own child. A year from today, ten years from today, or never. A woman, a man, or no one. I understand things in the world are changing. I do understand. How can I choose your life partner for you? It is, after all, your life."

Ved pulled away and wiped away his tears, smiling, despite the snot running down his face.

Prem took Ved's hand firmly in his own. "Wipe away your tears, Vedu. Everything is going to be fine. I'll make sure of it. You let me handle your mother and Disha's family. Don't bother yourself with the business deal or the engagement-party arrangements. But what about Disha herself? Do you want me to leave it to her family to break the news? The poor girl should not get hurt in this process. It's not any fault of hers."

Ved squeezed his father's hand. "No, Dad, she deserves better than that, and so does her family. They've all been nothing but kind, welcoming me into their family. More than that, Disha has become a close friend. I need to handle this myself. I'll talk to Disha and her family. I want to tell her personally and make sure she doesn't feel like she's to blame in any way; I'd hate myself if she does. She's become very special as a friend . . . we've shared so much. Let me talk to her and make her understand. And to Mum too. I promise."

CHAPTER 65

By the time Ved had left to pick up Carlos for the party, he still hadn't received a response from Disha. No text, no call. Nothing. Why wouldn't she just respond? Hadn't she just gotten mad at Ved for ignoring her attempts to contact him a few days ago?

Ved had always thought that when he finally came out to someone, he would feel like a burden had been lifted off his chest, a burden he'd become accustomed to without even realizing it. And, in his father's office, he *had* been relieved. He'd felt lighter and now was ready to face the rest of the world.

But as the hours dragged on, Ved was still carrying on the charade with Disha, which brought the weight right back on his chest, this time with the power to crush him entirely. He needed to talk to her, to tell her the truth. Even though Disha didn't know that Ved was gay, Ved *could* be himself around her, just like how he felt he could be himself around Carlos. That friendship had to mean something. It couldn't be worth losing just because Ved had been too scared to stop things before they got out of hand.

The car pulled up to the company guesthouse, and Carlos slid into the back seat, big grin wide across his face. Ved turned to look out the window, resting his head against the car door, willing the night to be over.

Carlos looked confused. "What? No kiss on the cheek today?"

Ved looked at Carlos, his eyes distant. "Huh?"

Suddenly, Carlos snapped, his face reddening, his voice sharp: "What is up with you today?"

Ved was still thinking about his earlier conversation with his father, replaying each moment in his head, and while he wanted to talk to Carlos about it, he knew he should wait until he had also told Dolly and Disha and Disha's family. He owed the full truth to all of them. No more promises about what he was planning on doing somewhere down the road. He wanted to tell Carlos that he had actually done it: he'd come out to everyone. Ved shook his head, as if to clear it, and came back to the present. "Nothing. I'm just distracted, that's all."

"That's all?" Carlos huffed. "You know, if you didn't want to come to the party, you could've just said so."

"No!" Ved squeezed closer to Carlos. "No, it's not that. I really am excited to go." His voice wasn't convincing.

"Are you?" Carlos demanded, seeing through Ved's words.

Ved slouched back against the seat. "Well, and nervous, of course. I've never been to an . . . event like this before." After a pause, he added, "I'm really glad that you're here with me."

The tension left Carlos's body. "I can't believe we're actually going together. When I first came to Mumbai, I thought I'd be going alone."

Ved pressed closer to Carlos. "Of course we're going together."

CHAPTER 66

Stepping out of Ved's BMW, they really looked like a couple that night. Purely by coincidence, they'd both slicked back their hair and dressed in jeans, collared T-shirts, and white sneakers. The only difference was that Ved wore a black shirt and Carlos wore a red one.

The party was at one of those trendy lounge bars in Lower Parel. What had once been a desolate mill area had been transformed into a hotspot for parties. Refurbished with lounge music, soft lighting, fusion food, and formidable alcoholic concoctions, it had become a new playground for the elite, replacing the old concept of a nightclub with its cooler, slicker vibe. Designer furniture, international DJs, molecular gastronomy. It was new money in old Bombay.

When they reached the bouncer, Ved paid the entrance fee for both himself and Carlos. Carlos hated that, of course, but Ved insisted that tonight was on him—his first outing as an openly gay man. Carlos, evidently sensing that Ved was still nervous, held his hand as they walked in. Ved automatically tensed and looked around to make sure no one could see before realizing that Carlos *could* hold his hand here. Without any shame.

Inside, the space was already packed with perfectly clipped beards, buzz cuts, tight jeans, and muscled bodies shown off by fitted T-shirts. Men who looked like runway models danced with queens dressed in shiny pink neon. Everyone was checking out everyone else, passing little knowing smirks and looks of flirtation. It seemed like they all were out to score, even if they were standing hand in hand with someone else.

Ved let Carlos tug him over to the bar. There was barely any room to stand among the people leaning over each other to get the attention of the two harried bartenders. Ved felt someone press into his back, closer than those around him, and turned to see a young guy with spiky hair and frosted tips. He was chewing gum and smiling. In the strobe lighting, his teeth seemed unnaturally white.

"Hey, handsome," he said, or rather, yelled, because the music was so loud you could barely hear your own thoughts. "Let me buy you a drink."

Carlos turned around and glared at the guy. "Fuck off. He's my boyfriend."

"Whatever." The guy walked away.

Ved raised his eyebrows at Carlos. "My hero."

Carlos rolled his eyes. "Well, someone had to defend your honor."

"My honor? What about yours?"

"That too. I want the people here to know that you're taken, that you're *my* date tonight."

Ved had never seen Carlos act so protective before. If he was being honest with himself, it was nice to have someone who cared enough to fight for him, who wasn't so willing to give into the free-love spirit of the night.

Carlos ordered vodka tonics. His was a double with a slice of lime; Ved's was plain and on the rocks with a cocktail straw. After handing Ved his drink, they both made their way over to one of the gray L-shaped couches. They clinked their glasses together and shouted "Cheers!" The ice-cold vodka and fizzy soda made Ved feel instantly buzzed. The warmth spread from his mouth all the way down to his toes. All of that previous tension that had locked his muscles melted away like it was nothing. He grabbed Carlos by the collar of his shirt and kissed him. Carlos gasped and threw his arms around Ved's neck, kissing him back and sliding his hand up Ved's leg.

Ved pulled away and leaned his forehead against Carlos's, cupping the nape of his neck. "I don't want you to leave Mumbai."

"I don't want to leave either."

———

Somehow in the time it took for Ved and Carlos to finish their drinks, the amount of people in the room had (at least) doubled, making the air feel stuffy and hot. You couldn't move your leg without bumping into someone, and the dim lighting wasn't helping. Ved knew that what he needed to clear his head was definitely another drink. He kissed Carlos's cheek and stood up. "I'm getting a refill. Do you want one too?"

Carlos nodded and kissed Ved's hand. Ved started wading through the crowds of people to get back to the bar. On his way, Ved was surprised to see several celebrities in the crowd, including big Bollywood directors, small-time TV actors, fashion designers, and models—all of whom likely faced the same struggle Ved was facing about coming out. He even felt like he'd seen two or three of the guys on Grindr, or maybe in a hotel room sometime over the last four years. Even though they might not have been able to be themselves during their day-to-day lives, they could be themselves right here, right now.

Ordering drinks, Ved was feeling the right combination of impulsive and tipsy, so he not only ordered two vodka tonics, but he also ordered a round of tequila shots with lime. When would he ever get the chance to do shots again? None of the people he knew would ever be caught dead doing tequila shots.

Carlos raised an eyebrow when he saw Ved bring over the tray of shot glasses. "Who are you?" he asked.

Ved laughed and threw back the first shot. "I guess I'm just in a good mood tonight."

———

It was a wonder how Ved was even standing after the countless tequila shots and the third vodka tonic. Carlos happily swayed on his feet. "Come on," he said, pulling on Ved's hand. "Let's dance."

Ved groaned and lay back against the couch cushions. "No."

Carlos pulled harder. "Ved!"

Much to his horror, Carlos was able to lift him up and lead him to the dance floor.

The last time Ved had danced—had really danced—was when he was a child in his bedroom mirror with music blaring from the radio while his parents were out for dinner. There was a reason he chose not to dance anymore.

"I'm going to look like a fool!" Ved yelled.

Carlos laughed. "Look around you, Ved. *Everyone* looks like a fool!"

He was right. Everyone *did* look like a fool, shaking their hips, raising their arms, jumping up and down. Ved started dancing, and surprisingly, he was having fun while doing it. The bohemian spirit in the air had infected everyone, it seemed. The music grew louder, and the room took on a faintly blurry outline. It didn't matter who was with whom or how anyone looked. What mattered was that they were all having a good time. Together, whether that be through dancing or laughing or kissing. Or maybe it was just all the alcohol. Either way, Ved was having the time of his life.

———

At some point, Ved and Carlos ended up back on a couch, though Ved couldn't be sure if it was the same L-shaped couch as before. They had to share it because the other half had been taken over by a famous designer, whose shirt was open. The guy from earlier with the frosted tips was right on top of the designer, kissing him deeply. Ved pulled Carlos on top of him, and Carlos started kissing Ved's neck before cupping his face to kiss him on the lips.

And no one cared.

No one spared them a second glance.

CHAPTER 67

Three days until the engagement party
Three days until Carlos's departure

Ved woke up smiling, his arms wrapped around Carlos. The sun was already on its way up into the sky, indicating it was well past 6:00 a.m. Ved felt at peace. He shut his eyes and just savored the feeling of being next to Carlos, of being able to lie here with his arms around him. If Ved inhaled deeply, he got the strong scent of Carlos's cologne. Ved gently removed his arms, careful not to wake Carlos, and arched his back like a cat, stretching. He should go get them some breakfast. Maybe he could make them eggs? Carlos would be so impressed to see him applying the skills from that weekend in Alibaug. Or maybe he could make something American? What did Americans eat for breakfast? Pancakes? Bagels?

Ved stood up to go ask Hari if he knew any recipes—and that's when he noticed the shouting. It was so loud, in fact, that Ved wasn't sure how he and Carlos had slept through it before. Ved couldn't make out exactly what was being said, but he thought he heard Dolly's voice. That couldn't be right. She never came over here unless she absolutely had to. And even if she were here, who was the other person shouting? Prem never raised his voice.

Ved tiptoed to the door and opened it a crack. It *was* Dolly, and the other person screaming *was* Prem.

Dolly threw a newspaper down on the breakfast table. It made a sharp slap. "Did you know about this?"

"I don't know what that is; the picture quality is so bad."

"Please. You know exactly what this is!"

"Don't these people have any sense about what they publish? Anyone clicks anything, and it gets printed in the newspaper! Anyone with a smartphone is suddenly a journalist!"

"Why was he here? Why wasn't he out with Disha? *My* son would never get mixed up in something like this."

Prem shushed her. "You're going to wake him!"

Dolly's voice got louder. "Oh? And your yelling won't?"

Prem began to speak again and then suddenly stopped, his face shifting from anger to worry. He had seen Ved standing in the doorway, one foot in his room, one foot in the hallway.

Dolly shook Prem's shoulder, her voice more furious. "What the hell are you looking at? Answer me!"

Prem nudged Dolly, and she turned. Seeing Ved, she, too, fell silent.

Dolly looked at Prem, her eyes wide, still clutching his shoulder.

Prem released a long breath. "Ved, please come sit."

Ved's heart started pounding. He was motionless, standing there like a stone statue in his ratty T-shirt and pajama pants and fuzzy bunny slippers. What was going on? Why was Mum here? Why was she fighting with Dad? Ved tried to blink the sleep out of his eyes. Maybe he just wasn't fully awake yet. That had to be it. It was the only explanation that made sense. "What's going on?"

Prem pulled out the chair nearest to him and patted the seat. "Sit, Ved."

As Ved sat, his heart began pounding harder. He felt his pulse reverberate throughout his entire body. Dolly turned away from him, sniffling, trying to hastily wipe her tears away with perfectly manicured fingers. Prem took her hand and nodded. She turned again, this time to face Ved, and slid a newspaper across the table to him.

Every worry line in Dolly's face seemed deeper. She was shaking, but somehow, she managed to keep her voice steady. "Ved . . . why were you at this party? Who is this boy with you?"

Ved looked down at the crumpled newspaper and felt dizzy. The walls zoomed in and out of his peripheral vision again and again, getting larger and smaller, smaller and larger.

It was a picture, a massive picture that took up the entire page, of a famous fashion designer. On top of him was the guy with the frosted tips. And just in the background, next to both of them, were Carlos and Ved kissing. Carlos was on top of Ved, with only the back of his head showing. Ved's face was blurry, though it was unmistakably him. The headline was bold, damning: DESIGNER CAUGHT HAVING SEX AT GAY PARTY.

There was no escaping the truth revealed in that picture. There was proof. Right there. For the whole world to see. Ved had been foolish enough to get caught on camera. It didn't matter that Ved's name wasn't in the caption or that the focus was on someone else. Anyone who knew him would recognize him in the picture. Ved wouldn't get the choice to come out. Not anymore. The newspaper had outed him already. Ved Mehra went to the Salvation Star party. Ved Mehra made out with another man. Ved Mehra is gay.

"Ved?" Dolly whispered.

What options did he have? What else could he do but come out to his mother? What else could he do but tell them about Carlos? This was it. The whole charade was over. He tried to open his mouth to speak. Then tried again. Then took a deep breath in for four counts, out for five counts, and tried again.

And he repeated almost exactly what he told Prem only the day before: "I'm sorry. I can't marry Disha or any girl. I'm gay."

CHAPTER 68

This time, Ved didn't brace for a reaction or worry about all the possible words that could come out of his mother's mouth. Rather, he slouched back against the chair, the fight drained out of him.

Dolly squeezed Prem's hand tighter. She had gone pale gray. Prem put his other arm around her shoulders to keep her upright and looked at Ved over the top of his gold wire-rimmed spectacles.

Another breath in for four counts and out for five counts.

"The man in the picture is Carlos Silva. He was visiting Jaipur for work. We met on a dating app right around the time I first met Disha. When he came to Mumbai two weeks ago, he asked if we could meet, and I said yes. I thought it would be harmless, that we could be friends, but . . . I've gotten to know him over the past few days." Ved cleared his throat, trying to make his voice sound stronger. "And I've come to care for him. To *really* care for him. I've never met anyone else who cares for me the way he does. With him, I feel confident enough to be the person I've always wanted to be."

Dolly broke away from Prem and walked closer to Ved. "How long?" she demanded. "For how long have you known that you weren't going to marry Disha? What about your fiancée? Did you not consider her feelings in all of this? What is wrong with you? Disha is lovely!"

Ved's voice rose too. "Mum, I've known I was gay since high school! Since middle school! I've known that I couldn't marry a woman since all the way back then! The only reason I even let things get this far is because of *you*. Because of both of you. You both forced me into this mold of being some perfect son who would not only run the company, but who would also marry the perfect rich girl, and it's *killing* me."

Dolly pressed her hand flat against her heart. "Vedu . . . I . . ." This time, she reached for Prem's hand. Just for a second. When they looked at each other, Ved could see the pain that passed between them. It was brief, but it was there. Ved saw it, and he felt his heart crack again. Guilt subsequently poured in.

"Ved," Prem began, his voice stronger than Dolly's, "we—"

Ved never got to hear what Prem was going to say because he started to cry. The tears rolled hot and slow down his cheeks, and he felt like he was choking on the lump in his throat. "Mum, Dad, I'm sorry. I didn't mean what I said. It isn't your fault that I didn't tell you sooner." Ved's voice was now nearly inaudible. "Please . . . I'm sorry."

Prem removed his spectacles and set them on the table. "Ved, I know I speak for both your mother and I when I say that we will always love you. No matter what." He took Ved's hand in his own, pressing their palms together.

Dolly swallowed, and though she tried as hard as she could not to cry, she couldn't stop the sobs that racked her entire body. She reached for Ved's other hand, squeezing it tightly, and took a shuddering breath. "I will *always* love you, beta." She squeezed his hand tighter. "You are my son. My one and only child. I was the first person to hold you when you were a baby. I saw you grow up to be the most handsome, successful young man. This doesn't change the pride I feel for you. I love you, and my love cannot simply be erased by this."

Prem met Ved's eyes. "What do you want to do next?"

Ved looked to Dolly, who nodded encouragingly. "I . . . I've been trying to call Disha. I need to speak to her, and I think . . . it's time for Carlos to hear the truth. I should tell him everything."

"Is Carlos here right now?" Prem asked.

Ved mumbled, "Yes" and looked down at his bare feet.

Prem gave a single nod of his head and straightened. He left the breakfast room. Dolly squeezed Ved's hand one more time and left too. They both stepped into Prem's study and closed the door behind them.

CHAPTER 69

Ved walked slowly back to his room and closed the door as quietly as possible. He leaned against it, taking a moment to steady his breathing. Carlos still lay on his side of the bed on his stomach. The sun shone through the window, making his hair seem a lovely light brown. Occasionally, he let out a soft snore that sounded like a kitten sneezing. He hadn't been kidding when he'd told Ved he could sleep through anything. He looked just as peaceful as when Ved had left the room. Ved hated to have to wake him up, but it was now or never. Carlos would be leaving in a few days. Ved knew that he had to come clean. Carlos would want the truth, would have wanted the truth from the very beginning, regardless of whether it made him angry or broke his heart.

He steeled himself, lightly shook Carlos's shoulder, and whispered, "Carlos?" After a few tries, Carlos turned on his back and opened his eyes, smiling. "Hi there," he said as Ved sat down on the bed.

The anxiety must've been clear from Ved's expression because Carlos pushed himself upward into a sitting position. The sweet, sleepy smile fell from his face. "Are you okay, Ved?"

Ved shook his head no and looked down at the sheets. Then he looked up, meeting Carlos's eyes. He had to say this directly to Carlos, to his face. "I . . . I haven't been entirely honest with you about my . . . life."

Carlos furrowed his brow. "What?"

"You know that I'm not out."

"Yes." Carlos nodded. "I already knew that."

Ved cleared his throat.

"Stop stalling, Ved."

Ved cleared his throat again. "Right, um, so I guess I should just say it because you deserve the truth and it's been unfair of me to keep you in the dark and I just don't want to live the rest of my life knowing I deceived you, even though our relationship will still be over in three days—"

"Ved," Carlos said, now beginning to show the slightest irritation. "Spit it out."

"I'm engaged to a woman. Her name is Disha. I met her around the time I met you—"

"*What?*" Carlos tried to sit up straighter but banged his head against the headboard.

Ved started speaking faster. "But I'm not engaged to her anymore, and I just came out to my parents because there was this tabloid that had a picture of us kissing at the party last night, so now everyone knows I'm gay."

Carlos's face was red. He strained to keep his voice at an even volume. "So you lied to me. For our entire relationship."

"No! I—"

"What would you call that deception, then?"

"That's not the point. The point is that I'm out *now*. I'm not getting married. I never intended to get married to a woman."

"Then why were you engaged to one?"

"I just wanted to make my parents happy."

"Oh, really?"

Now Ved turned defensive too. "What do you mean?"

"You say that you planned to break off the engagement."

"That's right," Ved said, sensing that he was about to fall into some sort of trap.

Now Carlos was yelling. "Wouldn't that have made your parents more upset than you not getting engaged in the first place?"

"I—"

"No, stop! It's a yes-or-no question!"

"It's complicated, Carlos!"

Carlos scoffed. "Complicated?"

"Yes!"

"Don't use that as an excuse, Ved. You need to own up to your actions. You seriously considered ruining both your life and your fiancée's life just to make your parents happy. I thought I knew you. You used me—"

"I wasn't using you! I would never do that." Ved's voice became pleading. "I care about you so much, more than anyone else. I didn't want to hurt you. That's the only reason why I didn't tell you. I told myself that I would end the engagement every single day. I just couldn't make myself do it. I tried. I really did. Please believe me." He reached for Carlos's hand, but Carlos immediately pulled away, as if he'd been burned.

"Don't touch me."

"Carlos . . ."

Carlos got out of bed and started pulling on his clothes. He avoided meeting Ved's eyes. "I'm leaving, Ved."

"Carlos, you *can't*." Ved tried to grab Carlos's arm. Carlos shook him off.

"What do you mean I can't?" His tone was incredulous.

Ved tried a different tactic. "But let's just talk about this. Please."

Carlos shook his head in disbelief. "I'm going to the airport, Ved. I'll find an earlier flight to Jaipur."

"Carlos, no!" Ved got out of bed to block the door with his body.

Carlos stopped in front of him. "Ved, move."

Maybe he should try a new tactic. "What about last night?" Ved demanded, the desperation evident across his face.

"What about last night?"

"At Salvation Star. After the tequila shots. You told me you didn't want to leave, that you wanted to stay here in Mumbai with me."

"It was different then."

"*How?* Tell me! How was it any different?"

"Because I didn't know that you were using me to fucking cheat on someone, Ved! Your fiancée! That you were engaged, for God's sake, *to be married*. That's what was different!"

"I wasn't ever going to get married!"

"Yeah, okay. You can tell yourself that, if it makes you feel any better. Now move out of my way."

Ved spread his arms against the door. "Please, Carlos, let's talk about this. Give me another chance."

"We just did, and I'm done with you. Move."

"I thought we made each other happy."

"We did. Not anymore."

Ved was about to protest again, until he looked into Carlos's eyes. They didn't look angry anymore. They looked lifeless. And then Ved knew that blocking the door wasn't going to bring Carlos back to him. He'd already lost Carlos.

So Ved did move aside. And Carlos stormed out of the room and down the long empty passageway, slamming the main door shut behind him.

CHAPTER 70

Ved threw himself down on the bed, trying to inhale Carlos's cologne, the smell of his skin. He couldn't feel anything. It was like his body had gone completely numb. He tried to cry and managed only dry sobs. He tried to curl up into a ball and failed. Instead, he stayed lying on his stomach, limbs spread across the entire bed. He tried to think of anything but the hurt expression on Carlos's face and miserably failed. The words he'd yelled at Carlos, the words Carlos had yelled back, seemed to echo around the room, bouncing off the walls and Ved's limp body. Ved could hear the pain in Carlos's voice, the anger, the desperation. And as they bounced around, he was reminded again and again of the mistakes he'd made, of how Carlos had been hurt by those mistakes.

He had contacted Carlos several times over the day, yet his messages went unanswered and his phone calls were ignored, and he was blocked on Grindr. Every time his phone buzzed, Ved's heart leaped with hope. Every time, he was sure that Carlos had decided to talk to him, to forgive him. Every time, he was crushed and felt even worse than before.

Now, when Carlos met the next guy, he would tell him about how his last boyfriend had been selfish and backward, how the bastard had been planning on marrying a woman, had been planning on doing that during their entire relationship. Just like what Ved had told Carlos about Akshay. And Carlos's new boyfriend would stare at him, shocked. Just like Carlos had stared at Ved.

Ved really was no better than Akshay.

He eventually fell asleep like that, miserable and longing for Carlos more than anything. When he woke up, the sky was gray and Prem was sitting at the foot of his bed. Ved groaned and shut his eyes again, trying to find sleep. At least in his dreams, Carlos was still here in bed with him.

Prem rubbed Ved's back. "Beta, how are you feeling?"

"Terrible."

"What do you have to feel terrible about?"

Ved mumbled into his pillow.

"Vedu, are you talking to me or to your pillow?"

Ved turned so that he was now lying down on his back. "Carlos hates me."

Prem's tone was still maddeningly even. "Why is that?"

"Because I was dating him while I was engaged to a woman."

Prem waited for Ved to say more.

"And he was right. I only told myself that I would find a way to break off the engagement. I don't think I would have actually done it."

"Why not?"

"Because I wasn't strong enough. The only reason I came out to Mum today and told Carlos the truth is because of the photo. Without it, I would be trying on shoes for the engagement party right now, and Carlos would be packing for his flight to Jaipur, and no one would know the truth."

"You're too hard on yourself."

"What?"

"Vedu, you *are* strong. Remember, you told me and called Disha well before this photo was published, and I know that could not have been easy for you, beta."

"I am still a terrible person." Ved's voice was flat. "I betrayed the trust of people who cared about me."

"You can't change the past. All you can do is set things right for the future."

Ved still felt numb, hollow from the loss of Carlos. "Okay."

Prem sighed. "Disha's father called earlier this morning to check if everything was going as per schedule. I told him you'd call him back."

Ved didn't move. "Do they already know?" When Prem didn't answer, Ved sighed. "I guess it doesn't matter." Sitting up, he continued, "It's well past time I set things right. I need to call them, and more importantly, I need to call Disha."

CHAPTER 71

After talking to Disha's parents for over an hour on the telephone—a conversation that was not easy to have, but Ved knew he had to get it done with the utmost tact and diplomacy possible—Ved retreated to the solitude of his room. Even though Dharmendra Kapoor had been furious initially, giving Ved an earful of expletives and threats for "hurting" his "precious baby" in this manner, Ved had remained calm and polite throughout, letting him vent his anger before slowly winding down to the realization that this was best for his daughter's sake. That breaking things off was in Disha's interest. That it was better now than later. Ved had made him promise not to breathe a word to Disha until he'd had the chance to tell her in person, to let her hear it from him first.

The blinds were now drawn tightly across Ved's windows, so he couldn't really be sure what time it was. He was now lying flat on his back across the bed and clutched a pillow, the pillow Carlos had used, against his chest. He was still wearing his pajamas. He was still completely devastated, willing the door to open, for Carlos to be standing there, ready to take Ved back. He stroked the stubble along his jawline, knowing his eyes must be puffy and in need of a face mask. Ved couldn't care less.

When the door did open sometime later, Carlos wasn't standing there. It was Disha. She looked terrible, too, wearing a faded gray sweatshirt and yoga pants, her hair in a low ponytail. She seemed tired. She somehow managed to force a smile when Ved sat up to look at her.

"Hi, Ved."

"Hi, Disha." Ved's voice dragged on the words. You'd think that saying two words after hours of silence wouldn't be that difficult, but you'd be wrong.

She held up a supermarket bag in one hand and two plastic spoons in the other. "I brought you some Honey Nut Crunch. Your favorite."

Ved looked down at the pillow in his arms.

Disha frowned, more out of concern than annoyance, and sat on the bed next to Ved. She handed him a pint of the ice cream and a spoon before opening a pint of Strawberry Cheesecake for herself. They sat like that for a while, silent and halfheartedly eating ice cream. Finally, Ved set down his pint on the nightstand and took both of Disha's hands in his own.

Deep breath in for four counts and out for five counts.

"We can't get married, Disha. I can't go through with the wedding." Ved's voice cracked, and tears collected in the corners of his eyes. It was a wonder he could even manage to produce more tears after what had happened earlier.

Tears collected in Disha's eyes, too, and she looked like she was about to throw up.

"I'm gay," Ved continued. "I've always been gay, and I've known that I'm gay for a long time. I should have never agreed to marry you, and I'm sorry. I'm so sorry. I love you, I really do, but not the way a husband should, not romantically." He forced himself to meet Disha's eyes. "I'm sorry."

Disha held his gaze. "I know you're gay. I've known for a while." She blinked rapidly, trying to prevent her tears from falling. "I'm not *that* dense, you know."

Ved rubbed his temples. "Wait, what? Did you see the newspaper article?"

"Yes, I did, but that's not how I knew. Ved, you never kissed me or touched me, and every time someone brought up our engagement, you froze. I knew. It's okay. You don't need to apologize to me. We were both just willing to make a sacrifice for our parents' happiness, the way they sacrificed everything for our happiness."

"No, Disha, you don't understand. I wasn't just deceiving you in that way. I have—had—a boyfriend. At the same time I was engaged to you."

Disha was silent. Ved reached forward to hug her. She stayed still.

"I've wanted to tell you. That's why I tried calling yesterday. The guilt was killing me. I didn't want to treat you that way, I swear—"

Slowly, Disha brought her arms up to hug Ved back. "Ved, you don't need to apologize." She wasn't crying anymore.

"No, I do, Disha, you need to understand the extent to which—"

Disha shook her head. "Ved, you have nothing to apologize for. *I'm* sorry. I . . . I was seeing someone too. While we were engaged."

Ved's jaw dropped.

"You remember my ex, Hemant?"

Ved nodded, still trying to wrap his head around what she was saying.

"Well, I continued going out with him after we grabbed coffee one time. At first, I just thought that we could maybe be friends, but then . . . I don't know." Disha paused, starting to cry again. "Things just turned into so much more than I could have imagined, and it all happened so quickly that I . . . the point is that I wanted to tell you too. I just didn't know how either. I thought that maybe if I avoided your calls, that would make me feel less guilty. I was being stupid. Avoiding you only made me feel worse."

"That's exactly what happened between me and Carlos. I knew he was handsome and funny and passionate . . . it's like you said. Things started moving so quickly. And . . . and I know it hasn't been long, only two weeks, but I really do feel like I've known him forever, and I think I might . . . love him."

"I think I might love Hemant too." Disha wiped snot away from her nose, laughing. "I can't believe it. We each fell in love with the other man."

"I spent every day trying to find a way to call off the engagement."

"Me too. I just couldn't find a way to do it without hurting absolutely everyone involved."

Ved lightly laughed. "Look at us now. Mission accomplished, right?"

Disha smiled. "Right. I would call this afternoon nothing short of a smashing success. After I told Hemant I was engaged and my parents spoke to you over the phone, I only cried for three hours."

"I only cried for two."

"Impressive." She tilted her head to the side. "How did my parents take the news?"

"Fairly well, actually."

"You're joking."

"No, I'm not. I told them exactly what I told you and apologized for deceiving them."

"And they just accepted your apology?"

"Disha, they want you married, but what was more important to them was that you would be happy. So yes, your dad did yell at me and call me a bloody liar and scorn me for letting the engagement get so far, but he wasn't really upset at me. He was upset that he had almost let you commit yourself to a life that promised less than utmost happiness."

"I can't believe that." She shook her head. "I guess I underestimated them."

"I guess I underestimated my parents too." Ved lay down on his back again, his voice more serious. "So what do we do now?"

Disha lay down next to him. "Well, after I told Hemant that I was engaged, he broke up with me. Of course he did. I don't know what I expected him to say. I think a part of me hoped that he would make some big romantic gesture and stop the engagement party so that I wouldn't have to be the one to disappoint Mama and Papa."

"Carlos broke up with me too. This morning. After I told him that I was engaged. He's probably at the airport right now, if not already in the air, already on his way back to Jaipur."

"Ved!" Disha sat straight up and pulled Ved up with her. "You still have a chance! You should be on your way to the airport. You need to leave right now."

"Disha, it's no use. You should have seen the way he looked at me before he left. I don't think he ever even wants to hear my name again, much less see me again. I betrayed him, I—"

"Yes, yes, we all know that what you did was wrong! Stop wasting time. Go make things right. Go convince him that you're willing to change, to be better in the future!"

"I can't fight for him. I already lost him."

"With that sorry attitude, you certainly have. I can't believe you're going to give up on someone who makes you happy. Out of what? Guilt for sins you've already confessed?"

"He's not interested in making me happy anymore. Why would he be? I actively made his life worse."

"You only say that based on his reaction in the moment to shocking news that you dumped on him. It's only natural that he freaked out. You need a chance to talk to him in a calmer setting. You owe it to yourself to do at least that. If you don't, what was the point of all the love you shared? It will simply be tarnished forever by this pain."

Ved looked at her. "You really think I have a chance?"

"You'll never know unless you try."

Ved started pulling on his sneakers and tying the laces. "You need to get Hemant back, too, then. If I can do it, so can you."

"No, Ved." Disha's voice was hard, devoid of all the hope it had held just a second ago. "That's a different situation."

"It's not different!" Ved grabbed Disha's shoulders. "You cannot seriously be advising me to go fight for my boyfriend *at an airport* when you're not willing to try to fight for yours. If he fought to get back together with you, after all these years, even after you broke up with him, he must really love you. It's like you said. We need to discuss the engagement in a calmer setting. The love you share with him has to count for something. Plus," Ved said, raising his voice to mimic hers, "'you'll never know unless you try.'"

Disha smiled, life returning all at once to her face, lighting her up. "Okay! Let's do it! Let's go fight for our boyfriends!" She jumped up and started pulling on her own sneakers.

Ved was about to run out of the door, but he stopped and turned back to give Disha a big hug. "I love you, Disha, you know that? Thank you."

Disha squeezed his shoulders. "Yeah, I love you too. Now go!" And she pushed him out the door, waving.

CHAPTER 72

An hour later, Ved sat in the back of his car, trapped in rush-hour traffic on the way to the airport. Chasing after Carlos had seemed like a great idea when Ved ran out of his apartment. It was only in the car that Ved realized there were some major gaps in his plan. For one, he was still dressed in his pajamas, and though Ved couldn't see much of himself in the car's rearview mirror, his bloodshot eyes were evidence enough that he looked as terrible as he'd felt earlier. Unfortunately, he had also left his phone on his nightstand, along with the remains of the pint of ice cream that had likely long since melted. This meant that Ved had no way of contacting Carlos to ask him if his flight had left.

Maybe that was for the best. Ved wasn't sure if Carlos would even respond to his texts at this point, and staring at the screen waiting for a response would be torturous. Then again, if he had his phone, he could at least look up the flight times. And most important of all, how did Ved plan on getting into the airport without a ticket? Should he just hope and pray that Carlos hadn't gone through security yet? Should he buy a plane ticket? Could he buy a plane ticket without his wallet? He did have his credit card number memorized, so he could try. Even if he did buy a ticket, should he buy a dummy one or one to Jaipur? And if he bought one to Jaipur—

Enough.

Ved closed his eyes and leaned his head against the warm glass of the window. He was going to drive himself absolutely crazy if he continued thinking like this. He couldn't afford to spiral again. He knew he should just focus on his breathing. That was what was most important, continuing to breathe in and out. If he found Carlos, great. If not, he would return home, clean up the mess he had left there this morning, find out the name of Carlos's company, and fly out to Jaipur in the morning with a fresh head. There was only one thing that Ved knew, and that was that Disha had been right.

Carlos was worth fighting for.

CHAPTER 73

Ved had never been a true believer in fate. Maybe "cautious believer" would be a better label for him. Whenever his mother had spoken about a plan being laid out for each human being, about fate being the driving force behind each living being's life, Ved had scoffed. He'd scoffed out loud. In his head, he had never been so sure. Sometimes, inexplicable things did happen, things that could only be explained by fate. Usually, when Ved heard about these things, they would bug him for a day or two. After that, he'd be able to forget that the occurrence had ever happened at all. He could reconcile fate as something that probably didn't exist. Probably. Any further examination of that belief made him uncomfortable. It was best to leave the whole matter alone.

However, when Ved drove up to the front of the airport and saw Carlos through the car window sitting in a coffee shop next door to the entrance just because he'd managed to look up at the right moment, he knew he would never doubt the existence of fate again.

"Stop!" Ved yelled, and the car jerked forward. Ved thanked the driver and ran to the coffee shop entrance, feeling his stomach drop. This time, he couldn't tell whether it was from nerves or excitement or some ungodly combination of the two.

Carlos looked up when the door to the café opened, bringing the sound of honking horns from outside. When he saw Ved, his eyes went wide.

Ved went to Carlos's table. Now, Carlos looked furious. He stood up and grabbed his duffel bag, leaving a full iced mocha latte sitting at the table. "No. I need to catch my flight."

"Please, Carlos. Just give me five minutes."

"Ved, I thought I made myself clear this morning. I'm not interested in seeing you right now."

"Five minutes is all I ask."

Carlos sighed and, after a full minute of silence, finally sat back down. Ved sat down in the chair across from him. Five minutes would be enough time for Ved to recite the speech he'd prepared in the car. More than enough time.

Carlos looked down at his watch. "Ved, if you have something to say, say it now."

Ved cleared his throat. "I know things went wrong between us, and I know that it's all my fault. I lied to you. I hurt you. And I will be sorry about that until the day I die. You *know* me, you *know* that I would never want to see you unhappy. I don't need to beg you to believe me because you already know how much I care about you, and I know it hasn't been long, but you've become the center of my world. I think about you all day and night, and I'm happier for it. I finally have someone who sees me as an equal partner and who can see me as the best version of myself, not as the worst version. I . . . I think I'm in love with you. Please don't give up on us. I want the chance to make things right."

Holding Ved's gaze, Carlos shook his head. His eyes looked as lifeless as before. "You don't love me, Ved. We've known each other for around two weeks. We were living through the honeymoon phase. Let's be realistic, sharing a life together is far more difficult than dinners and drinking. I agree that, given time, we could come to love each other. That's just never what this relationship was meant to be. It doesn't matter whether I would have chosen to stay in Mumbai or not. What do you think this is? *10 Things I Hate About You? Two Weeks Notice? Just Go with It?* This isn't one of those romantic comedy movies you love so much. Your big declaration of devotion is not enough to erase what you did. I'm not going to fall back into your arms."

Ved was gutted. He felt a deep pain in his chest. "But we make each other happy."

"Look, Ved." Carlos took Ved's hand, his voice gentler. "You *did* make me very happy. These past few days have been some of the best of my life. I thought . . . I thought you were going to be in my life for a long time."

Ved squeezed Carlos's hand. "Then stay! Stay here with me. We'll make a life together, you and I in Mumbai. I promise I'll cut back on work. I've been thinking, maybe it's time I resign and take up something that will bring me greater joy, a less hectic job, so we can spend more time traveling the world together. Enjoying our lives together."

Carlos looked down at their entwined hands. Without looking up, he said, "Put yourself in my shoes, Ved. Think about how you would have felt, finding out that someone you deeply care for, someone you'd been completely open with, has been deceiving you."

"Everything I told you about myself was true. You know me better than anyone."

"That doesn't excuse all the lies. It can't."

"I'm not asking for any of my lies to be forgiven. I know I messed up. I own up to that. What I'm asking you to do is to give me another chance. We can start fresh. And this time, with no more lies."

Carlos was still looking at their hands. "How can I possibly trust you again?"

"You *can*."

"I can't be sure of that. I asked you, multiple times in fact, what you were hiding from me, and you still kept me in the dark."

"I know, Carlos. Believe me, I do. It wasn't for my own enjoyment, or anything, like how you're making it sound. The lies ate away at me every day. They would taint every moment of happiness and embrace every moment of sadness. And being openly gay is still criminalized here; that was always at the back of my mind."

Carlos now met Ved's eyes. "So why didn't you tell me sooner? Why did you let this carry on for so long?"

"I . . . I knew that if I told you, I would lose you, and I couldn't bear that."

"You're right about losing me."

"Things will be different if you stay. I came out to my parents and I broke off the engagement. There's nothing else for me to hide."

Carlos looked at his watch again. "I really need to go, Ved."

"Think about it."

"Think about what?"

"Think about our relationship, what we could be in the future. Please take the time to think about your feelings for me. I know our relationship is worth fighting for, so I'll be here waiting. If you ever realize the same thing, come find me."

Carlos looked pained. "Ved . . ."

"Just think about it."

Ved stood up with Carlos and hugged him tightly. "I'm really going to miss you, Carlos." He was desperately trying to hold back the tears, but his shaky voice gave him away.

"I'll miss you, too, Ved. Take care of yourself."

Carlos left to go board his flight.

Ved stayed standing in front of that table in the coffee shop for a long time after. He watched Carlos through the glass windows, slowly wheeling his bags through the terminal entrance, dipping into his duffel bag to show his passport to the authorities, and then slowly disappearing amid the mass of people. Ved hoped that Carlos would turn around one last time and wave, just so he could see him again. But he never did.

CHAPTER 74

Ved: Mum, is everything okay?

Dolly: Of course, Vedu.

Ved: I just haven't heard from you since our, err . . . argument. Last week.

Dolly: I just needed time.

Ved: I know, Mum.

Ved: Well, how is your kitty group? Are any gurus coming over this Friday?

Dolly: Yes.

Ved: Can I come over on Friday too? I'd love to see you.

Dolly: I can't believe I was so unapproachable.

Ved: What?

Dolly: Why couldn't you tell me? What kind of mother was I, If you kept this part of yourself from me?

Ved: It's not your fault, Mum. I was just scared.

Dolly: Scared of what? What were you so scared of that you couldn't tell your mother?

Ved: I didn't want to disappoint you. Let you down after all that you've done for me. As your only son, I knew you wanted to see me with a family and children, the grandchildren that you've always wanted.

Dolly: You can never disappoint me. I'm sorry if I didn't show that to you before, but I will now. You can confide in me.

Ved: Thanks, Mum. That really means a lot to me.

Dolly: I've started going to therapy.

Ved: You what?

Dolly: Don't tell anyone.

Ved: Why?

Dolly: It was time. I've spent too long letting negative emotions build up inside of me.

Ved: I'm really proud of you. But what about all those fortune-tellers you've had over the years?

Dolly: Oh, that! They were also very helpful, beta. But I couldn't share my secrets with them because they are so gossipy and would blabber to the world. Imagine my plight if people found out about . . . ?

Ved: I love you, Mum. You are a beautiful and strong woman.

Dolly: I love you too. Thank you for telling me that you're gay, Vedu.

Ved: There's something else I have to tell you . . .

Dolly: Okay, please don't tell me you want to move to another country; that will kill me!

Ved: No, no, I could never leave Mumbai. I . . . it's about my work, and I wanted to talk to you about it before I spoke with Dad. But you have to promise me that you won't say anything to him. He has to hear it from me.

Dolly: Beta, just tell me. God promise, I won't tell anyone, including Prem.

Ved: I'm planning on resigning from Mehra Electronics. I've been thinking about it for a while. I know, I know, you'll talk me out of it, but I have wanted to resign for a very long time. I don't want work to become the sole focus of my life, like it did with Dad. I want to enjoy living my life, making work just a part of my day. You know how it is with the company—it's a huge responsibility. There's no getting away from the late nights and all those reports and presentations. I'm done with it. That's not the sort of life I want to live.

Ved: I hope I haven't disappointed you and Dad. I know you were keen that I launch Mehra Productions, expand the company into new territories. Take it forward. But that's not what I really want.

Ved: Mum, you there?

Dolly: I'm here. My therapist has asked me to take five deep breaths before I respond to anything.

Dolly: Vedu, follow your heart. I am fully behind you, my child. You are, after all, blessed with superb genes, being my son, and a Mehra. Your name means 'divine knowledge.' I know that whatever you do next, you will do with great success.

Dolly: Vedu, are you there, hello?

Dolly: Hello?

Ved: Wow, Dollyji, now I need to take a few deep breaths. I never expected this!

Dolly: You will find the right time to tell Prem. All will be fine. I know it.

CHAPTER 75

It was as if Ved had entered an alternate reality, in the best way possible. Everything was the same, except now, Ved didn't feel the weight of trying to hide who he was. It would take a long time to come into, he knew. For now, that guilt of being gay, the burdens of secrecy he'd grown used to? Gone. Of course, that ache from missing Carlos was always with him. That, he knew, would take an even longer time to get over. But that lightness, the way he could finally breathe easily, made life . . . well, it made life more worth living.

Ved had been worried to go back to the gym and work, or really, to step outside the house after the tabloid article was published. He'd expected people to stare, whisper, and give generally strange looks when he walked past. But people didn't treat him any differently. The picture didn't mean that Ved would live in shame for the rest of his life.

Even Ved's relationship with Prem, which had been defined by distance for years, now felt easier. Prem often made a point to spend time with Ved over the weekends, whether that be briefly over breakfast or taking a walk together through the park. During the day, Ved also received frequent texts on news reports regarding the case against Section 377. The date for the verdict was fast approaching, with several members of political parties now even championing the change. There seemed to be an overwhelming majority of Indians who wanted Section

377 removed, from celebrities to lawyers to businesspeople speaking out publicly.

Ved was sleeping through the night, and Sheetal's cucumber face masks were working wonders on his skin. After Ved had returned to work, she had gifted him with a giant pack of them, with a wink and the note: "For date night, boss." Now there were no more compulsive hookups or late-night ice cream binges standing in front of the freezer. He'd gotten rid of Grindr for good. Ved was feeling better about himself, dressing in brighter colors and even experimenting with prints. Plus, he went out for brunch with Disha every Sunday. At their rate, they would make it through every brunch spot in Mumbai by the end of the year.

He still missed Carlos, of course. Ved had found one of his T-shirts hanging behind his bathroom door. Carlos had accidentally left it behind one of the times he was over. On the days he especially missed and longed for Carlos, he would take that shirt out of his drawer and hold it close to his face, inhaling the scent of Carlos's crisp lemon-and-fig cologne. However, the ache had dulled. Ved had stopped staring at Carlos's phone number or their stream of text conversations, trying to telepathically will him to initiate contact. It was no use. If he chose to contact Ved again, great. Ved would be overjoyed. If he didn't ever contact Ved again, at least Ved had tried. He knew he couldn't force Carlos to come back to him. And Ved was slowly beginning to see that perhaps happiness could come from other sources. Maybe Carlos wasn't the only reason Ved had been happy all those weeks ago. That being said, Ved still texted Carlos every single day.

Ved: Hi Carlos. How's life in Indonesia?

Carlos never responded.

CHAPTER 76

It was time. Ved felt ready to organize a family dinner. The last time he had eaten with both of his parents at once in the same room had been well over a year before the divorce. Right now, all these years later, it seemed like everyone was finally willing to at least try to get along. The last time they had been together at home was deeply emotional with his coming out, but Ved appreciated how supportive they had been of him. It had been a form of healing, for all of them. He now wanted them to be closer as a family unit, the togetherness he had craved all these years.

Ved had looked forward to the dinner all day, even going to the trouble to take out the fine china plates that had never been used and to light tall candlesticks. He bought a bouquet of lilies for his mother and waited by the door for her to arrive. Expecting Dolly to arrive on time proved to be naive. She arrived fashionably late, a full forty-five minutes after the time Ved had texted her to be there. She walked in smiling, her arms laden with bags and bags of food. She gave the bags to Hari and leaned in to kiss Ved on the cheek.

"Mum, I thought we were getting takeout Chinese food? What is all this?"

Prem looked up from the couch, where he was reading *A Suitable Boy*. "Dolly, you brought food? I can't say that I'm surprised."

Dolly laughed. "No son of mine is eating Chinese takeout food when his mother still has two arms to cook."

Ved decided that now wouldn't be the best time to mention that he ate takeout Chinese food every Friday night in front of the TV. "But, Mum, what are we going to do with all the food we ordered? We even got the vegetable Manchurian specifically for you."

"Oh, Ved, don't be ridiculous. Just put the food in the fridge. It should last for a couple days. Now, let me go heat up all the food with Hari."

———

Dolly, in true motherly fashion, had prepared a vast spread of Ved's favorite foods: mutton kebabs, *roti canai*, fish in green curry, *besan* omelets, and, for dessert, homemade *kesar pedas* coated in roasted pistachios.

The Mehras passed around the plates of food, and if it weren't for the slight awkwardness in the air, Ved could have almost been fooled into thinking he was right back at his childhood dinner table. He didn't mind that the burden of conversation fell onto him during the long stretches of silence. Everyone was eating together. That was what mattered to him.

"So," Ved began, "it has been really hot this month. Abnormally so, don't you guys think?"

"I agree," Prem said. "It's global warming."

"Well, I don't know what the science is," Dolly said, raising her finger, "but what I do know is that the bloody AC in my apartment isn't nearly strong enough to withstand such temperatures. I've called the air-conditioner repairman three times, and still, I feel no change."

"Dolly, I'll give you the card of our air-conditioner repairman. He is very good. I'm sure he'll be able to help you."

"Yes. Please remember to do that."

More silence punctured only by the sounds of chewing and Fubu's occasional bark.

"So," Ved began again, "the election is coming up."

"Vedu, please," Dolly said. "Let's not discuss politics during dinner. Tell me, have you gone out on any dates lately?"

Ved choked on his bite of food. "What?"

"Well, darling, I don't expect you to die alone just because you're not marrying Disha, and I would like some grandchildren while I'm still young."

"Grandchildren?"

Dolly rolled her eyes. "Yes, grandchildren. Ved, you need to get with the times. As if gay men cannot have children. You know *Elton John* had two children with a surrogate?"

Prem nodded. "Yes, they spoke about it on the news."

"Mum, what was it your therapist said about respecting boundaries?"

"I *am* respecting your boundaries, Ved. I just don't want you to end up alone. You did say you were happy with that boy—what was his name?"

"Carlos."

Dolly smiled. "Yes, Carlos. What happened to him? Why aren't you two still dating?"

"It's complicated, Mum."

Prem set down his fork. "You can talk to us, Ved. What happened between you two?"

Ved set down his fork, too, and looked at his parents' faces. Dolly took Ved's hand and Prem nodded encouragingly. "We broke up." Ved forced his voice to remain steady. "After I told him I was engaged to Disha."

Dolly sighed. "That's a shame."

"Did you try to contact him again?" Prem asked.

"Yeah, I have. I text him all the time. He just never responds." Ved couldn't stop his voice from shaking now.

Dolly exchanged a look with Prem. "Darling, do you want to tell us more about him? My therapist says talking to people you trust can truly help."

"I don't even know where to begin."

Prem took Ved's other hand. "Wherever you feel comfortable."

Ved took a deep breath in. "Carlos . . . he loved traveling. He even had this blog where he documented all his adventures, called *Curious Carlos* . . ."

———

After dinner, the three of them moved to the couch in the living room. Prem poured three generous glasses of bourbon, and they sat like that for a long time, sipping their drinks, stuffing themselves with crispy pakoras. They were silent, though this silence was different from the silence before. Now, the silence felt warm and comfortable. Ved could have stayed there like that for a long time.

———

Ved: I ate the most amazing pakoras today. Made by Mum, of course.

Ved: Did you ever try them while you were in India?

Ved: If not, boy, did you miss out.

Ved: You'll just have to make a point to eat some next time you come here.

Ved: I miss you, Carlos.

———

The next morning, Ved was feeling ready to talk to Prem about something that had been on his mind for a long time. He got dressed in a loose T-shirt and jeans and walked down the hallway to Prem's office.

He didn't even feel nervous. That is, until he stepped right in front of the office door.

The door was smooth, dark wood, so dark that it was nearly black. The wood itself was rustic. If you ran your hands down it, you could feel the grooves of the tree's rings. Looking up, the door seemed to stretch high into the sky, which was ridiculous. Of course that was ridiculous. Ved was over six feet tall. He should be the last person to be intimidated by the size of the door. Nevertheless, there was something intimidating about this specific door. After standing there, waiting for Prem to sense his presence through the thick wood, Ved gave up and knocked. Prem opened the door for him with a smile, and Ved stepped into his father's office. The interior looked pretty much the same as Prem's office at work—the same glass desk, the same bookshelf, the same wide computer monitor.

Prem gestured to a small couch in the corner and sat down next to Ved. "What brings you to my office, Vedu?"

Ved looked at Prem. "There's something I need to tell you."

Prem laughed. "What is it this time?"

"I've decided to quit the company. Effective immediately. This job is not making me happy. I need to find something that I love to do. I already packed up my things, so I won't be going in on Monday."

Prem nodded. "Is that all?"

Ved furrowed his brows. "You're not upset with me?"

"Why would I be upset with you?"

"It's just . . . I thought that you wanted me to inherit the company after you retired."

"I do want that."

"So . . . ?"

"Ved, I don't want to bring any more unhappiness to this family, and especially not to your life. I thought I made it clear to you. I want you to do what makes you happy. If this job doesn't make you happy, so be it. There's nothing I can do about that."

Ved hugged his father. "Thank you."

"You're welcome. Now tell me, what is it that you love to do? I can set up whatever it is with our contacts."

"No, Dad, I don't know yet. And if you're the one who sets up the job for me, I'll never be able to find out. I need to do this on my own."

"Very well. Find your passion. You can always come back to our company if you want."

"Thank you."

———

Ved: C, I just discovered a new Baskin-Robbins flavor called "Fresh Litchi," and I think "Honey Nut Crunch" might have some serious competition.

———

Ved: Dollyji, I told Dad that I'm resigning. He was supportive, just like you said he'd be. You both are constantly surprising me these days. Why didn't I know I could trust you from the beginning?

Dolly: Vedu, you know you can trust me with anything. I'll always be there for you. Last evening, that silly Sheila aunty tried to make a big deal about you and that newspaper clipping at our kitty party. I told her to get lost. That I stand by my son in every which way.

Ved: Mum, you didn't!

Dolly: Who does she think she is? Trying to talk ill about you. Anyway, she apologized this morning. It's all okay now.

Ved: Aww, you're the best, Dollyji!

CHAPTER 77

Later that day, Ved began his job search by speaking to the Mehra Electronics headhunter. Ved figured that if anyone had a good grasp of available jobs, it would be someone his father had hired. However, the headhunter was of no help. During their entire call, he kept asking why Ved, who was so good at his job, wanted to leave a multimillion-dollar empire when so many young men would kill to be in his shoes. According to him, Ved's decision to quit was equivalent to "career suicide."

That's what made Ved decide to turn to the internet. He scrolled through LinkedIn for hours. Not a single job caught his eyes. By chance, while researching a company specializing in graphic design, Ved came across a retweet on Twitter: "A start-up NGO for HIV prevention is looking to hire a full-time youth counselor immediately. Send your résumés to the link in our bio." That seemed interesting. Ved researched the NGO more and found that they also had a hotline for members of the LGBTQ+ community. Ved was sold. He immediately sent in his résumé and crossed his fingers.

He knew how much that hotline could help. If he'd been able to talk to someone about his sexual confusion, especially during his teenage years, someone who would have guided him or simply listened, then maybe Ved would be in a better position today. Just because his choices had already been made didn't mean he couldn't help others make better choices in their futures.

The next day, Ved received an email asking him to come in for an interview, despite him having no experience as a counselor. Ecstatic, Ved immediately showed up at the office. It was boxy and small, and the central hallway was so narrow that you had to walk down it single file, but Ved absolutely loved the place. It wasn't even vaguely as fancy as Mehra Electronics or half as well paying, and so what if he wouldn't be lunching with movie stars if Mehra Productions took off? At least he'd found a place where he felt he could make a real difference. He was going to help other gay people so that they would hopefully never feel as trapped and desperate as he once had. That had value, far more than all those product presentations and monthly reports. Ved's hard work would finally mean something, would contribute to a goal greater than making money. Ved would be going through a special counseling training course before the job began. He also offered to handle the NGO's account books on the side, which was what really sealed the deal. The hours were easy, from ten in the morning until five in the evening. It would give him enough time to figure out what his other passions were. Who knows? Maybe he would take up writing or painting or even baking. The possibilities, for once, felt endless.

As a bonus, there wasn't a dress code. Ved was told he could start on Monday, and he couldn't wait.

———

Ved: C, just started a new job as a youth counselor at an NGO that helps people with HIV and those within the LGBTQ+ community.

Ved: How's your job going? Are you in Indonesia right now?

CHAPTER 78

After Ved's first day at his new job on Monday, which went really well, he contacted a broker. He knew it was time for him to move out, to have his own space. Bigger, smaller, fancier, cheaper—Ved didn't care. He had enough of a fat bank account to pay for whatever he saw fit. What he wanted was to move into a place that he could call home. Not that moving out meant Ved intended to sever his connection with his parents. Not at all. In fact, they now met every Friday night for family dinner. Strangely enough, Ved now saw more of Prem than he ever had when they worked together.

Over the next few days, he visited many apartments in Bandra and Khar. They were designed for expats or CEOs, with tall spiral staircases, marble flooring, Murano chandeliers, sliding mirrored cupboards, and Buddha artwork on the walls. They felt more like hotel suites than apartments, which was definitely not what Ved was looking for. After two more rounds of apartments, Ved finally settled on a place in a leafy by-lane of Bandra. It was simple, sparse, and cozy. The bedroom barely had any space for a bed and wardrobe, let alone a desk. Yet it contained a small balcony of potted plants and a washer and dryer. In other words, it was perfect. The coziness of a balcony with bright-yellow walls and lush green trees reminded him of his grandfather's Mumbai cottage where he and his parents had spent so many weekends.

Ved signed the lease without a second thought.

———

Ved sent a picture.

Ved: Can you believe the view from my new apartment, C? I can actually see trees.

CHAPTER 79

Six weeks later

The first piece of mail Ved received in his new apartment was an invitation printed on thick creamy white cardstock in an iridescent gold envelope. It was inviting him to Disha's wedding in two months. After receiving it, Ved immediately called Disha.

"Guess what I just got in the mail?"

"Please tell me you're coming!"

"Whoa, how did you assume that I meant your wedding invitation? What if I'd been talking about my electric bill?"

"You know, I think I liked the sullen version of you better."

Ved bit his lip, trying to keep a straight face, even though Disha couldn't see him. "Oh, that's too bad."

"Uh-huh. So, are you coming?"

"Of course I'm coming! If this invitation is any indication, I should be expecting quite the event."

"Don't get your hopes up too high. The party planner we hired has been informed that she's only allowed to communicate with my mother. Mama claims that my wedding will be even better if everything is a surprise. She doesn't want me to be stressed."

"How's that going?"

"Terribly, of course. I'm too much of a control freak to not know what's going to happen during my own wedding."

Ved laughed. "I agree."

Disha laughed too.

"Disha?"

"Yeah?"

"I'm really happy for you. You deserve nothing but the best. And you're blessed with the nicest parents, really. Your father messaged me the other day to say he hopes everything is fine between us, that he would like me to always be a part of your family in whatever way possible."

"Really? He didn't mention anything to me."

"He really cares about you. You're one lucky girl, Disha."

———

Ved sent a picture.

Ved: Guess who just successfully made an omelet all by himself?

Ved: I know what you're thinking, Carlos, and you're right. It is pretty impressive.

Ved: What can I say? I learned from the best.

CHAPTER 80

Two months later

From a mile away, you could tell that a mega wedding was taking place at the Kapoor mansion in Malabar Hill this weekend. The place was lit up with thousands of fairy lights painstakingly strung in trees along with marigolds. The sides of the roads were lined with rose petals that somehow remained bright red throughout the night. Luxury cars were parked across the compound, including Beemers, Jags, Mercs, and Rolls, all so shiny and new that they put Ved's six-year-old BMW to shame. Classical Indian music boomed from strategically hidden Bose speakers, and the entire entrance to the mansion was flanked by two massive sky-high bejeweled Swarovski peacocks to welcome the guests.

A tent over the lawn was crammed with posh, well-dressed people. Ladies with bouffants, shimmering jewelry, and flowing silk saris laughed with men in custom-made designer suits. Kids ran around wearing Indian paisley-embroidered sherwanis, and harried-looking maids chased after them. The combination of perfumes and colognes was potent enough to make Ved cough when he stepped inside.

Ved couldn't even spot his parents in the melee. What caught his eye instead were the massive chandeliers spaced across the tent's ceiling and the gold water fountain gushing in the center of all the people.

That, and the rows and rows of silverware dishes laid out buffet-style containing food from all corners of the world: Italy, Japan, Spain, Mexico, America, and, of course, India. Waiters dressed in black-and-silver livery walked around with trays in white-gloved hands. One had caviar dumplings. Another had champagne *pani-puri*. What had Disha been talking about? This was one of the coolest, most lavish parties Ved had ever been to.

"Ved. It's nice to finally see you. I missed you at family dinner last week."

Ved turned around to see his father. "Hi, Dad, sorry about that." Ved reached in for a hug. "How are you?"

"Fine, fine. How's everything with the new job?"

"It's great. I'm really enjoying my work."

"And your apartment is fine?"

"Yeah, Dad. I love it."

Before Prem could say more, Dolly walked over and kissed Ved on the cheek, leaving a red lipstick stain. She smiled and rubbed the stain away with two bejeweled fingers. "How are you, darling?"

"I'm doing well, Mum."

"Tell me, have you received any important calls lately?"

Ved shook his head. "Should I be expecting a call?"

Dolly smiled. "No, no. Forget I said anything."

Ved gestured around him. "This is some party, right?"

"I wouldn't expect anything less from the Kapoors. Now you see what I meant when I told you these people shit gold?"

"Mum!"

Dolly laughed. "Well, it's true. They flew in top chefs from all over the world to cater, the flowers were grown in Amsterdam, the fountain made in Italy, the crockery imported from Wedgwood; even the napkins were monogrammed in Paris."

"I've certainly never attended a party like this."

"It gets better, haan. Apparently, they've flown in some sort of international VIP guest especially from America. Top secret."

"That sounds like something Disha would love."

"Speaking of . . ." Dolly pointed to the other side of the room, where Disha was waving to them.

Ved waved back. "Mum, you'll be okay if I go talk to Disha?"

"Go have fun."

Disha ran forward the rest of the distance and hugged Ved. She stepped back to look at him. "Why *hello*, Mr. Handsome. That's a great suit."

Ved laughed. "You shouldn't be the one talking. Look at you! I'm assuming the only person who could have made such a gorgeous dress is Disha Kapoor."

Disha gave a twirl, the Swarovski crystals on her dress twinkling in the light. "I'm glad you like it. It only took me hundreds of hours to make."

"It paid off."

Disha started to pull Ved toward the packed dance floor. "Dance with me?"

"You think Hemant will mind?"

"Please. He loves you almost as much as I do."

"Disha, you know I'm not a good dancer."

She smiled. "It is my wedding day. If I ask you to dance, you will dance."

Ved groaned, but he did dance with Disha. The song was slow, so he put his arms around her waist, and she put her henna-adorned arms around his neck. They swayed with the beat.

"You look happy, Disha."

"I should hope so. This is the happiest day of my life."

Ved focused on making sure he didn't step on Disha's feet.

"You know that you'll find love again too. With Carlos or with someone else."

Ved met Disha's eyes. "How are you so sure? I haven't even been able bring myself to go on a single date these past few months."

"Because I know you, silly. You're a total catch. Give yourself some time."

"Thanks, Disha."

They continued swaying until the song was over, and right after, the lights dimmed. Suddenly, the air was rife with excitement. "Namaste, Mumbai!" came a booming voice over the speakers. "I'm so happy to be here on this special night!"

"Oh my God!" Ved and Disha said at the same time.

"Is that—"

"There's no way—"

They both turned to the stage, and standing right there was the international queen of pop in all her grandeur, wearing a silver dress and matching thigh-high boots. She had a big red bindi in the center of her forehead. Disha started moving toward the stage. "Come on, Ved!"

Ved was about to follow until his phone started vibrating. He pulled it out of his pocket to see who was calling and stopped dead in his tracks, answering immediately.

"Hi . . . yeah, it has been a long time."

CHAPTER 81

Ved stumbled outside the party, his heart pounding. "Hold on a second. I can't hear you over all the music."

Carlos laughed. "Are you clubbing without me?"

Ved paced the length of the lawn, wishing he could sound as relaxed as Carlos did. "I'm at Disha's wedding."

"Well, it sounds like—"

Ved couldn't stand it anymore. "Why are you calling, Carlos?"

"I miss you too."

"You *what*?" Ved struggled to breathe.

"I miss you."

"Why? I've been texting you for months. What changed?"

"Your mother contacted me."

"She *what*?" Now Ved really couldn't breathe.

Carlos laughed again. Why was he being so casual? How did he manage to remain calm when Ved was breaking down? "I have my email address on my travel blog, and a month ago she sent me this long email telling me how breaking up with you was a mistake I would regret for the rest of my life."

"She said that?"

"Yeah, she did." Carlos's voice turned more serious. "She was right, Ved. I didn't see that at first, and don't get me wrong, I'm still not sure whether I can trust you, but I want to try."

"You do?"

"I do. Are you free for a cup of coffee next week?"

EPILOGUE

Several months later

It was 5:00 p.m., and Ved was walking home from work. There was a slight chill in the air that felt nice after being in the warm office all day. Like every Friday, Ved stopped at Candies and ordered two of their famous chicken mayo sandwiches along with two cold coffees. Since the weather was so nice, he took the long way home through the winding road close to the sea. Many couples sat on rocks by the beach, while a few people dressed head to toe in Nike jogged on the sidewalk border. A few people walked their dogs, and a group of Japanese tourists took selfies of themselves by the sea. There was a sense of calm in the air.

Work was great. Now Ved went home feeling fulfilled, like he'd done something meaningful with his day. Twice a week, he took evening cooking classes at a nearby studio, and every morning, he worked out. Except now, Ved didn't go to the gym. He used a treadmill that stood in his living room, which was great because it allowed him to watch the news while working out. He even had a group of friends from work whom he grabbed drinks with during the weekends, often at Toto's. Of course, he also continued going to brunch every Sunday with Disha. Hemant sometimes joined them too.

At home, he had some errands to take care of before he could relax with his sandwich and some Netflix. Emptying the trash, ordering another round of cleaning supplies, feeding Fubu, paying the cable bill, paying the electric bill. Oh, and paying the newspaper bill.

Stepping into the apartment, Ved smiled and said, "You're home early."

"Yeah," Carlos said, "I couldn't resist. It's been a long week." He kissed Ved's cheek. "Please tell me that one of those sandwiches is for me."

"Yep. I also got you a cold coffee."

"I think I might be in love with you."

"Really?" Ved kissed Carlos. "I couldn't tell."

They sat down together on the couch, Ved wrapping his hand around Carlos's shoulder, gently caressing it to comfort him. He watched him eat for a few moments before asking, "So, how are you liking the new job?"

"It's amazing work. I never thought I'd ever get the chance to design my own clothes."

"You always had it in you."

Carlos leaned his head against Ved's shoulder. "Well, you were the first to see it."

It had been almost four months since they moved in together, and Ved couldn't be happier. Carlos had gotten on a plane right after their call during Disha and Hemant's wedding. It had taken both of them some time to get back to the way things were before, but now, Ved could wake up every morning, ready to seize the day. And so could Carlos.

"So, I have a surprise for you," Carlos said, smiling.

"What is it?"

"Before I tell you, I want you to know that I already took the liberty of booking plane tickets and a hotel room for the weekend, so there's no going back."

Ved shoved Carlos's shoulder lightly. "Carlos!"

"We're going to Goa!"

Ved stared at him, his mouth open.

"Surprise! It's on me, from my first paycheck."

Leaning forward, Ved kissed Carlos deeply. "That is an excellent surprise."

"I knew you'd like it."

"When do we leave?"

"Next Friday, so you'd better start packing."

———

On Monday, Ved entered the conference room to run a counseling session. Framed on the wall was the front page of *The Times of India* on the day the Supreme Court unanimously overturned the colonial-era ban on gay sex. He stared at it for a second, feeling a familiar pride rise up in his chest. Today, the room was filled with about twenty teenagers, all seated in a semicircle. Usually, the office would be lucky to have eight people come in.

Ved stood next to the whiteboard. When the kids saw him, their chatter died down. Ved gave them a bright smile. "Hi, everyone. How's your Monday morning going?"

He heard some muffled words.

Ved nodded, as if they'd all spoken. "So today's chat is about coming out." He looked at each kid. "How many of you are out to your parents?"

At least three-fourths of the kids raised their hands. Ved was taken aback. "Wow. Are you *sure* some of you aren't lying?" he joked. "No, I'm just kidding. That's great! Why don't we go around and share some of our coming-out stories?"

Ved took a seat in front of the semicircle. "Does anyone want to go first?"

The kids looked down, shuffling their feet, avoiding Ved's eye contact.

"Hey, no problem. I can share my experience first to get things going." He paused. "What you all may not know is that I once almost married a woman . . ."

DOLLY'S SPECIAL GLOSSARY

(Because mothers know best!)

Besan omelets: Savory pancakes made from chickpea flour. They serve as an excellent partner for any curry dish, if you're not interested in spending hours making bread. After an already-long day in the kitchen, I know I certainly don't want to be doing that.

Beta: A term of affection that mothers use to address their children.

Bharta: A dish made by grilling eggplant pieces over an intense open flame and then mashing those pieces into a mush. Don't be afraid to hold your eggplant over the flame. The smokiness of the vegetable is what makes this dish truly special.

Biryani: A spiced rice dish. The types of spices and the add-ins really depend on who's cooking. I like mine with a nice boiled egg and plenty of dried fruits.

Chai: Black tea boiled with milk and various spices. My version includes cardamom, ginger, and black pepper along with plenty of sugar.

Chicken tikka: Pieces of chicken that are marinated in a spice mixture and then grilled. If there aren't char marks on the meat, then it hasn't been prepared correctly. Never forget to squeeze some fresh lime or lemon on the chicken right after it comes off the grill.

Chutiya: Asshole, idiot, imbecile . . . take your pick.

Cutting chai: A half order of chai, often prepared stronger than a regular glass would be. Served in distinctive short and fluted glasses.

Dal: A curry made of lentils. The variety is vast, depending on the type of lentil. If you're ever at a restaurant, you should order black dal. Trust me.

Gulab jamuns: Fried balls of milk and flour soaked in a sugar syrup. Unlike jalebis, which are eaten dry, gulab jamuns are meant to be eaten piping hot with the accompanying syrup. Sometimes I add a dash of rose syrup to my sugar mixture.

Jadau: A special, intricate style of crafting Indian jewelry.

Jalebis: A circular sweet made of fried flour and soaked in sugar syrup. Messy to eat and frighteningly high in calories, but oh so worth it.

Ji: Attached to the end of names as a sign of respect. Naturally, all well-raised children would use this when addressing their parents.

Jootis: A shoe that is typically made of leather and is extensively embroidered with metallic thread.

Kaju katli: A sweet made primarily of cashews and cut into rhombuses. Often found with silver foil. No Indian gift is complete without a box of these.

Kesar peda: A soft sweet made with milk and saffron. Can be spotted a mile away by its vibrant yellow-orange hue.

Kulfi: Many call this frozen dairy dessert a "traditional Indian ice cream." Much better than gelato, I promise.

Ladoos: Made from flour, fat, and sugar, pop these yummy round shaped sweetmeats into your mouth and forget the word "calories."

Mithai: What we call Indian sweets. No happy occasion is complete without them.

Naan: Traditional Indian bread stretched into a long, ovular shape. No curry dish is complete without a piping-hot stack.

Pakora: A spiced fritter usually filled with vegetables. One of my personal specialties, along with lots of cheese inside it.

Puja: Hindu prayer ceremony. I always conduct a brief one in my apartment every morning in front of my collection of deities, but I attend larger ceremonies at the temple for special occasions such as weddings.

Roti canai: Another type of Indian bread, this one being flakier and lighter than naan.

Saab: Used to address a boss as a sign of respect.

Salwar kameez: A tunic-style dress worn with a pair of pants that are wide (like harem pants) and narrow at the ankles. One of the staple Indian outfits worn by women of all ages. I, myself, own no less than twenty-five, each in a different color. After all, you wouldn't want to be photographed in the same one twice.

Sherwani: Traditional Indian dress for men that resembles a long coat. Often heavily embroidered and worn with a pair of pants. No groom at an Indian wedding can avoid wearing at least one of these, though God knows they try.

Vada pav: The Indian veggie burger, consisting of a white-bread bun stuffed with a fried potato cutlet. A popular street-food choice that comes with a variety of chutneys.

ACKNOWLEDGMENTS

This book would not have been possible without the gentle guidance and editorial astuteness of my agent, Priya Doraswamy of Lotus Lane Literary. To see what started out as a casual conversation six years prior actually being published today, with many moments of uncertainty notwithstanding, is a testament to her unwavering belief. Aashna Moorjani, masterful apprentice at Lotus Lane Literary, my heartfelt thanks in expertly chiseling the narrative at every step and, like an alchemist, making it shine of gold.

To everyone at Lake Union Publishing, I am greatly indebted to your faith, trust, and championing of this book. All my gratitude and love to every one of you. Editor extraordinaire Chris Werner, your care, understanding, and attention to detail have helped steer this book to be the best version of itself. I could not have asked for someone better to work with. A shout-out of thanks to Bill Siever, Jill Kramer, Nicole Burns-Ascue, and their wonderful teams for the masterful copyediting and proofreading. And Krista Stroever, a very special thanks for your laser-like gaze in ensuring that all the missing gaps had been filled.

Last but not least, to my special circle of friends who ensure I stay sane with their madness. And my family, especially the late Pinky aunty, I am extremely thankful for your love, support, and emotional nourishment through it all.

ABOUT THE AUTHOR

Photo © 2020 Dhiman Chatterjee

Farhad J. Dadyburjor has been an entertainment and lifestyle journalist for over twenty years. Born and based in Mumbai, India, he has held several senior editorial positions, including at *DNA* newspaper, as launch editor at the international men's magazine *FHM*, and currently at *The Leela* magazine. He has also written for numerous publications and has a blog of his own. His debut novel, *How I Got Lucky*, was a satire on India's celebrity culture.